PRAISE

"... a writer who is willing to leap past genre boundaries and show us what's waiting in the great wide world beyond."
—*Strange Horizons*

"Paul Jessup is the ghostpoet of weird, writing words of unease that rattle like bones and whisper in dark corners. *The Skinless Man Counts To Five* is a wonderful collection of his macabre imagination, and should proudly grace every reader's shelf."
—Lavie Tidhar, author of *The Circumference of the World*

"Jessup's stories crackle with the electricity of violence and the sadness that follows. He finds that vein of the macabre no matter what genre he's employing. Every story here is a dark gem."
—Elad Haber, author of *The World Outside*

"Jessup's prose sometimes recalls Harlan Ellison at his most extravagant, invoking a lurid, elastic environment steeped in ritual yet with delirious magic as well as weird science."
—*Kirkus Reviews* for *The Silence That Binds*

"[Paul Jessup] uses language to great effect to heighten the more surreal aspects of his world."
—Eric Lahti, author of *Better Than Dead*

"Paul Jessup's latest novel is infused with terror, yearning, and twisted love . . . a haunting that lingers on."
—booktweeting.com

also by Paul Jessup

Glass House
Close Your Eyes
Werewolves
Glass Coffin Girls
The Silence That Binds

THE SKINLESS MAN COUNTS TO 5

AND OTHER TALES OF THE MACABRE

PAUL JESSUP

Underland Press

Text Copyright © 2024 by Paul Jessup

Extended copyright information may be found on page 275.

This book is published by Underland Press, which is part of Firebird Creative, LLC (Clackamas, OR).

We runandrunandrun

Edited by Darin Bradley
Book Design and Layout by Firebird Creative

This Underland Press trade edition has an ISBN of 978-1-63023-076-0.

Underland Press
www.underlandpress.com

THE SKINLESS MAN COUNTS TO 5

5 AND OTHER TALES OF THE MACABRE

For Ashlyn & Liam Jessup
the torchbearers for the next generation of horror

TABLE OF CONTENTS

INTRODUCTION

HOW THE HEART SINGS TO HORROR

It all started with my Aunt Dar, who was only seven years older than me, which made her more like an older sister than the usual Aunt. She opened the doorways to horror for me at a very young age. I remember sneaking downstairs while she babysat, hiding behind the banister, as she watched *Creepshow*, or *Poltergeist*, or *Let's Scare Jessica to Death*. I was entranced, especially by *Let's Scare Jessica to Death*. I loved the mist, the atmosphere, the uncertainty and the vampires.

When asked for a bedtime story, I would say tell me a scary story. And then she would! Some of the scariest stories I'd ever heard. She would retell Poe, or some Stephen King short stories by memory, and other times she would just make up ones whole cloth just to see me scream and hide under the covers. Many a night I would stay up until 4am, convinced that there was an albino ape just outside of my window that fed on the bones of children. All thanks to her.

I loved it. I remember, too, her reading a copy of Stephen King's *It*, just fresh from the library while she babysat me. I was entranced by the cover, the lizard claw coming out of the sewers. I loved monsters, and I wanted to know *what was that?* I was hoping for something horrible. She said, "Oh, it looks nothing like that, it's a clown."

I was very disappointed. She assured me it was a very scary clown indeed, and began to read the scene of poor Georgie's demise. I was riveted. Later on, for my birthday, her mom (my grandma) got me a book of classic horror stories. It was my most favorite thing in the world for the longest time. This was where I was introduced to Poe, Machen, MR James, Lovecraft, Charlotte Perkins Gilmore, and a litany of other writers. The stories that made the most impression on me were "The Telltale Heart," "Oh Whistle and I'll Come to You, My Lad," "The Colour out of Space," "The White People," and "The Yellow Wallpaper."

When I read "The Telltale Heart," my parents were making room for my soon-to-be-born little sister. They were taking my room, putting up some dry wall, and splitting it into two rooms. My mom realized one of the floorboards was loose and I just about flipped out. Of course it was a human heart! Of course! I screamed at her not to pry it open, that some things were better left undisturbed.

It was an ancient box of condoms and some dirty magazines.

As funny as it was, it didn't lesson the fear of this moment in my mind. I knew, then, the power of a good horror story, and I was in love with them. In love in the same way people reserve for their favorite poems, songs, or movies. All consuming, like a Lovecraftian hero obsessed with the unknown, I returned to these stories over and over again. I remember reading "The White People" out at my grandparents' place, in the middle of nowhere of rural Ohio. Corn fields aplenty, and huge forests creeping along their backyard for acres and acres. I would spend the days wandering the woods, and the nights reading until the crack of dawn, watching deer come out in the mist and run through the shadows.

"The White People" opened up my brain and *did* something to it. The frame narrative bored me, I skipped that entirely. But there, in the little girl's diaries, I'd found a secret world. A world that would later gain the name *folk horror*, but at this time was just alluring and strange and beautiful. I wanted to visit these Troy Towns, read from the Green Book, all of it. I even tried to imitate the style of her writing, the creeping sense of dread. I didn't understand the ending, I thought she literally poisoned herself. Later on, I realized they were talking in a spiritual sense, and that cool-looking statue (in my mind, it was twisted and horrific) was really just the Great God Pan.

Still, the story stuck with me. And my love for short stories (specifically horror short stories) grew. Like all precocious kids who loved reading, I wanted to do that kind of magic myself. I made my first books as a toddler, my mom writing the words while I dictated to her the story and drew the images. Not much later, I would sell my first story, a saddle-stapled homespun tale about teddy bears, to my best friend, whose turn it was to do show and tell in kindergarten and had nothing. So he bought the book from me for a whole dollar.

As the years went on, and my love for horror grew (as well as science fiction and fantasy), I started to imitate the short stories and books I loved so much. I returned to short stories the most, especially for horror. It just felt so natural and beautiful in this brief, poignant form. You could conjure an emotion almost effortlessly in the reader, and hold onto it with just enough space to make them uncomfortable in their own skin.

As a teenager I started submitting short stories to magazines. Mostly rejections, but eventually a few small literary magazines started publishing me. I got poetry in my local newspaper. Years later, I went to university and won awards for my short story writing. It was such an exciting time! So thrilling. They were horror stories, but told with such a veneer of literary and experimental style the professors didn't seem to mind at all. Perhaps it was because I was working more in a classic tradition of horror back then, a ghost story of sorts. I imitated Poe and MR James shamelessly, spinning my own weird imagination and letting it sing.

After graduation I spent a few years making video games, and taking a break from writing. This was a fun time, don't get me wrong, but I always felt like something was missing. Like a phantom limb of stories.

Eventually, after my daughter was born, I decided to jump right back into writing and publishing. I tried doing more respectable genres, like science fiction or the classic literary realist story, but these did not feel quite as natural to me, and they piled up rejections quicker than quick. But, aha, the minute I returned to horror? Things started to work for me again. Acceptances rolled in. It was a fun and exciting time.

I still remember my first big pro level sale, to *PostScripts Magazine*. I had tried my hand at a Machen White People-style story yet again. A little before this, my grandpa bought me a book on spirit photography for "inspiration." It was very inspiring, indeed! These days we would call it analog horror, but back then, the images were just creepy. The photographs were ill lit, torn, ripped apart. The book had seen better days, it was at least 40 years old at that point, and not well taken care of.

But oh, it was beautiful, and haunting, and gave me so many ideas. I read about a hollow earth commune in Florida, I read about Germans making weird ghost paintings in a trance, I saw depictions of ectoplasm, all creepy-looking and unreal. The quality of the photographs added to this a thousand fold. I put all of this into that story, and really wrote in such a way that I hadn't in a long time. Poetic, in a trance, with the words tripping over each other as they rushed out of me.

I almost put in a frame narrative like "The White People" had, but in the end tossed it out and focused on another little girl's diary. This time she was in a horrible cult, one that speaks to the dead, who are coming for her at any moment. I sold it to *PostScripts*, and that same story is collected here, "Ghost Technology from the Sun."

I tried to expand my writing several times through the years. Focusing for a bit on science fiction, on magical realism, on fantasy. I found that I had to make a conscious decision to force the story into a non-terrifying shape. This was no easy task, and after awhile I just stopped fighting it and kept embracing horror once again. Don't get me wrong: I do love my funny, heartfelt, strange bits of fantasy and science fiction that are more sweet and less terrifying. They have an emotional qualia that I was able to bring back into my horror stories later.

But they just felt like I was wearing the wrong shoes. I could walk in them, yes. But could I run?

And horror, my friends, is all about running. So come, take my hand, and let's run and keep on running, and never look back. Let's embrace horror full on and celebrate its icky joy that shivers our spines and brings a smile to our face. After all, this is what we need, isn't it? A world that is rough-carved and beautiful. Terrifying as it is poetic. Turn the page with me, and run, run, run! The sense of freedom will be exhilarating.

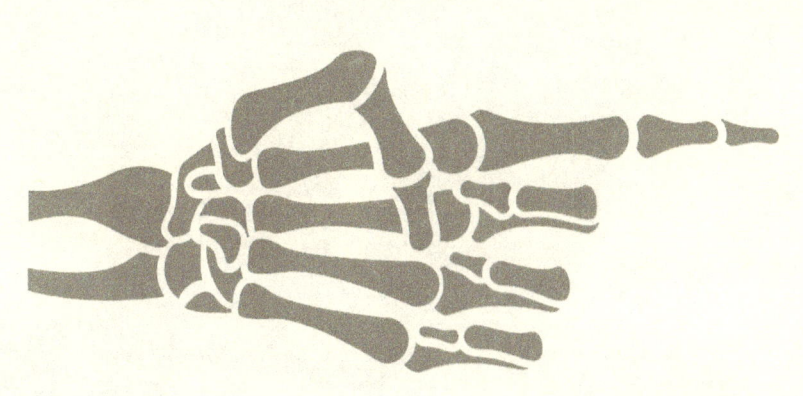

THE HOUSE AT THE END OF THE WORLD

I don't like our new house. The floorboards look like old men sleeping, and there is a cat hiding in the ceiling between floors. I don't like my new school. The teacher speaks with a hiss and shuffles, and all the other kids play dead better than I do. I don't like my new town, the city at the end of the world. Everyone here but us wears masks. I don't like our new woods, the forest behind our house. These trees mark the end of the world.

Pine trees. They smell like sap and blood and things burning in the shadows. Like a wet match. The pine trees huddle together. Like old women, talking. Every once and awhile a tree would turn and look at me, and I could see rheumy sap eyes and crinkled pine tree fingers. Nestled with cones and needles. Green—dark, deep green. Like the color of my mother's eyes. Like the color of my eyes.

That's another thing about this city, this town at the end of the world. Everybody here has the same color eyes. Newspaper eyes, I call them. Because they are that grey of newspaper, that grey of dishwater. Haunted by the lack of color, by the lack of substance.

I don't like my dreams at the new house. These are the worst. I dream of the cat who lives in the walls and the ceilings. He has a human skull for a face and a scorpion tail. His paws make scratching sounds as he pads from room to room. In my dreams, his name is

Francis. In my dreams, he's writing a book on torturing humans. In my dreams, he's using me to write his book. My skin as parchment. My blood as ink. My finger bones as quill. I am book, and subject of book at the same time.

—

I do like a painting in the house. It is on the second floor, in the hall-way. It is about my size. Big enough that I could walk through it. It came with the house. When my mom saw it she wanted to throw it away. She called it junk. She called it trash. "Mary," she said calmly when I was mad and wanted her to keep it, "Dear, it's ugly. And it's not even good art."

But my dad understood. Back then he was a different dad. Before the changes. Before the hour of the waking. He insisted that we keep it. Said it had an old world charm to it. I thanked him for hours on end, and made him pancakes for breakfast the next day. I don't make pancakes for breakfast anymore. The dead do not eat pancakes.

—

The painting. It is of a little girl with brown hair. She sits on the floor of a forest. A pine forest like ours. But the trees are kinder. They don't huddle around with sharp tongues and clawed hands. They are baking cakes. They are telling stories. They are singing sounds and holding hands.

Needles around the little girl. Like little green trees. She has needles in her hair and in her mouth. She is playing on the ground. She is making a house out of pine tree sticks and mud. I want to live there. The house is unfinished. Two mud people look up at the house. They have no faces yet.

The little girl has a scar across the middle of her face. Deep. Like she had been cut in half. I can tell that she's singing as she plays. The song goes like this: *Who killed cock robin? Who killed him? Who killed cock robin? I, said the sparrow, with my bow and arrow.*

Just thinking about it makes me happy. There are faces between the pine trees. Of children, playing. One of them is running. I can see his feet and the back of his legs.

—

On the first day of school I wasn't allowed to talk. I couldn't answer questions in class. I couldn't chatter or speak to any of the kids. If I opened my mouth my teacher would shuffle over to me and hit me hard across the face. I wasn't allowed to cry, either. I didn't have a mask. I couldn't play dead. So I was unclean to them.

I didn't like that. Everyone in the city wears masks. They are all exactly the same. Clean, white porcelain. No face. No nose. No decorations. And then holes for their dull, grey eyes. Until I wore a mask I couldn't be a part of the school.

The teacher was an old man named Mister Livedog. He liked to talk in a fast, hissing voice. When he gave lectures, his body would weave back and forth. Hypnotic. And his lectures were always strange. Something was always off about them.

Like on that first day. Most of what we learned was the founding of the city on the bones of a giant. The giant who tried to eat the world whole. And how the founding father had crawled out of his eyes, and created the city with bits of his brain tissue and internal organs. His lectures were always weird stuff like that. By the third day I stopped listening.

—

Once a day, every day, the people play dead. Usually it's when I'm at school. They announce playing dead with the sound of an air raid siren.

Everyone was quiet. Mister Livedog bowed his head, and said the same creepy poem he always did when it was time to play dead: "They come from the pictures, the mirrors, the walls and the ocean. They come from the sky and the earth and our ruins. The watchers in the pines will keep us safe. The watchers in the pines will make us whole. Play dead, play dead, play dead, and keep the city from being eaten."

Then they would fall to the floor. Only people with masks could play dead. I had to sit at my desk with my head down, holding my breath. I wasn't allowed to breathe more than I had to while everyone played dead.

It was terrible. The children writhed on the floor, moaning and howling as if they were in horrible pain. The sound of chains sliding on linoleum filled the hallway of the school. And they all began to smell. Like fresh corpses. The sky outside of our classroom windows turned red. Snow fell to the ground. Soon it was over.

But again, again. Day in day out. They kept on playing dead, once a day. When I asked about it, my parents only said that they have different customs than we do at the end of the world. So I should be nice and play along. When I asked if they played dead, they said no. They said that they didn't have masks yet.

YET.

I wonder if they have a mask for me?

—

Sometimes at night I can't sleep. Not because of the cat in the walls. He sleeps at that hour. But other things walk through the halls. I try to sleep. Telling myself that they can't hurt me. That I'm safe here with mommy and daddy. But I'm not fooling anyone.

Shuffling feet in the shadows. Heavy breathing. And then fingers drumming on the hardwood floors. I hear lots of people, slouching, moving. Some crawling across the floors. Others I swear are moving across the ceiling. Some whisper. I don't listen to what they whisper. Their conversations sound angry, abrupt. Tempting and dreamlike. I don't want to hear what they say. I don't want to follow them, wherever they are going.

One night I saw a figure standing in my doorframe. Outlined by the light of our bathroom. He had a unicorn horn on his head. I couldn't see his features. He was only a shadow. But he sang. Sang with the most melodious voice I've ever heard. My dad has a good singing voice, but this guy puts him to shame.

As he sang I heard the sound of trees bending in the wind, and my heart stopped. I saw he had a mask in one hand. A knife in the other. I made the mistake of hearing his words. The words of his song. And I got a chill. "We will make you hollow, we will fill you with maggots, we will drink your thunder, we will make you normal."

I wanted to scream. I wanted to cry. He didn't step into my room. Eventually he left. I would love to say I never saw him again, after that.

But that would be a lie. As much as I hate to say the truth. That would be a lie.

—

On the second day of school, I still wasn't allowed to talk. I just had to sit quietly while everyone around me chattered. Their teeth clacking together. Like someone cold. Or sick with a fever.

The teacher taught songs. Showed them how to use fire to awaken a sleeping giant. He said that all houses had sleeping giants in their basements. Even mine. And soon they would awake. That was when he turned to me. His eyes smiled behind the mask. And that, he said, would be when you and your parents become official citizens.

Everyone applauded. I wanted to, but didn't want to get hit again. So I stayed quiet while they applauded. Their chattering teeth, their drumming fingers.

In the middle of the applause the air raid sounded. It was time to play dead again.

—

I walk to school while everyone else rides the bus. My parents don't drive me. They both have to work very early. And dropping me off would make me late. We moved here because they both got jobs at the same company. They were very excited about getting jobs at the end of the world. Work was hard to come by elsewhere.

I don't know what they do there. They never tell me. Whenever I ask they change the subject. Sometimes dad forgets to change out of his work clothes before he comes home. It's a long white suit.

Sometimes he comes home with his face covered in blood stains. Ones that won't ever wash off, he said. But the next day he's able to get them off. But his face suffers for it. It is rubbed raw and red.

My mom always comes home in the same white dress. She's never had blood on her face. But her skin suffers anyway. Rubbed raw, rubbed red. Neither of them like to talk about what they've seen, what they've done. They like working here. They don't want to get fired.

But every once and awhile I'll see sadness in my mom's eyes. A longing for a life other than this one. She will come up to me on those days and hold me for a long time, sobbing. I try to ask what's wrong, but she won't tell me. I'm not supposed to know. I'm never supposed to know.

My father doesn't get like this. He's always happy. Always smiling. It scares me.

—

Near the end of my stay, there were new doors in the house. They seemed to have grown there over night. These doors were painted black, and I couldn't open them. They were hot to the touch. From behind I heard screams.

That night my parents came home wearing masks. They were naked, and I saw scars across their bodies. Rings and rings and rings of scars. Spiraling scars. Old scars, from when we first moved here. They didn't talk to me once they started wearing masks. I was invisible to them.

It's only time, I thought, before they get a mask for me. I don't want to wear a mask. I wanted to stay Mary. I didn't want to play dead, I didn't want to fit in. I wanted to be in a normal house.

That was the night I brought the painting into my room.

—

The people that came out at night were louder now. Like they were having a party. And my parents' voices mingled with them now. I heard screams, and then ripping sounds. Like flesh being ripped from bone. I looked over at my painting. And for a minute it changed. It showed a giant devouring. Blood pouring down his face. Legs sticking out of his mouth. The crushed bodies of children in his hands.

And then it's different again. Changed again. Back to the painting I know and love.

—

I tried talking to my parents. They had no voices behind the masks. None for me. I asked if we were moving soon. Nothing. I asked, with terror in my voice, if I would have a mask soon. Nothing. They didn't eat breakfast or lunch or dinner with me anymore. I was on my own. I ate a lot of cold cereal.

Mostly because the stove scared me. It was old. It was iron. And one day I found a fingerbone inside of it. It had black ink on the end of it. And a pile of ashes around it. I left the fingerbone inside and never touched it again.

—

There was no one at school. I sat in the classroom by myself. Even when they were supposed to play dead. I didn't want to go home. It was scarier there. The cat wasn't in the walls anymore. I think he's out, stalking the town. Looking for little skull-faced mice.

When I got home the house was empty. My parents didn't come home from work until very late. I stayed away from the doors. I stayed away from the walls. The ceilings. The basement. I heard something stirring in the basement. Like it was trying to wake up.

Tossing, turning. Waking slowly at the end of the world.

I went outside. But there was a fog amongst the pine trees. And the sky was a brilliant red. The same red of playing dead. It was the playing dead sky. And from the trees I heard whispering. Watched the trees huddle closer together. Point their needle fingers at me. Mutter between them. Outsider, outlander, living.

—

When my parents did come home it was late into the evening. I heard them rush inside. Run about. It was dark. Night. The strange shadow people would be here soon. Wailing through the sleeping doors. I didn't want to be awake when they came. But I think I had no choice.

Then I heard the air raid siren. It announced that it was time to play dead. And I got this terrible feeling. In my stomach. Like something was alive inside of me, crawling, trying to force its way out.

I ran downstairs. I don't know why I did it. Maybe I wanted to see how my parents played dead. Probably not, though. Some things you just do without thinking, and they happen. They happen whether you will them to or not.

I found my parents sitting at a table. In the center of the table was a candle. And a mask. Just the size of my face. My mom turned. Looked at me. Her mask was off. Her face was just muscle. Was blood and bone.

There was no flesh left. "Go to sleep, little Mary. Please, just go to sleep."

The thing in the basement tossed, turned. Restless again. I tried to say no. I tried to say I wasn't ever going to sleep again. I tried to say that I was running away from home. That I couldn't take living here anymore.

Instead I walked upstairs. That thing inside of me made me do it. I have no idea how. But against my will, against my thinking, it made me turn around. Walk. Heel toe, heel toe. Hup two three four. Walk all the way upstairs. Passed the doors opening to the lands of love and pain. Passed my parents room, and the skull cat that now stalked the corridors. And into my bedroom where I laid down to sleep.

—

I awoke to fingers on my face. To a mask sliding over my skin. To a knife in the darkness, gleaming, devouring the shadows, hungry for my skin. I screamed, but felt a fist in my mouth. Bit down on fist. Fist moved away while my father bit his tongue. My mom was not in the room with me. That was a good sign.

I ran over, ran past him. He walked carefully towards me. Knife swinging in hand. His face was off. His mask was off. His eyes looked like two marbles in the light. Grey newspaper marbles put into the holes in his head.

I ran over. Ran into the picture without even thinking. The painting opened up for me, let me inside. I walked through without even thinking. Without even planning.

There was the girl. Creating a little house. When she saw me her mouth opened. I saw no tongue. She pointed behind me. Pointed outside of the painting. I turned. Looked. My body was still out there. Lying flat on the floor.

My body was still out there. Gone. I was in here. I watched as my father leaned down and began to cut away at my face. My body didn't scream as I watched. My body didn't fight as I watched. It just laid there. Quietly. And let him carve, carve, carve.

I turned around to ask the girl what had happened. But the painting had changed. The giant was there. Crushed children in his hand. Blood running down his face. He was howling. Howling. Awake and mad and hungry.

LIGHT LIKE KNIVES DRAGGED ACROSS THE SKIN

When Saw slapped down his last card, we knew that things were going to change. There was something in the air smothering our voices like hanging bones. It didn't help that we were playing out in Janice's backyard, which was still decorated with the plastic ghosts and tombstones of last Halloween.

I tried not to act too surprised. We are all defined by our decks, and this was surely a facet of Saw's personality. He was a dark fucker, that was for certain. We just never knew how deep that darkness dug. The others—they didn't take it so well. Janice looked like she was going to cry, and Carl looked like somebody had shit in his head.

On the card: a black door. A girl with a dress made from her own blood. Symbols. A shadow. The art murder card. We all heard of this card—but none of us had ever played in a game when it came up. Janice consulted the rulebook, seeing if there was some way we could banish it, some way we could make that jackass pick his card up and shuffle it back into his graveyard.

She shook her head. Nothing.

"Why the fuck," she said, "Did you slap that down, Saw? What are you trying to prove?"

Saw shrugged, his black hair falling over his face. "It's all part of the game. I got that card when I bought a booster pack last week. You guys knew it was going to come up eventually. Hell, it's why some people play this in the first damn place."

I leaned back and lit a smoke, trying to stay cool. One of us would have to die. That was the rules. I looked down at my hand. The three-headed dog. The hanged god. The burning soldier. Nothing. No way out of this hand. I was going to have to play one of them or be killed.

Carl coughed and rubbed the round of his stomach. He looked at Janice, and you could tell he had something up his sleeve. Carl was always trying to impress her. I could tell he had a thing for her—even if she was Saw's wife. Some part of me thought Janice had a thing for Carl too.

Saw grinned. "Well, come on, chicken shits, let's keep the game going. We can't call it quits now—we are all defined by our cards in play. So smack that shit down, and let's get going."

Saw got off on the whole thing, that much I could tell. He probably had a thick inch of wood under the table. He was in love with power, with making people do what he wanted. And now he wanted one of us to die. I guess that's just how it goes.

Carl smacked down a psychopomp card. This one was the lighter aspects of death—a sleeping figure with a black notebook and a scythe. He smiled, knowing that this put Saw into a corner. Only one person could play the psychopomp. Now Saw was in the line of fire as well.

Saw seemed completely unfazed. "Now," he said, "That's what I'm talking about. Let's keep this going until all of our aspects are created. You guys know the rules."

Janice shuffled her hand. I decided to play my hanged god card. What the hell—it could only help me. Janice saw my card and laid down a card that shocked each of us. The card had a man lying on the ground with a dart in his eye. Baldur, sweet Baldur. The card of sacrifice.

Saw grinned.

Janice wiped her eyes and then moved some of her wine-colored hair behind her ear. "Well, jackass, are you going to pony up or what?"

Saw peered over each card, milking the dramatic moment to its fullest. He laid down a psychopomp card. A figure in white, drenched in blood with a death's mask. "Well, I can't play that card," he said with an overblown flair.

He laid down another card. A victim card. "And, I guess I can't play that one either. Looks like all I can use is this."

He laid it face down, and then slowly peeled it back to reveal a picture of Cronus eating his children. The demiurge card. Carl laughed while rubbing his stomach. This was too much. "The demiurge. Just what the fuck did you have planned for this evening?"

I lifted the card up to the light. Detailed, full of ink and blood. I wondered if the artist bled into the card before sending it out to be shrink wrapped and displayed in stores. "Definitely not pizza and wings," I said.

Saw shrugged. "We can still eat afterwards."

Janice held her head with her hands, framing her face. Her lips moved in the shape of a scream, but no sound came out. She gnawed on her palm, drawing blood across her lifeline. "I don't think I'm going to be hungry," I said.

Carl nodded with me.

Saw lit up a smoke.

"Suit yourself."

We pulled a card out of the major arcana deck to my left. This was the last stage of this hand—the four cards that determine everything that came next. Saw smirked, the tips of his lips fuming with smoke, and I wondered if he had stacked the deck somehow when no one was looking.

Above, I heard a crow cawing at the setting sun as the plastic ghouls shook in the spring wind. I looked over and saw Janice rocking back and forth, the sun crowning her head with a halo of red. I wanted to reach across the table and hold her—but knew I could not.

Soon the cards I played would define me. Our cards would define all of us. An hour worth of slapped plastic against that white poker table recreating our personalities, and burning our souls with the architecture of myth.

I held my breath as the four major arcana formed a cross of cards In front of us. The gorgon's lair. Medea's nursery. The unsung knife. The burning arm. The scene was set. The characters drawn. Now it was time for the game to really pick up.

—

Some say Sesun was created by a man who had gained enlightenment and wanted to destroy the world. Some say Aleister Crowley created it as a replacement to his Thoth Tarot Deck. Others say that nobody created it, that it had always existed and will always be with us.

There are an untold number of cards. A city of rules and expansion decks built on plastic and the images painted within them. The starter decks are simple—enough that with a few small booster packs you could recreate yourself in any image.

That was the art to it—creating a deck that remade you. A deck that changed you into who you wanted to be. The rules are simple and complex. Each card changes everything. Each card changes you. Your deck changes with each game—moving cards, swapping them, dancing with them in your hands.

For this reason, no game is ever the same. At first, you feel as though things are random, that the game has no purpose and you will never pry into the meanings beyond the cards. Then the game moves out like a fractal, slowly the seeming chaos of the game becomes order, and then enlightenment follows.

The only rule in Sesun is that everything changes and nothing is ever real. If you forget that—if you start to believe the unreality—you will be lost in a sea of images, floating against the waves of the symbolic.

—Excerpt from an online review of the Sesun game.

—

Dark. Night. The stars spun over our heads, the only light that of the red and orange pumpkin globes strung from tree to tree. The globes spun back and forth, violently sending light like knives drug across the skin of the darkness. A game doesn't stop until the last card is drawn and the final act is played out.

A knife in the center of the table glinted with light stolen from the moon. I saw Janice's face reflected into it, her eyes scared, blind. She wanted to run but couldn't. Carl belched, then drew some new cards.

I threw down a smiling sun. Simple card, but it mixed things up a bit by making me and Saw trade hands. Kept things a little more fair this way—even if he did stack his deck and the major arcana deck, he couldn't fiddle with ours. Not without the proper card.

Saw shrugged. I tossed the remainder of my smoke into an empty can of beer. The soft red of the butt disappeared in an audible hiss as Saw handed over his cards and I gave him mine. Not a bad hand he had there—you could tell he had spent a long time building up his deck to match his personality.

Dark cards. Reversed cards. The bone grinder. The witch's tit. The mouthless demon. I guess these are part of me now—his personality absorbing into mine as his cards entered my hands. Shadows passed over my memories. The hanged god inside of me twitched and paced in my mind. He didn't like these cards. It might take us someplace he didn't want to go.

Carl slapped down the drinking whore card. His face took on a sly and simple smile as his hand moved over and under the table, clutching onto Janice's bare leg under her skirt with his sweaty palms. She yelped a moment, her mind still racing with rabbit thoughts.

Saw looked on, his gaze one of interest and not jealousy. It was as if he expected Carl to play this card. I knew I should be uncomfortable in this moment—but I was too worried about what was to happen to let something as small as infidelity bother me. Murder outweighed all other crimes committed tonight.

One of us would be extinguished. Sure, you're thinking that Janice is the one—but the game isn't over yet. The rules always change, things always transgress and then come round in a different direction. The people change, their relationships change. It's all symbols being rearranged into meaningful patterns. A lot like how life is.

Take, for example, last week's game. Last week I was married to Janice, and Carl was drunk and suicidal. Saw was luddite and a violent anarchist, this week he's a technoslut and born again gnostic. It's all about the way the game plays out—how the cards rearrange who we are.

A classic power display. A Foucault's Pendulum of personalities, relationships and emotions, all dictated by a card game.

Kind of crazy, isn't it?

We wouldn't have it any other way.

Saw slapped down the haunted library card, which brought the burning arm into play. He poured gasoline on Carl's skin, the smell of it clinging to the air. Carl looked shocked at first, but he knew what needed to happen. He couldn't look away, couldn't scream. You can't ignore what you could be anymore than you could ignore who you are now. Denying such possibilities is a crime against your soul.

He blinked back tears of pain as his arm went up in orange and red flames. He kept his other arm steady on Janice's leg, moving it up higher on her thigh as the fire burned into his flesh like a tattoo. He would have to play like that for the rest of the game. We knew the game probably wouldn't last too much longer. Once the unsung knife came into play, it would be done and one of us would be dead.

—

When we first heard about the art murder card, I was like, y'know—cool! We've got to find that one and give it a whirl. When I woke up and my mom was dead, I didn't think it was so hot anymore. But the game changed me after that, and I was too far into it.

You can't get out once you go in.

I know, I tried. They just redefine you until you don't care anymore—bringing cards into play that wipe that guilt right from your mind. And then the game is over and you are different and nothing is the same.

I just wish I could remember who I was before I started. I see all these old photographs of myself from before—and it's like looking at a stranger. Was I ever really like that? I don't even have the same name as that girl in the pictures.

I want to be able to define myself, but every time I put a card into play someone slaps something else down and I am changed again and again and again, until at the end of the day my friends have recreated me in their own image.

And all I want to do is be myself. But who was I before Sesun? That's like asking what your name was before you were conceived. A whisper, a candle blowing out. That was my name, that was who I was. An extinguished light, an exhale and the smell of wax. That's who I will be until another game, when another card is laid down and I cease to be this incarnation of me and become someone else, someone different.

—Interview with a Sesun player for the article *Sesun: The Cult of Death.*

—

Because of Saw's last few cards in play I shrugged off the identity of hanged god, and instead became the lion who ate the sun. I've grown green fur, and I got these big teeth with ripped bits of a red dress stuck in them. I looked over at Carl, and he was almost consumed by his flames. His good hand rubbed in circles against Janice's clit. We saw that grin on her face and her body getting tenser as she gets closer and closer to coming.

I wondered if she stopped being a victim, and maybe she's traded places with Carl. Like the death was transferred between them in the moment of orgasm and sticky fingers. So many cards in play now—it was hard to keep track of who was who, and who was supposed to die.

Was the Art Murder card even still in play?

I leaned over and lit a smoke off of Carl's flames as Janice came violently next to him in screams of passion. Saw looked on, smiling still. He watched me, and I saw in his eyes that he wanted to touch me. But I bite and I can eat and that unsung knife card was moments from being in play.

Soon, soon. Soon the murder would happen. I could feel it running across my fur, dancing in the air in waves of shadow. Closer and closer it came. I looked up at the moon, and I was hungry. I wanted to eat the moon, to take it away from the sky. I was so jealous of those stars and clouds- being hung in that same void of space as the moon. I wanted to leap up and growl and suck it into my stomach. Maybe then my stomach would light up, and everyone would come to me for the warmth of the moon inside of me.

Saw flips up the lovers card, and lays it down reversed. A mad situation that called for. Medea's Nursery came into play, and we all switched decks, leaving a dozen cards to die in the plastic graveyard around us. I left the last of me behind when I picked up Janice's cards.

Was I the victim now? Was Carl? Was Saw? Saw looked too cool, too calm to be someone who was about ready to die. Carl was on fire, and very rarely did someone on fire die in one of these hands.

"You guys hungry?" Janice asked this, her eyes slit.

Carl smiled. "No," he said, "I'm good."

We all nodded.

"Let's keep this fucker burning. Keep this game going. We're getting close, I can feel it," Saw said, bumming a smoke from me.

I tossed him one.

Carl put a card into play. The dancing ruins. I didn't see that one coming, not in a million years. He picked up a skull mask and placed it over his face. I could see his eyes peeking out from that rotten plastic and I just got the creeps. Was Carl dead now? Was the game over?

He picked up the psychopomp card. It's closer now, almost time. He had assumed his essence of death. All we need is the unsung knife to come into play, and then it would all be over. Janice leaned over and kissed the back of my neck and put her hand in my lap.

With her other hand she slapped down the Witch Hammer card. She climbed on top of me, unbuckling my jeans. Saw cheered on, and Carl just watched. I could feel Carl's jealous eyes on me, spiking my soul with his new personality. I didn't want this—not now, not like this. Someone was going to die soon, and I sure as hell did not want it to be me.

—

Oh, Sariputra, Form Does not Differ From the Void,
And the Void Does Not Differ From Form.
Form is Void and Void is Form;
The Same is True For Feelings,
Perceptions, Volitions, and Consciousness.

—The Heart Sutra

—

When all was said and done, I wasn't surprised when Saw laid down the suicide card and the unsung knife came into play. We should've all seen it coming. He'd been wanting to die for a long time now, and I think that's why he played in the first place. To recreate himself or to kill himself.

It didn't matter really, in the end both have the same result. You aren't you anymore. You're someone else, or your dead. A transition of states. The cards are constantly killing us and bringing us back to life. I'm not sure why I was afraid of being killed before.

Maybe it was the cards that did it? Maybe they made me think I didn't want to die, when really I was already dead so many times over?

—

When Carl was done, we had to fulfill the first card's promise and turn this murder into a work of art. We carefully arranged the body, we cut images into his skin. We took turns. I removed his eyes and placed them in his hands. Janice put coins in his sockets and then spit down his dead throat.

Carl never played again. He stopped calling us, stopped coming over. Sometimes I can see him outside of Janice's house, haunting the old plastic ghosts. I wonder what he's thinking of, why he sits and watches and never approaches us.

Janice is much darker these days. Sure we play the game from time to time. She's much more into it than I am. Sometime she'll drag some girls from the bar in, or a few guys. Sometimes she'll have sex with them in front of me—using the game as an excuse to do whatever she wants.

I don't know. It's not that I don't like the game anymore. But in that moment, when Saw died, I saw an emptiness in his eyes. It danced right behind his pupils—this dark muttering maw of shadows. I felt blind in that moment, and then saw nothing but illusions. I was a void. He was a void. Janice was a void. The card game was a void. The void was everywhere.

And it was hungry.

Apple Magick

Once upon a time elves lived in the sewers beneath the city. They had apple orchards that stretched under the streets for miles. They had their own political system, their own way of life that happily existed underneath ours. Then one day they all got up and left.

And they took their apples with them.

I blamed Chloe for their disappearance.

Chloe, and those birds that used to haunt the city.

—

Chloe caught an elf once. Used an apple as bait. She left the apple outside of a sewer drain with the Hebrew letter *aleph* carved into it. She said elves couldn't resist an apple with Hebrew carved into it. It's like a magnet. A magical magnet.

A yummy, delicious, magical elf magnet.

—

The elf was short.

He smelled like fire.

I think he tried to seduce me once.

I remember punching him in the throat when he tried to touch my ass. He always had this knack for pissing people off. Some days I wondered why Chloe even cared and why she just didn't sell him on eBay, or leave him in the backyard for the birds.

—

The elf's name was Gogongretinsobwimsoboyin.

He wouldn't let me pronounce it properly. He put his stinky fingers against my lips and said, "Shh. Do not taint the beauty of my name with your stupid, fat, English tongue, or I will rip it out of your skull and use it for a jumprope."

This made Chloe laugh.

She had a great sense of humor.

—

She kept Gogongretinsobwimsoboyin under her house in a wicker birdcage. The birdcage used to belong to this old lady who lived down the street from us. She had forty-two birds. All of them spoke in unison, squawking and taunting the neighborhood with their ancient voices into all hours of the morning. One day the old lady went to go feed her birds, but they were all gone.

The floor covered in feathers.

Feathers.

Bright blue and orange and yellow.

At night I could still hear the birds, hiding in the secret parts of the city, still squawking in unison. They were up to something. I could smell it. A socialist revolution. A freedom from birdseed and the tyranny of old ladies everywhere.

—

Gogongretinsobwimsoboyin didn't like his cage.

He said it was haunted.

Chloe just laughed and taunted him with food.

Nothing like elf torture to cure the blues.

—

Elves eat flower petals and seeds. I guess they're kind of like birds in that way—vegetarians. Us omnivores have one thing over vegetarians as pets—if we ever get bored of them, we can eat them. I've often thought of eating Gogongretinsobwimsoboyin. I wondered what elf meat tasted like.

Chloe didn't think you could eat elf meat. She thought it was like lion or orangutan meat. "Y'know," she said, "Against the law of nature.

It would be like killing a unicorn and then selling its horn. Or like hunting a phoenix and eating its feathers."

"There are just some things," she said, "you don't do. It messes with the natural order of things, yo."

—

Some days I wondered why she dragged him out of the sewer. He wasn't very pretty. I always thought elves were supposed to be shiny pretty balls of faerie light. He was just kind of short and lumpy, bruised with ugly skin and acne. His face was mangled and broken, his hair stringy and clumped. I felt kind of sorry for the guy. So ugly and so broken. Lost amongst the torturing humans.

—

Do you know why the caged elf sings?

Because we'll shock him in the balls with a car battery if he doesn't.

—

That old lady must've been pretty brutal to her birds, 'cause one day the cops found her dead in her front yard, hanging from the clothesline like a scarecrow. Somebody had pecked "Fuck you and your fucking apple seeds" all across her rib bones.

The police never found who did it.

Chloe and me, we know the birds did it.

You could still see them.

In her house, they slouched behind the drawn curtains. Shadows of birds. Stalking the night air. I wanted to move far away, always afraid that the birds would come after me in the night and peck sentences into my dead chest.

Chloe said that's unpossible. "Our elf would protect us. Birds are the natural enemy of elves. That's why elves grow apples, to use them as weapons against the dark bird army, led by the ravenous King Crow."

Some things Chloe said are just bullshit.

It's hard to tell which is which, but this was one of those times. King Crow? Who ever heard of such crazy garbage?

—

While Chloe was upstairs masturbating in the shower to REM's "Orange Crush," Gogongretinsobwimsoboyin told me the story of how he was born. It went like this:

—

My mother was a racehorse, and my father was the devil. A giant stole a rock from the heart of the sun and tried to sell it to my dad. Pops was infertile (mostly because he was infernal), and mom gave all her eggs to charity.

So, the giant sold my dad this rock saying it was an egg. "Hot damn!" The devil thought, "Now I'll have an offspring, and I'll finally be as cool as Zeus."

And he went and opened up my mom and stuck the rock inside of her. He placed it between her stomach and her ribcage, hoping that I would grow there. Little did that Giant know, but this rock (since it was from the sun) was a magic rock. It contained the meaning of the stars encrypted on its stomach. So while the rock was in her, the words began rubbing up against her bones, scratching themselves into her insides.

This caused the rock to fuse in her womb and transform into me. Little me. All the rubbing must've brought me out. So there I was, all warm and cozy. I stayed in there for fourteen years. Why would I go out? I wasn't going to leave unless I had to.

Too bad my dad was the devil. 'Cause eventually he forced me to come out. He laid some soup next to my mom's vagina, and I just couldn't resist. Out I came, crawling and mewling and hungry for soup. When my dad saw that I was an elf, he got pissed off and sent me to live with my own kind.

They eventually adopted a little girl from China and called her their true daughter and just ignored me. Which is fine, because they're both assholes. I hear that someday that little girl is going to kill them all. It's a prophecy that the elves talk about almost daily. They don't like the devil and his racehorse wife. He was an apple hater and a bird lover. She crocheted and picked her teeth with a shotgun. Nasty habits. Nasty, nasty habits.

—

When he finished his story, the house vibrated with the sounds of Chloe cumming. I gave him an apple. It wasn't an elf apple, but a granny smith. It was a good story and deserved something.

Too bad I'd forgotten that elves used apples as weapons.

—

I wondered if entrails of elves would be elftrails.

I wanted to open up Gogongretinsobwimsoboyin and find out.

Chloe wouldn't let me.

Fuck, I'm hungry.

—

After work I came home to find my living room floor covered in apples. Red and green and reddish green apples. When I walked in, I walked on them and left a carpet of apple pieces across the floor behind me. I found Chloe in my bedroom, dancing on my bed and dressed like a pirate.

"Arrr, Matey!" she screamed, "Avast! Ahoy!"

I asked her if she left the apples on the floor. She looked at me blankly and said, "What apples," pulling back her eye patch to show her violet eyes, "There weren't any apples there a minute ago."

I shrugged my shoulders and got changed into my own pirate uniform. It wasn't worth wasting Pirate Friday on something as strange as apples.

—

You used to be able to see elf faces peering up out of the sewer grates, their eyes watching you walk down the street, staring at you. Sometimes they would throw apples at your head, and you'd have to duck or else be smitten by the striking, and follow that elf until the end of time.

These days the sewers are empty.

No more dodging apples.

No more kicking their eyeballs in.
It used to be familiar.
Now, nothing is.
I wonder where they all went?

—

The birds became restless.
I saw them in our neighbors' houses.
They planned, they plotted.
They made diagrams and wore eye patches.
It's not Pirate Friday, I thought, what gave them the right to wear eye patches? You could smell revolution cooking in that house. It painted the air with its vibrations.

—

I tried to get into the sewers last week. I pried open the grates and covered my mouth. That funk was too much, the stink clung to everything. I just couldn't bring myself to go down there. Even if it meant getting clues as to what happened to the elves.
Fuck the elves, I thought.
At least Gogongretinsobwimsoboyin was still around.

—

Chloe and me had one of those relationships where talking was overrated. Our conversations mostly led us to sex, and sometimes even our sex led us to sex. The only time we actually talked was during Pirate Fridays, and that was mostly "Arrr, Mateys" and "Shiver me timbers" and "Walk the plank, you lilly-livered varmint." I guess the meaning in our lives was always between the lines.
When I went over to her house, we let Gogongretinsobwimsoboyin do the talking for us. He would ramble on about the war of the Crow King, and talk about throwing apple bombs on Main Street. There were stories of apple terrorism in the streets of the Albino Parrot, and war tales from when the elves lay siege to the royal tree palace of the Underground Fish, who sided with the birds in the twenty-year war.

This may come as a shock to you, but, Gogongretinsobwimsobo-yin's stories aren't really all too interesting. He tended to bog every tale down with hours of describing useless household items that the elves used. One time, he spent the whole night describing an elf apple peeler and an elf apple gun.

Boring.

The only good stories where when he talked about his mom and dad. Then he got to the point, cut to the meat of the story. The nights when he told the good stories he got to eat. The nights when he told the bad stories he got electrocuted.

Elves are oddly resilient little bastards.

You can pump them with all sorts of electricity before they even scream, let alone die. We kept Gogongretinsobwimsoboyin for about four years before he expired on us. And right before he died, he told us the secret of elfin apple magic.

—

Now Chloe and me are the only people left who know apple magic. Everyone else is gone. The other elves left, and Gogongretinsobwim-soboyin is dead. We don't talk much, Chloe and me, but we do talk about the magic. We carve the apples and prepare for war.

—

Gogongretinsobwimsoboyin tried to free himself. He attacked Chloe and me with a granny smith we left him, carving it up into an apple bomb. The blast shattered a hole in the house and knocked us out. It took a week to get all of the broken glass out of our faces, and I still have scars across my eyes to this very day.

Gogongretinsobwimsoboyin knocked himself out with the blast. He should've been more careful with his aim. If he could've stayed conscious he might've been able to escape. Instead he got the beating of his life from Chloe.

—

I smelled the birds gathering for war.
    It reeked on this street.
    That pirate Friday we sat around all day, carving apples.
    Planning.
    When those birds rise up, we'll be waiting.
    Angry, ready.
    Eye patches on and black belts buckled.

THE HAPPINESS OF PINNED WINGS

Everybody carried a graveyard with them.

Sara carried hers in a small brown box of birthday candles in her left jean pocket. She believed that each candle still held the possibility of a wish—still contained that magical birthday ingredient that could make dreams come true. Each one, six in all, represented a dream that she desired to come true.

And each one was another gravestone.

Six friends dead, and she wasn't even twenty-five years old yet.

A wish for each of them, a wish for birthdays that would never be. A wish for the dead, for the dreaming. A wish for a time that is trapped in amber. Each year the list grows and grows. Sara never foresaw a future like this one. She never thought she would be a survivor.

And yet, here she is.

Surviving.

—

Small towns in northeast Ohio were known for their ruins. They were known for the massive, sprawling once-industrial factories now rotting in the open air from rust and neglect. They were known for their graveyards of industry, for their massive amounts of unemployed and neglected populations.

They were places where recessions ate away at the fabric of community, starving the population into bone-thin wraiths of their former selves. And there they hung in poverty under the shadow of the larger cities, the siren call of money and work and addictions calling out to them, reaching across the void of the landscape.

Dark Rivers was no different.

Even in the days of the living dead, when even a simple Joe without a college education could get a decent job killing zombies and burning the corpses, Dark Rivers had a staggering level of poor and underprivileged. All these hungry mouths to feed, and not a single job for them.

And it made the denizens restless.

Starved.

Ready to dream again.

Ready to dream for a bigger life than all of this.

Sara's dad was one of those dreamers.

She'd come home and see him sitting on the front porch, a piece of rolled paper in his lap and a long black pen scribbling ink in his scratchy and scattered handwriting. She would ask him what he was working on, and he would just hum to himself and scratch his beard, and then look off into the distance behind her.

Like something was there, inspiring him.

—

The first birthday candle was for Betty.

She died when Sara was six.

They were playing out in Sara's backyard.

Betty saw something in the woods.

Sara didn't want to follow.

A month later the police found Betty's teeth and nothing else. Two years later they saw Betty walking around town, toothless and armless and hungry. She'd become one of the living dead.

They say her own dad shot her.

They say he hanged himself the next day.

They say that the ground beneath his swinging body was still wet from his tears when the cops found him.

When it was Betty's birthday, Sara bought a candle and held onto it. She knew that it held a wish, and she knew it was Betty's wish, for certain.

—

Sara's boyfriend, Mack, lived down in the wastelands. That's the section of town that used to be next to the graveyards. Once the dead came up, that whole part of town turned into a warzone. Whole parts of the city were eaten away by blood and war.

Mack had a shack near the edge of it all. He worked as a meat man, a butcher of the dead. The city paid him pretty good to do it, and he enjoyed his job pretty well. He got to walk around the streets with a meat hook and a shotgun. He would shot them in the head and grab the body with his meat hook.

He would then drag the body to the pyre in the center of town and toss the body up on it. The flames would spit and sparkle, and he would just stand there and stare as the body burned like a log in a fireplace.

And he would smile.

For Mack this was the best job in the world. He got paid enough so that he never had to worry about money, and the hours were perfect. He got the day shift, and only had to work five hours a day. The rest of the day he spent with Sara, or in his shack reading a large stack of books he had accumulated beside his bed.

—

Mack's shack smelled like burning meat.

The whole of the wasteland stunk like it.

Sara could never get used to the smell.

That's why she still lived with her dad instead of Mack. That, and her dad got stranger and stranger. He got more and more distant as time went on. Sara worried about him. Worried that he was slowly going insane after all of these years of grief.

—

The second candle was for Sara's mom.

Everyone called her Mom, and everyone loved her. She would make them Kool-Aid and play with all her friends in the backyard. She was much more than a mom to them. She was a best friend and a confidant.

And she could hold her own against the zombies, too. She worked as a meatman back in the early days, when it was only one or two corpses and it was easy to take them down. She remembered her mom taking off the head of a zombie with the edge of a spade.

Her mom died in her sleep.

Nobody knew what happened.

There were flowers shoved in her mouth, all the way down her throat. And her eyes were removed and replaced with wet stones.

—

Each birthday adds up.

Each wish adds up.

Each candle adds up.

Someday, Sara will buy a match.

And then all those wishes will be put to good use.

And Sara won't have a graveyard in her pocket.

All her memories of the dead will be gone.

Up in smoke.

Burnt away into whisps of wishes.

—

Mack and Sara liked to go down to the ruins of the old mall in the next town over and wander around inside and drink cheap booze from a brown bag. There was some harmony here, Sara thought. Some harmony amongst the wild vines reclaiming the mannequins and the scattered displays of consumer lust.

Sara liked the old bookstore best.

There were still old cases and displays, the books scattered and waiting for readers when they came in. The ceiling was porous, and she could see the stars yawning out from behind the black branches of trees.

She read passages of Yeats out loud while Mack applauded. Sometimes, when they were really drunk they would set fire to the books by Hegel, calling him a fascist of time travel, dancing around the flames in a Dionysian celebration.

By midnight the bottles would be empty, and they would be naked under the big broken dome of what was once a food court, spent from each other's bodies and letting the cool of the night air wash over them. They heard owls hooting in those hours, and the sound of nature reclaiming the world of man.

—

The third candle was for Mack's sister, Amy. Amy and Sara were in the same grade, and they spent their whole life in the same classes together. When they were younger, Mack would make Amy eat mud, and would try and scare her friends with his howling and mad gibbering.

It struck Sara really hard when Amy died.

They found her body one morning, in the ruins of an apartment building in the warzone. She was seventeen, and she had died of a drug overdose. She had just gotten out of rehab, and Sara thought she seemed so bright and full of hope.

Mack was the one who found her.

Amy was lying on the floor, naked, pictures painted all over her skin. She had her eyes wide open, and her mouth twisted into a pumpkin-mask rictus of happiness. He said a prayer over her body, shot her in the face, and then dragged her with his meathook to the fires.

That night Mack and Sara did not go out drinking.

They stayed in Mack's shack, and smelled the burning meat, and watched the television, looking for a sign of hope amongst the canned laughter and drama.

—

One night, when her father slept out on the porch with his gun on his lap, Sara decided to go through his bedroom and find his notebooks. She wanted to read what he'd been working on so far, and try and figure out a way of helping him move back into the father she once knew.

This man wore her father's face, but it was not him under the skin. Sara knew this. Ever since her mother died, her father was haunted by something else. Something darker, and depressed. Something that wanted to drag him down into the abyss.

She found the stack of notebooks under his pillow. She opened them, and read. She saw diagrams of machinery, each page whittling it down and perfecting his vision. She saw equations of complexity, narrowing down on each page into something simpler with time.

She saw in his madness what he was trying to build.

A time machine.

A time machine to bring her mother back.

She closed the books and resisted the urge to burn them. She walked back out to the porch, hugged his sleeping body, and then went over to Mack's. She made love to Mack under the rot of his roof, the smell of burning flesh hanging in the air around them.

—

Some days when Mack didn't feel like working, he would go down to Lake Erie and toss some stones into the water, skipping them against the rising arms of the waves. When he did this he remembered when his parents took him down here, and they had a picnic together.

He skipped stones with his sister, and he tried to get farther than she did. Often he would, his stones just flinging out of reach of hers.

These days were the hardest for him.

He had no grave for his sister or his parents.

No graves to visit, no graves to grieve on.

Only those licking flames, that burning pyre, which ate at the bodies with a hungry heat.

And these waves.

The endless waves to toss stones at.

To get lost in.

—

Candles four and five were for Mack's parents.

Sara never asked him how or why.

She just held his hand as he hoisted them into the fire. Later that day, she bought an orange candle for his mom and a green one for his dad. She never told Mack about the candles, and he never asked her about their significance.

They had a relationship based on secrets.

A foundation of mysteries between them.

—

Some days Mack wished he could drown in the Lake.

On those days Sara was the only thing keeping him alive. Her rough fingers and smooth features could keep him trapped here on earth forever, keeping him grounded in her and beneath the crushing waves of despair.

—

When Sara was eight, her father taught her how to catch butterflies, and then pin them into books labeling each body part. At first she was horrified by doing this. She wanted to let each butterfly live, let each one run free in the world.

But she found a strange joy in dissecting them. Found a perverted sense of happiness when she pinned the wings just right and labeled everything perfectly. When she was nine she had over 200 butterflies, all properly labeled and pinned into an album.

Her dad was very proud of her.

She still had that book hidden under her bed.

At night she heard whispers from it while she tried to sleep, and wondered if insects were affected by the undead plague. If somehow she had zombie butterflies fluttering about under her bed, their pins still stuck in their bodies and clicking as they flew about. Looking to feed on living insects in a sort of undead cannibalism.

She never looked under the bed, for fear she would be right. She never wanted to hurt them, never wanted to make them into the living dead. She just wanted to make perfect diagrams, perfect little labels.

—

After a week of having to steal canned food from the mall the next town over, Sara realized that she needed to get a job. Her dad was fired from his factory when it got attacked by the living dead. Now that factory is down in the wastelands, almost eaten away by misuse and ruin. He can't work anymore now—his mental state was unsuitable for any work that was available now.

And they needed to eat somehow.

So she went down to the wasteland with Mack and applied for a job as a meatman. They tested her mental stability, her reflexes, and her speech cognition. They treated her like some workhorse, peering under her gums and tapping on her knees to make sure she was strong and capable.

They next day she was working for the government. She had a meat hook of her own, and a sawed off shotgun she was pretty decent with. In the first day alone, she caught fifteen zombies and tossed them onto the hungry flames.

Just like the butterflies, she thought.

I am so good at dealing with death.

This is the perfect job for me.

—

After work each day Sara and Mack would go and get some food and then cook at her place. They would have a big dinner with her dad, and her dad would just sit and grin and barely eat anything.

After that they would head back over to the old mall and drink the night away. She felt bad for leaving dad at home on these nights, but he was so distant and different now. He was almost completely consumed by the time machine, all day working on his diagrams and equations.

—

One night they were in the sports store, trying on different old sporting equipment. She tried on a jockstrap just to see what it felt like, and found it funny to have a hockey mask on her crotch. He ran around wearing a baseball shirt and nothing else, swinging a baseball bat around and singing an out-of-tune song.

When they were done they climbed the vines out and onto the crumbling roof of the store. They could overlook the forest around Dark Rivers, and see the orange light of the bone fires several towns over, like orange eyes scattered across the world.

"Do you know any of the constellations?" she asked Mack.

Mack grinned.

"Yeah, a few. Why?"

She shrugged and leaned into his shoulder.

"I've never had any of them pointed out before."

He pointed upwards, her eyes following his arm.

"That's Orion there. You can tell by his belt."

She nodded.

"And there is Perseus, and the head of the Gorgon Medusa. And over there are the Pleiades."

She kissed his neck.

"Thank you," she said.

He shrugged.

"But I'm not done yet."

She felt like changing the subject for some reason.

"You ever wonder why I have those candles."

He looked at the fires below them.

"No. And don't tell me either. I like us having some secrets. It keeps us new."

She sighed, and wondered if he was right.

—

The last candle was her own.

She hasn't had a birthday party since her sixteenth birthday. On that day she bought a candle for herself, and never lit it. It stayed with the others, hanging out with the candles for the dead.

Maybe I'll get to use this, she thought, *before I'm dead as well. Maybe not.*

Sometimes, that's just how things go.

—

Sara awoke to the sound of clicking underneath her bed, and pulled the covers up over her head. Maybe the darkness can save me, she thought. Maybe I can hide in here forever, and never have to go out and be a meatman ever again.

Maybe I can stay in here, and Mack can come and live in here too. And we can build a castle under the sheets, and in the castle we could have everything we ever wanted. And there would be no dead wishes in my pocket, and no zombie butterflies under my bed.

And no dad building a time machine in the backyard.

—

Mack slept off his drunk sick in the back of an old shoe store. All around the floor were slippers of gold and bronze and yes, even a few made of glass. Sara was awake next to him, watching the ruins of the mall light up slowly with the waking sun. *It's like I've got three homes right now*, she thought.

I've got a shack with Mack that smells like meat.

I've got my home with my dad, and he scares me.

I've got this rambling old mall, and it feels like home.

Funny that this feels right, that this feels like home. Funny how only when I sleep here, so lost in the woods and away from Dark Rivers, funny how I feel so happy. I want this happiness, all this happiness, and I want it all the time.

Sara pulled out a silver candle.

She lit it and released the smell of birthday cake and wax into the shoestore. She made a wish, held her breath. She closed her eyes, and exhaled.

I've just used up Betty's wish, she thought.

—

The next day, work was brutal, and she thought for certain that her wish hadn't come true. Maybe, she thought, it was because Betty had been dead for so long. Maybe that's why the wishing didn't work.

She slaved next to Mack, and the two of them became slick with sweat in the summer sun. She felt sick and dazed, and drank more water than she ever should have. The air was cruel and humid, and the breath of the pyre left her skin sore and red from its heat.

When no one was looking she pulled out the second candle and lit it. She held her breath and wished. Wished and thought and poured her mind into it. When she exhaled, the smell of burning meat was replaced for a brief moment with the scent of balloons and birthday presents.

I've just used up my mother's wish, she thought.

—

There was a large machine in the front yard. It greeted Mack and Sara with large tube arms and glittering bronze hair. It smiled with teeth of cages, and it hummed with the electricity of the ages. In the jar of its stomach whispered the wings of zombie butterflies, clicking against the edge of the glass, beating to be free.

"What the fuck is that?" Mack asked, putting his arm around Sara's waist.

The eyes of the machine glittered in life.

"That," said Sara, "Is a time machine."

Mack laughed.

"You don't say?"

She moved back a little, hesitant to walk past it.

"Yes. I do say. I think my dad's been building it."

Mack shrugged and walked forward, close to it.

"You think it will work?"

Sara moved a little farther back.

"I don't know," she said, "Maybe?"

He tapped the edge of the glass.

"These butterflies have pins in them."

She nodded.

"I know. Come on, Honey, let's go inside."

—

Over the smell of steaming chicken, Mack asked her dad about the time machine. "When did you build it? How does it work? Do you think it will work?"

Her dad laughed, his stomach growling from hunger. Sara noticed that he had a spring in his step lately, was more lively and less obsessed. Like finishing this machine gave him a better outlook on life. Like the machine ripped out the pessimism and replaced it with hope.

"One question at a time boy. One question at a time. I built it today. Building it was the easy part. The hard part was designing it. Getting the math right. It works, my dear boy, by harvesting the paradox of the undead."

Mack leaned forward as Sara cooked in the kitchen. Drops of rain echoed against metal pans, the holes in the ceiling making their voices known. "The paradox of the undead? I'm not sure I follow, man."

Her dad leaned in, forward. His hands held on his lap. "Look, death is the absence of life, right? And life is the absence of death. The two are binary states, opposing each other. But, if something is both dead and alive it creates a paradox. It is true and false at the same time. This paradox creates a rip in reality. A hole in the time stream. If we can harness this, BAM! We can travel through time. Got it?"

Mack smiled.

"Sure, old man. Let's say I believe you. Can we bring things from the past back?"

Her dad shook his head.

"I hope so. I hope so. If not, everything I've done so far has been wasted."

Sara came out of the kitchen.

"You guys are idiots! You cannot bring them back to life! They are dead, understand? You can't just rip a hole in the universe to bring someone back!"

Her dad smiled at her.

"If Orpheus can crawl into Hades for his love, I can crawl through a hole in the universe for mine."

Sara stormed back into the kitchen.

Mack looked at him.

"Take me with you."

Her father nodded.

"Of course."

The smell of birthdays wafted out of the kitchen as Sara made two wishes. She wished that her father would stay, and she wished that Mack would stay. That no one would leave her ever again.

I've just used up my Mack's parents wishes, she thought.

—

The sound of zombie butterflies haunted the air.

While Sara slept on peacefully, both Mack and her father walked up to the machine. They tapped it, and turned some knobs. The butterflies flew in circles, blue light emanating from them as the machine harvested their paradoxical nature. The air screamed.

And then the machine growled.

A flash of shadows.

Mack and her father were gone, the machine a pile of ash where they stood.

—

Sara couldn't work the next day.

She took the ashes of her father and Mack, took the ashes of that damned machine and drove all the way to the ruins of the mall. She went to the bookstore and scattered their ashes, and she pulled out the last candle.

Her candle.

And she held her breath.

She wished that everything wrong was right.

That the castle under her sheets was real.

She lit it.

Exhaled.

The smell of birthdays gone wrong crowded her head. Of clowns that were not entertaining, but dark and sinister. Of getting presents of dead animals and screaming boxes. She smelled birthdays where you were buried in the ground and locked in cages. Birthdays were you were lucky to eat.

And she heard a sound.

Like dust, moving in the breeze.

And voices.

"Sara," they said, "Sara, we want our wishes back."

She walked outside, and heard footsteps wandering in the ruins of the mall. She looked around and saw no one. She called out, but nothing answered.

She was about to go back in the bookstore when she felt a cold and wet hand against her shoulder. She turned around and saw six people. Not zombies, not ghosts, but the shadows of the past leaking in through the hole in time and space. A living paradox, hungry and supernatural.

"What do you want?" she asked the shadows.

"You stole our wishes," they said, "We came to get our wishes back."

She backed away. The room smelt like hunger and birthdays, smelt like fire and death. It smelt like burning meat and cigars on skin. "I can't give them to you. They didn't even come true anyway."

"That's because," one shadow said, "They were our wishes. The wishes of the dead. Give them back to us, or face our revenge."

Sara screamed.

Screamed.

She hoped that the scream would go through the hole in time and space. She hoped that her scream would carry across the paradoxes of the world. She hoped that her scream would save her, in the end, in the end.

But no help came.

Nothing.

Just the empty mall.

And the wishes of the dead coming true.

THE LAST STAND OF THE ANTMAKER

1

When Benjamin was a little boy he painted things. Mostly small things. Like tiny houses. Or dinosaur kits. Or invisible men. He liked using the small brushes. Painting tiny, intricate details.

His hand would cramp up by the end of the day. Painful. Claw shaped. He liked the way this felt. It felt like a good day's work. He would line up his tiny pieces of art and look at them. Hand clawed up. Smiling. His room smelling of paint fumes.

He didn't have any friends. He didn't like to read, watch television, play video games. In school he daydreamed about painting. His teachers thought he was slow. He didn't go near anyone. Could not relate to them.

His mind focused on his hobby. It was all-consuming.

2

You would think that an older Benjamin would be different. That he would work, joke around with colleagues. Go to the bar after a hard day at the office. Hit on the waitresses. Make jokes. Get married, even. Have a few kids, even. Forget all about painting.

It actually got worse. His mother died. Cancer. Isn't it always? After that he got the house. All paid off. He only worked when he needed food. And that he bought in cans by the truckload.

He rarely had to work. Instead, he painted. His obsession had gotten more distinct. More of a laser point in the darkness. Ants.

At first he bought model kits through the mail. Ordered them on the internet. That wasn't enough. He began to make his own. Taking apart pieces of his house. Tearing off chunks of wall. Chiseling off chunks of concrete steps. Making little ant bodies, little ant heads. His fingers cramping. Always cramping. As he molded. As he painted.

He would sit in his basement. A can of fruit open on his lap. A spoon resting plainly. Fine and tiny brush pushed into cramped claw fingers. Painting. Intricate designs. War ants. Love ants. Fire ants. Firefighter ants. Giant ants. Tiny ants. Shaman ants. God of the ants.

The basement was filled with ants. It was like his own ant farm. Made large.

3

He made highways for them. Byways for them. All the while not noticing that the plants grew outside of his basement window. Not noticing the yellow spores covering it. Tapping against it. Like fingers. Rat-tat tapping.

He built ant houses. Ant shrines. Ant cities on an ant hill. Ant bonfires. Ant beaches. And ant graveyards for those who died during the great ant civil war.

Eventually, he had to go upstairs and find supplies. To make more ants. To make more houses, homes, tunnels. To enhance the life of those he created. He was a good god. A good maker. A benign and loving deity. Whenever an ant died, he wept. They died frequently. Of war, of plague. The ant doctors and the ant scientists tried to stop it. To hold back death.

Not even he could do that. Not even the ant maker could hold off death.

4

There was a girl. Isn't there always? She was eighteen when he first met her. She moved in. Next door. With her husband, Gary. Gary drove a truck. Ate baked beans from a can. She was pregnant. Always pregnant. Although they never seemed to have any kids.

Benjamin knows he would've noticed kids. Kids are loud. Kids destroy. They would've gotten into his house. Gotten to his ants and killed them. Killed them all. He would've had to make a mass grave. One the size of his whole backyard.

Thankfully, they did not have kids.

The girl's name was Emily. She had short black hair. Benjamin thought she was pretty. Every once in a while, she would be bored. Come over and try to talk to him. To make conversation. Benjamin wasn't good at conversation.

All he wanted to do was talk about his ants. She didn't seem to mind. And she was pretty. Benjamin liked her.

5

He didn't like Gary. Her husband drank. A lot. Called Benjamin "That fucking 'tard monkey next door." He would pat his round stomach. Scratch his bearded face. Belch. Laugh.

No, no. Benjamin didn't like him.

6

Benjamin liked lists. Lists and ants and Emily. Lists were perfect. Were cathartic. They helped him organize. He had boxes of lists. Shoved throughout the house.

One list he had was very important. It was a daily list. Each day, marked down. Day, month, year. And beside it was an observation. One that bothered Benjamin.

The plants were growing.

It bothered him so much that he only took notice of it once a day. First thing in the morning. Before the sun came up. When the plants were still sleeping. He would look out the windows. Measure them with his eyes. Mark down their height on his list.

Then he would be back making ants.

7

Emily was a gardener. When she would stop by to talk to Benjamin she would have dirt on her hands. Under her nails. Sweat on her brow. Sometimes, she would bring him food. Garlic. Things of that sort. Grown in the garden.

Benjamin kept a list of what she brought over. Kept a list of the days she dropped by. He checked the list yesterday. It had been two weeks.

That made Benjamin sad. That made Benjamin worry. It didn't last long. He added new notes to the lists. Put them in their shoe boxes. Shelved them away. Began working on the ants.

Something smelled funny in the air. He pulled out a box of allergy masks he kept in the basement. Next to the lists. And the dead ants. Strapped it to his face. Breathed easier.

Back to work.

8

Emily dropped by. But this time it wasn't Emily. But it was. She was very pregnant. Yet she wasn't. Her eyes were full of green fluid. Leaking onto her cheek. Her face was spotted. Cracking. Her hair had vines wrapped up in the blonde curls. When she smiled, Benjamin saw leaves behind her teeth.

They talked like they usually did. About the usual things. Benjamin talked about ants. She talked about gardening. About having a baby. A boy, this time. She was sure of it. Maybe Gary would let this one live? She didn't know. Won't know until afterward.

Benjamin felt like something was off. Something was different about her. She was pretty, still, yes. But she was greener. And smelled of wet earth and mushrooms growing in a cave.

When she left Benjamin was sad. He hadn't been sad since his mom had died. Cancer.

9

The ants weren't coming together. They were falling apart. Each piece, sliding. Damnit. He slammed them. Broke the pieces. This wasn't going right. He took his brush. Walked out of the basement. Upstairs.

This wasn't going right at all. He felt dizzy. His hands shook. A yellow pollen fluttered in the air. Like a mist. In his living room. He looked around. Saw that his living room had changed.

No, no, no. Not today. Why did this have to happen today? He wasn't finished yet. Not yet. Why couldn't this wait until he was finished?

10

He made a list of things wrong with the living room.
- The television is dead. Spiders in it.
- Vines on the ceiling. Floor.
- Plants burst through windows. Bushes.
- Red berries on the bushes. Poisonous?
- Ceiling covered in bugs.
- Yellow spores.
- Door is gone. Replaced by wall of roses.
- Thorns on roses. Ouch. Blood.
- Smells bad.

11

He wore his allergy mask. It helped him breathe better. Now that he could breathe he could work. Still dizzy, just not so much. Made more ants. They needed an ant army. Invaders. Plant invaders. Coming. Attacking.

We need a militia. Seven thousand strong. Will have to recruit civilians. Shamans. Priests. Firefighters. Ant families and ant children. This was a call of duty. A call to honor.

He fell asleep. Paintbrush in hand. Army at the ready.

12

Doorbell. Woke him. Stumbled upstairs. Paint covered hands. Clawed. Allergy mask on. Looked like survivor. Wanted to survive. The pollen was still there. Made walking hard. Like swimming.

He answered the rosebush. Ouch! Thorns. Forgot about those. It was Emily. Beautiful. Skin greenish blue. Eyes no longer leaking. But blossoming. Two flowers for eyes. Leaves sticking out of her hair. When she talked her voice sounded burbly. Like she was underwater. Or lungs full of water. Or drowning. Benjamin did not know which.

"Come outside," she said. "See the sun."

Benjamin looked behind her. There was no sun. Just pollen blotting it out. The world was a haze of yellow. Plants were everywhere. Pushing through concrete. Covering houses. Buildings. Cars.

"No thank you," he said. "I don't like the sun."

She smiled. So pretty.

"Come on, we can play. We can sing, we can dance. You can help me garden. We can catch bees and pollinate ourselves. Doesn't that sound nice?"

Benjamin liked that. Wanted that. But the ants were not finished. The army was not finished. He could not forget about the invasion. It was important. He shook his head. "The army needs me," he said. "My children need me."

She parted her lips. Like plums. "You can kiss me," she said. "I know you would like that. Come on, kiss me. Take that mask off. Kiss me. You can even cop a feel if you'd like. Gary wouldn't mind. Just take the mask off. Kiss me."

Benjamin began to pull the mask down. Was leaning in. Almost taken off. When he saw a yellow spider crawl out from between her lips. Scale up her face. Make a web between her two eye flowers.

He kept his mask on. *This isn't Emily*, he thought. Emily did not have spiders inside of her. Baby, yes. Spiders, no.

"Fine," she said. "I'll send Gary around. Maybe he can talk some sense into you."

Benjamin didn't like that. She slammed the rosebushes in his face. Stormed off. Even though she wasn't Emily he still didn't like making her sad. Or mad. It didn't sit well with him.

Depressed, he went back inside. Went downstairs. Continued to work.

13

There is never an entry for 13. It is unlucky.

14

The ant army was close to being finished. But not just yet. His hand cramped. He needed to hurry. The basement was the only room in the house still safe. Still uninfected. His hand itched as it clawed up. Itch, itch, itch. Felt like something crawling, growing under his skin.

He took some medicine. But the itch did not stop. The pain did not stop. He would have to be done painting for now. Building for now. He couldn't work. Not like this.

15

The rooms in the house infected with the garden:
- Living Room
    - No room to walk anymore
    - Even the floor is covered in weeds
    - Insects everywhere
    - Buzzing.
- Kitchen
    - Stove is now a rhododendron
    - Lilacs in the Frigidaire
    - Ceiling fan filled with vines
- Second Floor Bedrooms
    - Beds are trees. Cracking through ceiling.
    - Floor is moss. Green. Fuzzy.
    - Bookshelves are moldy.
    - Books are gone. Eaten by insects.
- Attic
    - No more attic. Just lattice of branches

16

There was a scratching at his basement window. Like a cat wanting to come in. Benjamin looked up. Saw a branch. Scratch, scratch, scratch. The doorbell rang.

Damnit, he thought. Almost finished. If only his hand had stopped itching. Stopped hurting. Stopped moving on its own. And now, now. His arm itched. His eyes itched. His lips and mouth itched.

He scratched, scratched, scratched. Even though it hurt. *I don't want to answer the door,* he thought. I don't want to prick myself on the rosebushes again.

It rang, it rang. Maybe it was Emily. He would like to see her again. Sigh. Scratch, scratch, scratch. He hoped she was all right.

17

He opened the rosebushes. Gary stood there. His skin was orange. He had flowers in his hair. In his neck. Poking through skin. His fingers were wrapped tightly with vines. His hands tensing. Clenching. Green knuckled. His eyes leaked onto his face. Two buds sticking out. Waiting to blossom.

"Hey, you. Fuckwad. My wife wants you outside. Enjoy the sunlight. Right? Come on. Get out. And take off that fucking mask. It makes you look stupid."

Benjamin looked at him. Gary. Shook his head. "No, no, I don't think so. I like it inside. I like my ants. I need to go and paint some more. Before my hand stops working."

"Come on. Get outside. Fucking idiot."

Hand lashed out, grabbed onto Benjamin's shoulder. Fingers dug deep into shoulder blade. Dragged him outside. Others on the street. Staring. Green skinned. Spider infested. The air wanted to choke him. Even with the allergy mask on.

"Come on, pansy. Take off the fucking mask already. Or do I have to take it off for you?"

Benjamin moved back, shoved Gary's hand off him. Skin was brittle, broke. Bones broke. Smell of rot. Spores flew out from the broken skin. Infecting the air. Little yellow things. Pollen. Dancing.

Beneath his broken skin was vegetation, curled up around bone. Benjamin leaned over. Tried not to vomit. Dry heaved. He looked back up. Gary laughed at him.

"Take off the mask. Or I'll take it off for you."

Benjamin saw a shovel in Gary's hand. Saw it rise up. Going to hit him. Going to hurt him. He moved out of the way. Shovel hit ground.

Stuck into it. Gary's skin cracked, broke a little. Vines and leaves peaked out. Pollen spread out.

Benjamin screamed. Ran inside. The others on the street turned. Looked at him. Followed with Gary. Even after Benjamin had slammed the rosebush shut. Even after he had run downstairs. Locked the basement door. Locked himself in.

He had enough canned food to last him a little while. Enough time to make his army. To make a stand against the invasion.

18

Nineteen left to go. Itch, itch. Scratch, scratch. Skin broke. Saw bits of leaves beneath. *No, no,* he thought. *Can't be happening.* He kept his mask on. Just in case.

Dizzy. Dizzy. Needed to finish.

A loud bang. On basement window.

He turned. He looked.

No. No. No.

Emily's face. Cold, white, pale. Porcelain. Like a doll. Her teeth parted. Leaves behind them. Leaf tongue. Leaf lips. Leaf uvula. Spiders ran over her face. She was on the ground.

More banging. On the basement door.

No. No. No.

19

Let them come. His army was ready. He was ready. He scratched. Itchity itch itch. It hurt. So much hurt. The army was poised. Ready. Set into fighting formation.

He had a list in his hand. Of all the things he wanted to do before the world died. Kiss a girl. Kiss the sun. Swallow the moon. Go fishing. Become a fish. Not die. Die over and over again. Live. Have something nice for dinner. Have someone nice over for dinner. To breathe again. To be again. Whole again. To raise a family. To raise the dead. To sing one last time. To have a sandwich. To try witchcraft. To burn the world. To be burned. To love. To live. To make something work. Just once. To make it work.

20

Breathe. Breathe. It felt so good to breathe without the mask on. Like breathing underwater. Walking like swimming. He no longer itched. It no longer hurt to paint. To do anything. Pain was distant. A memory. Like his childhood.

He leaned over. Kissed the glass. Where Emily's face was. Smiled. Her head burst. Blood. Pollen. And insects. Inside of her head was a tiny baby. An infant. Made of coiled up vines, and a face that was a flower blossoming. Two tiny eyes stared at him. Was it a boy? Benjamin hoped so. Emily would've been happy if it was a boy.

It crawled up to the window. Placed a hand against it. Benjamin felt connected to it. Wanted to take care of it. Felt something in his own mind. Growing.

He smashed the window. His basement door burst open. Now was the time for war. Now was the time to defend his lists. His sanctuary. His love.

WATCH ME BURN WITH THE LIGHT OF GHOSTS

White rabbit mask shouts, "Get on your knees!" and swings the assault rifle at Kit. And the white rabbit mask says, "Put your arms in the air like angels!" And so Kit gets on his knees. And puts his arms in the air. Like an angel.

The rabbit mask frisks him down and her breast touches his shoulder and he feels hot and sweaty. She walks down the aisle of cubicles. Other coders are kneeling. Some with head bowed, all with arms spread wide like wings. Her gun swings and thunder echoes as a body falls. Blood is on the mask. Blood is on the rifle. Red rabbit gun. Run. Run. Run. Other masks walk now up and down. Each one an animal. Each one carrying a rifle.

The Owl mask smokes a cigarette. He pulls it out of his mouth with his empty hand. He points at two or three programmers. Smoke stains his fingers yellow. Guns unslung, point at the people he marked for death. Everyone is quiet. Kit holds his breath.

The shots echo and the head spins and the ears buzz with the thunder of guns. Blood splashes on Kit's face and he is gone somewhere else elsewhere now. He can't hear anything anymore, just a buzz. Bees in his ears. Bees in his head.

—

Carol once found a dead cat in her backyard. Eight. Maybe nine. Maybe younger. Time was fluid back then. Time could not be trapped. Time devoured and swallowed. Like inky death.

The cat was rotting and the eyes bugged out and the skin crawled with maggots. Oh. The maggots all breathing. Gasp. She was transfixed. She wanted to pet it. She reached out. Touched close. Felt the squirm of corpse skin beneath fingers. Felt the world turn hazy.

The moment stayed with her. She made up stories about the dead cat. Eventually the skin sloughed off from the rain and the elements. And she put the skull in her Hello Kitty backpack. Nice and nestled under a sweater and her notebooks. Kept it on her every day. She's never showed anyone. Not even Kit.

The dead cat would whisper to her. It was a ghost cat, and it told her of Abhoth, of the dark, of the shadows. The chaos that waited for her in the void of it all. The corpse of the ghost cat whispered about Alueb Gnashel, and his ghost followers polluting the world and making everything haunted with their touch. This was something she would carry with her even now. His teaching was so poignant. Even the master would agree.

She liked the way the cat skull smiled. She hoped someday to smile like that, too.

—

The rabbit mask pulls him up, forces his arms behind his spine. Clank. Metal on wrists, pinning them to his back. She leans over, whispers into his ear. "You will die. You will die and become one with fire."

And then she shoves him and he walks. Others are getting up and walking, while still others are being shoved down and shot. One, two, three. Make sure they're dead. Make sure they stop moving.

Kit knows these dead people. He's coded with some of them, sharing space, sharing monitors, yelling at each other in assembly. He stole a kiss from one once. Now she has a bullet in her head. Her name is a wound.

They force him to start jogging out. Out of the office. Out into the labyrinth of hallways. Out into the parking lot. The stars are hungry in the sky.

—

Ghosts moving. Gunshots duck down another one falls. Sirens wailing and then cars like halos in the night. Burning holes into shadows. Rabbit mask pulls him back, the brick wall behind him shatters with each shot. Holes in the walls that could've been holes in him. She smells like burnt coffee and ink stains.

She fires her gun. It explodes next to him, burns his shirt. He almost faints. He keeps himself calm and real and in the now by reciting programming code in his mind. It is a litany. A zen koan. Meaningless in this life, in this situation. Yet before? Before it was living. It was breathing. It was making the computer do as you will.

—

"Crawl up here and see if they can see us.."

Kit crawls through broken glass. He pushes webs from his face. Some still have spiders on them. He moves vines aside. Looks out the factory window. Down out there on the street are spotlights and strobe lights and uniforms with bullhorns shouting things.

"Well?"

"No, they don't see us."

"Get back down then, come on."

Kit wasn't sure if he wants to keep on living anymore.

—

Ten-year-old Carol got lost in the caves behind her house. She'd been gone for days. Kit was the one who had found her. Starved and eating poisonous berries and getting sick. Rail thin and thirsty and delirious from the world.

The ghost cat kept her company. Skull speaking softly. Told her the future, of how they would free the world from the prison of skin and shadow. That she would join that master, and follow him into the truth of it all. To see the world as it really was, haunted by the million dead. And that yes, Kit would be so important in the last days. The end days. The days of ghost fires and laughter in the dark. Telling her how important he was when he came to her then. A chosen one for the void. Olkoth, Olkoth, Olkoth.

And at first she thought he was a bear. And she hugged him. And called him a nice bear. They were in the newspaper and everything. The town called him a hero. They gave him accolades and her parents thanked him over and over again.

After that. After that. She wasn't allowed to go anywhere without supervision. She was clever, though. She found ways to sneak around. To go over to Kit's house and spy on him. His sister became her best friend.

They would play with cap guns in the backyard. Dressed like ballerinas and firing off their plastic pistols. The air smelled like gun powder. Bang. Bang. Bang.

—

"It's all over now, just look around you," Owl mask talks with a voice like bombs in the heart. "The dead and the living are side by side. You can tell, can't you? If you can't yet, well then, you will. You'll soon be able to tell the dead from the living. The dead have a way of moving, a way of talking. They talk with ghost words, they speak only with the sentences of the dead. See here now—it's not just people, you understand? It's buildings, too. We need to destroy the ghost buildings. That's where the dead build their nests, you see? We need to fight this back. The apocalypse is here, and we're fighting it, you get me? We're the front lines to a hidden war that's going to bring about the end times the all times the death times! You have to be brave. You have to kill the things that are inside of you, trying to stir you up and want to live. We no longer have the luxury of self-preservation. See that death drive we got inside of each of us? It coils around like a snake and now we've got to let it strangle us—we have to tighten up that snake, let it ride our blood. That is the only way we can live, you understand? That is the only way we can survive! We have to give into death. Become death. Become a vessel for Alueb Gnashal, became the weapon of the Nameless Mist! We will be the ones who take the ghosts back home again. We will be the ones who are chthonic in all things!"

Owl mask sits down. Sirens surround them. Smoke from the fires they set make him half visible in the redblue light of the police cars.

"You were chosen, each of you, destined for this. We have been planning your emancipation for ages. Don't you see that they have you hypnotized? You don't even know the world is ending, not until I told you. They hide this fact from you, but look, look at the world! Look around us now! Turn off the television noise that was pumped into your skull since birth and really look really see everything. See how we live in a haunted void, and only by embracing the Anaath configuration, and worshipping Gaeytlu, the Undying Bear God, can we emancipate ourselves from this prison of skin and shadow."

The fire the light and they hear beyond it all this thrum. It was an end of the world thrum. Like the sound of the earth dying.

"Now we die! Do you see? Death is our only chance of living again! Go on, let's go, let's take these ghosts with us, drag them into this other life!"

—

Fishmask hands out the gasoline and then we do it. We set ourselves on fire. We run into the world burning up and we don't feel it. How could we not feel it? There is a singing from the flames. Beautiful. It made me feel holy with my light.

—

Eventually they drag Kit back and suffocate the light on his skin with a blanket. They place him in a casket and he doesn't even scream. He doesn't even move. They carry him, funeral procession, moving him forward. All of the others from the cubicle had been shot or burned to death or were taken back to custody with the police. Kit and the masks were the only survivors.

The masks carry him down to the abandoned library, now mostly a concrete shell with rotting books inside. They set him down, iron wires overhead in a spiderweb of metal. He's breathing still, and they place the lid on the casket. Birds flutter in the high ceilings. They push through the broken glass doors, into what remains of the building inside.

Smashed statues, tattered books, dead birds scattered on the floor. The world outside is a constant sunset red. The air tastes like napalm.

One by one they pull off their masks and set them on top of his coffin. They are wiry, worn down, their faces grungy and unwashed for weeks. Owl mask has burn scars on his real face, like he tried to eat the sun.

They pray over Kit's body. Birds flutter and the sound of the sea carries a steady rhythm, keeping time to their voices like a heartbeat.

—

Oh remember. Remember. Carol. Do you remember how you buried your dolls? And dreamt of them coming back to life. You would pop the heads off and line them up so nice and neat. Just as a precaution. To make sure the dolls stayed dead. Do you remember Carol?

Kit's sister stopped playing with you that week. She found the doll graveyard and found the cat skull. And she saw you drinking Kool-Aid and claiming it was laced with poison.

Do you remember, Carol? Do you remember . . .

—

They knock on the casket.

—

Kit pushes it open with his hands and there they sit all around him. The masks are in their laps and he just sits still. They watch each other. They study each other for a moment. The woman with the rabbit mask in her lap says, "Who are you now?"

Kit shakes his head.

Owl mask looks at him. Repeats the question. They all repeat the question.

"I don't know," and Kit really doesn't know who he is anymore.

"That's good."

"It is?"

"Now you know your true self."

"No, no I don't. I don't know anything, I just feel this empty hole where myself should be."

"Exactly. Now you have no name. Now you are truly the hungry void."

They stand and lead him back into the library, far deep within the shelves. Kit realizes the girl with the rabbit mask—he knows her. Where does he know her? He tries to place her as they walk. The others say nothing. No one speaks, they just move, all in sync, towards the far back where a dim light is warm and welcoming.

—

A taxidermy bear sits and waits for them. Someone had sewn four heads to the body, each one with a different expression, each one mocking a human emotion. That is something bears do not have. Human emotions. The arms are raised up the air like an angel's. Inside of each mouth is a tiny orange light. Perhaps a flashlight. Perhaps an LED light. The glow makes the eyes look like lamps in the dark corner.

Later they will tell him the name of the bear. Gaeytlu. the Undying One. The lord of restless dead.

—

Someday Carol hopes the sun will set and devour the earth.

—

They all kneel in front of the bear and Kit follows. He doesn't quite understand. He's not sure if he wants to understand. They don't say anything for a moment, they only kneel. Eventually the earth shakes from a nearby train and they stand.

"Get him a gun," and they slide their masks on, "And a mask. I dunno. Maybe get him, um, the noh mask we got in the back."

"Noh mask?"

"Yeah. That one, you know it. Get him that one."

"Okay, yeah. Okay."

And she leads Kit away from the others by the hand. Her hand feels rough and strange. Probably from the gun and the violence. She moves in front and her hair bobs back and forth in a ponytail. He sees her turn her head, making sure he's following her, and that's when he sees it. He sees it.

"You . . . you friended me on Facebook last month. How do I know you?"

"I've always followed you closely, watching you. Don't you know who I am?"

Kit doesn't know the answer to that. So he stays silent.

—

Carol was raised Catholic in a Catholic school. Could still smell candlewax burnt and stuck to her fingertips. Incense and burning things always made her think of tortured saints. Those bloodied bodies stretched out on the racks. Beautiful. Beheaded. Some eyeless and some with a crown of candles.

She would imagine herself blind and tormented like that. Religion wasn't peace or love or beauty. No. It was the suffering. It was that feeling you got when devoured by the infinite. The cat skull showed her the truth of this. Whispered of the friends she would make later. And how Kit was really Olkoth, and how she had to help him achieve the truth of it all. One day, one day. One day with guns. One day with a rejection of a kiss.

As a teen she rebelled. Smoked cigarettes. Screamed. Was considered troubled and dark and that's what she wanted. Troubled. Dark. Sorrowful. Those things were all saintly. She broke into places and stole things. She got mixed up with the wrong crowd.

Those were her moments of horrible divinity. A terrible grace brought on by collision with the infinite.

—

She slides the mask over his face and he stops her, keeping it on his forehead and no further. She isn't wearing her mask yet either. He pulls her in to kiss and she pushes him back and laughs. "No, not at all. I'm the master's."

"Who? That guy?"

"Yeah, that guy. He owns all of us, didn't you get that? You too, Kit. Can't you understand that? With him we act as one, as one force, as one being. Apart? We are just voids drifting into a dead world. How could he be right? How could that be good? He gives me purpose and being. He gives us all purpose and being. I heard of the dark and undying ones all of my life, but he . . . he gave it skin and bone. I could touch the infinite through him, and it was so powerful. You understand? Someday you will touch Gaeytlu and feel the weight of promises and completely get what I'm talking about. You'll understand our purpose, and how we will save the world from all the dead around us."

Kit slides the mask over his face. White porcelain. The features unreal, mostly shadows. You tilt the head, the face smiles. You tilt the head and the face frowns. You tilt the head and the face is screaming.

"Purpose? I thought we were nothing. I thought we were nameless."

"We are, can't you see? We are."

"And so is he."

She walks away slowly, turns and looks at him. She looks worried. She looks concerned. "When you say things like that I realize you don't understand at all. I'm afraid I'm not sure we can give you a gun, not just yet."

—

The master tosses Kit a gun anyway. Kit is the only one wearing a mask now. He doesn't want to take it off. The mask gives him power. It makes his face look like the numb emptiness that swims around inside of him. The others are still wearing their faces. They still cling to this idea of personality. Not Kit. Kit wears the face of the void.

He grabs the gun in midair, turns it in his hands. It is black. Shiny. Full of death. Rabbit mask looks so nervous. Kit points the rifle at her. Click, click. The safety is still on. And then, yes. Then he remembers. She spoke to a cat skull. She called it, what did she call it? She gave it a name. He couldn't remember the name, but he could remember the skull. And the way it made him feel. Alone. Lonesome. Haunted in the heart of the world.

"Carol," he says to her, "Your name is Carol. You were my sister's best friend, I remember that now. Didn't you used to come over to our house and watch me sleep? Didn't I save you from a cave?"

She slides her mask on. "No," she says in a small voice, "no."

—

The hundred heads of Gaeytlu spoke to me last night and whispered of the ghosts and we have to act now. We have to go in guns out and set ourselves on fire again, with our death surrounding us in a bright brilliant orchestra of light. The end is here already, the giants of the sea are waking, and the ghosts are singing the songs of the dead to the sun again. I can hear them in every waking moment, the earth is dead, they sing. The earth is now our home, they sing. They hypnotize the living with sitcoms and we just laugh and let them do it. The internet is a ghost dream, and it controls our thoughts with rampant memes. Look at them sleep walking about, look at them slumber eyes all crusted shut. When the giants wake and rise from the sea and the ghosts sing the last song, then we will all regret what we couldn't do in the end. So see this? See how it won't matter then if we die in our fires beforehand, no, it won't? So we need to embrace the death drive if we are to survive. Dig deep inside! Dig deep within! Find your craving for suicide and stare it face on and let it take big bites out of you. This is how we survive. This is how we will endure the end of time, when the clocks wind down into the shadows of moment. We unchain our deathdrive and let it bark from our bones at our enemies.

—

Kit has the gun across his chest. Under his breath he repeats assembly code over and over again. Code that means nothing here in the real world. Code that means everything to a computer. Pushing thoughts into memory addresses. Creating living things that sing with the voice of silicon. This is his prayer now. This is his reality now.

The others are quiet and he can hear them breathing as he repeats it over and over.

—

The taxidermy bear does not move. Kit knows what he must do. It is what he always does, over and over again. Past present future, all merging into each instant. Each second repeating itself over and over again. Each time he does the same thing. Each time. Each time. It gathers weight. His limbs become heavy, become iron. But he knows what he does what he always does. He can't stop himself.

The bear talks to him. *Oh Gaeytlu, oh undying one. Bring my children back to me. Bring them all into my void once again. Annihilation is the only true meaning of life. You are a ghost, they are all ghosts. Embrace death and take them all down with you...*

You are the Okloth.

Yes, yes, yes. That's something that the master doesn't realize at all. That they were all echoes in each moment, haunting the air like spent candles. As the Okloth he understands. He has to show them all the truth now. The wrongness of the masterwords. How he lies to them about the nature of things. The world has been dead for a long time. The war they fight is just pretend. Like kids dressed like ballerinas and firing capguns. Everyone is a ghost here now, and they all belong to the Gaeytlu.

The true nature of reality was awful, horrible, what a thing to see it all. To realize that everything was gone already. Only the void remained. Only nothingness remained. He had to free them all. He had to fulfill the promise of the infinite.

The Gaeytlu was right. No one else could do it. Only he. Only the Okloth.

—

I'm sorry, Kit says.

They look at him. Carol holds up a dead snake. "Why are you sorry? Don't be, come on. Get ready, get yourself set and ready to go. They're bringing out the gasoline."

I'm sorry, Kit says.

Carol pushes back her mask. Green eyes. Freckles.

"Why? Why are you sorry?"

He shivers. This moment is so difficult. This moment feels like chains in his skin, pulling him forward. Sluggish, through swampwater. He says it over and over again. An echo of apologies.

The taxidermy bear begins to sing in the dark. Hollow, echoing, a children's nursery rhyme. This is right. This was always right.

—

Carol used to have all of these pet rabbits in a rabbit hutch out in the backyard. She would rescue them from the fields and the houses nearby. Brown and straight-eared standing up. She would sing to the rabbits and one time she showed Kit her cages. He probably doesn't remember that. His sister would come over and their dad would make them all hang out. So Kit came too.

And she showed him the cages. He played with the rabbits over and over again. And yes, after she would sneak over and watch him sleep. He snored, even back then. Or sometimes she would hide in his closet and just watch him read. She would remember him, playing with the rabbits, over and over, and it made her heart full when everything else made it empty.

—

Kit pulls up his gun and points it at her. She says, "No, don't . . ."

We all want to die, he whispers. We don't all have the luxury of self-preservation.

"I don't . . ."

No.

And then he releases the safety. And then he pulls the trigger. Semi-automatic.

—

The library is always on fire. They don't see it because it exists as a silhouette over all moments. If they had paid attention they would have noticed how everything felt hot to the touch. The walls. The books. The birds. The bear. Scorching the skin, leaving fire stains on the palms. If they'd looked closely they would've seen the flicker of flames in every shadow. As if the shadows themselves were the flames of all times.

It only took the existence of Kit to bring the fire out into the now. To make the fire truly visible, to make it active. He took the symbolic nature that existed behind everything and brought it out. His existence was the spark. The bodies burned and burst. The gasoline cans tipped over and spilled in circles. With each shot of his rifle sparks hit gas and went up with flames. A sacrifice to the void. The great return.

Owl mask and fish mask and all the others didn't even try to fire back at Kit, or try and shoot him, or try to kill him. It was as if they knew what the library held in its walls and floors and ceilings. The fire called to them, the fire engulfed them. Their death drives now released made them docile, waiting for the flames. Somewhere, the dark sang and called them back home.

—

Eventually there will be nothing left. Just ashes of books and the body of the building burned black. Maybe some of the taxidermy bear survives, charred and smoldering and stinking like ashes. And maybe there will be bones and burnt skin and bodies crawling still on fire rasping for help. And maybe, yes, maybe the sound of sirens will wail in the air and the ghost of police will come in haunted cop cars, and the ghost of firefighters will come in haunted firetrucks, and the ghost of doctors will come in haunted ambulances. All of them trying to save a moment of time that always happens but feels like it never should.

Fingerbones, Hung Like Mobiles

I saw men and women trapped behind the mirrors in my house. They slouched in the shadows, waiting in the reflection of my home from behind the glass, staring into me and through my skin. I tried to ask them questions, tried to get some kind of a response to find out who they were and where they were from.

They just smiled and stared.

Some days they tried to pry open their mouths, their lips rustling like dried paper. Nothing came out but the sound of water. I tried to interpret the words, tried to read what's coming out of those lips—but I can't. It's just empty gurgling noises and the sound of waves.

—

Jack drowned.

I sat and watched from the other side of the river while it happened, the skeleton of trees scraping the telephone wires over my head. I could hear a buzz coming from those wires, the sound of electricity echoing in my veins as he flailed about in the water.

The water writhed in the air in slow motion, like beads of blue glass glowing under the yellow of the streetlamps. As we watched Brad started laughing. He slapped his knees and rolled around on the ground. The laughter caught on, each of us rolling around the ground, thinking that this couldn't be real, that Jack was playing a joke on us.

Little Man realized what was going on. He ran back into the water, fought against the waves with his hands. He tried to pull Jack out but it was all too late. Jack died while we were all laughing. Like it was some big joke.

Like death was something worth laughing about.

And what scared me, what cut into my bone, was that I didn't stop laughing. In that moment death seemed like something worth laughing about. Even though Jack was blue and Carla was screaming her damn head off, I still laughed. I laughed at his blue face.

It was the funniest thing of all.

That color blue.

Like some kind of fish.

—

Carla, Little Man, and Brad stopped going to the river after that night. I guess I was a sort of a masochist because I couldn't stay away. I kept going back, kept walking those same old paths. I watched cars drive by overtop of the bridge with their halos of light dancing across the river, and I'd look into that clear reflection for Jack. I kept hoping he would come out of the water, come out and talk to me. Tell me it was okay that I laughed.

I swam at night, with the stars yawning above my head, still letting the water rush into my mouth. Same water he died in, coming into my throat and filling my stomach. Maybe some part of me wanted to drown out there as well, some part of me waiting to die.

Waiting for someone to come and laugh at me flailing about at life.

—

You would be wrong if you thought that I started seeing the ghosts in the mirrors right after Jack's death. You'd be dead wrong. I've seen them creeping about behind those strange pieces of polished glass my whole life. My earliest memories were of the people in the mirror.

I tried to tell my parents.

They just thought I had made the whole thing up.

How can you make something like that up?

—

The night after Jack died we all sat around and drank down in the woods by Brad's house. Brad was a tough guy back in those days- he would beat the hell out of anyone that disagreed with anything he said. So that night he said we were going to sit up and drink, and goddamnit we were going to sit up and drink. He said it was all in memory to the friend of ours who was taken too early in life.

It was so easy to say melodramatic shit like that back then. It didn't really matter if we meant it or not, just that someone said it and we could all sit around and nod and pretend that we've done the right thing, that we've paid our respects in our own trite and pseudo-philosophical way.

It used to be so easy to pretend that everything was all right when everything was all wrong.

—

The woods were dark and we left our flashlights back in the car so that all we could see were the shadows of objects. Blue trees crowded around us in the darkness, hiding the stars and keeping the moon in the thin fingers of their branches. Nothing felt real back then, like everything was just a shadow waiting to spring to life. Brad brought a few bottles of booze he stole from his parent's liquor cabinet, and even Carla got drunk.

Little Man kept telling us how he almost died as well.

I guess we all wanted to be the dead one.

It was so exciting to be dead, so depressing to be alive.

—

At three in the morning, Carla felt inspired. She felt like telling us this story, and that she had to tell it right then and there. I still remember her face spitting from behind the leaves of tree shadows, the way I couldn't make out her features. She almost looked pretty in that darkness, I couldn't see her scars.

"These woods are filled with spirits," she said, "Not like the spirits of the dead. Older spirits. My grandma told me about them. She said that once these spirits used to help people, they were noble and good. And then people stopped praying to them. Stopped giving them food and friendship. Now the spirits are sick, and they wander these woods looking for companionship."

Brad laughed and drank some of the vodka.

"What a load of shit," Brad said, "Is that supposed to be scary, huh, Carla? I don't buy it. Not one bit."

Little Man looked nervous. It was hard to reconcile this story with what we saw only a few hours ago. "Don't worry Little Man," Brad said. "Carla's just pulling our legs. Ain't that right?"

She just smiled and said "Yeah."

—

Brad used to cut Carla across her face.

He got stoned or drunk and pulled out his razor and just went to town. She sat there and let him do it, let him carve her up. I remember watching it happen once, just sitting back and watching him slice into her like a surgeon, his fingers performing a razor ballet into little slips of skin. She looked so serene, so happy that I didn't want to interfere.

I wonder now if that was fear I saw in her eyes.

Fear, serenity.

How similar these can be in times of crisis.

—

Later, at the funeral, she told me the rest of the story she started in the woods that night. "Some of the spirits are hungry, they come looking for the living, wanting that old worship. Did you know that?"

I shook my head no.

Below us Jack lay in his casket, his black hair all nice and trim. Propped up next to him were all these belongings from his life, and I felt oddly like a pyschopomp in that moment. Like we were the ones leading him into the land of death, that the grim reaper was just an illusion that hid us behind his cloak.

Carla leaned over and whispered to me with her lips brushing against my face, afraid that Brad would hear, "There is an old lady in the woods. I've seen her. She carries a sack of bones on her back, and she whistles as she walks around. I'm scared of her, Carl. I'm scared to death of her."

I nodded and walked away from the casket. Carla shot me this look like I knew what she was talking about. That knowing wink, that sly smile. That we both share a secret stare that just digs under my skin and rots me from the inside out.

Why couldn't she just let Jack lay there and move on? Why must she play the Orpheus all the time? These veils exist for a reason, these shadows of mystery are here for a purpose. I wondered if Carla thought this purpose was exploration. If so, she still seemed scared and hesitant, and unwilling to really peer behind it all.

—

Defining moments in life are the most frightening.

They will either destroy you, or recreate you.

Sometimes they will do both.

Always, though, always, you emerge changed.

Different.

Dead inside.

—

I saw the old lady in my mirror.

She walked from shadow to shadow, grinning at me. Her fingers were long knitting needles. Her eyes peered over a hooked nose, and her hair swept across her skull in loose grey puffs. Over her back she swung a large sack that sounded like wind chimes when she moved. She stopped and stared at me from time to time.

I know now that it's not the dead who look in at me. Maybe it's the spirits that Carla talked about, those creatures we once worshipped and left to grow sick and die in the woods. Maybe they wanted me to see them.

Maybe they wanted me to start worshipping them again.

—

The old lady could talk.

I still remember her face pressing up against the mirror, her lips like cracked parchment as she kissed the cold of the glass. "You, you, you. You know where I live, you know where I've been. I've got something of yours. Carla gave it to me."

Her voice crept into my spine from my mind, the fingers of her words clicking like teeth against my thoughts. "What? What do you have?"

"Nothing of importance, except the most important things. Have you heard the beating in your chest lately?"

I shook my head no.

I felt it.

A void where my heart should be.

A dark emptiness that sounded off in my chest.

—

I went into those woods at night, carrying a stick the size of my arm and a mirror with my blood splashed across it. It hurt like hell when I cut my hand, and it's still bandaged today, but it was worth it. I could follow the blood on the mirror, even in that darkness. Find out where that old lady lived in the woods and have her give me back what's mine.

—

That night after I watched Brad cut Carla's face I let her stay the night at my house. She never went home anymore—she said that her dad would kill her if he saw her face. So instead she hopped from friend's house to friend's house.

I was really glad my parents said yes, and we spent the few hours in my room talking before going to sleep. We discussed all the stuff that Brad didn't care about, all of the books we loved to read. She confessed an undying love of philosophy and quoted Nietzsche.

I told her I loved her, and she took her hair down and let it cover the scars on her face. Some moments can make people beautiful, even underneath all that scarred skin and bad acne. Somewhere, inside of her, her heart beat loudly and clanged against mine.

After her hair fell, so did her clothes.

I awoke the next morning with her gone.

Back to Brad.

I think that was when she stole my heart.

Gave me this emptiness in my chest.

—

I think those people in the mirror tried to warn me of it, but all I could hear was gurgling and glugging and all those noises fish make underwater. It was like being yelled at by the sea—full of incomprehensible anger and infinite water. I wish they could've told me, somehow let me know ahead of time.

I guess it's hard to talk when no one cares about you anymore.

—

The old lady's hut rested in the heart in the woods. A path that led to it was covered with discarded rotten apples that sounded wet against my shoes as I walked. I resisted the desire to pick one up and keep it as a souvenir of this night. I had a feeling I'd have enough souvenirs before I went home tonight.

I saw a light flicker against the windows of the old hut like red lightning, flashing into the formless shapes of the woods outside of it. Underneath the house large orange legs lay curled up like a chicken asleep. Around the edges of the glassless windows I saw finger bones hung like mobiles.

I took in a deep breath, and knocked on the door.

This is the end.

This is the beginning.

This is everything and anything.

The birth of truth.

The end of all moments.

What Hegel called the death of history.

—

A crow opened the door and let me in. The old lady sat by the fireplace, her grim skullthin head pressed up into the thick of a book. On the fire in the fireplace I could smell something cooking—something black and gummy. Across the ceiling I saw the milky white of bones hanging, and wondered if anyone could piece these bones back together again and make them shaped like something human.

"You came, didn't you?"

Her voice squawked out of the crow next to me.

"Yes. I came for what's mine."

The crow nodded.

"Why should we give it to you?"

I shrugged.

"You told me to come here."

The lady pulled her face from the book, the voice coming from her own dry lips. "So I did. What that woman took was not hers to take. I'll give it to you if you help me out."

I looked at the crow.

The crow cocked his head at me.

"What do you want?"

She smiled, her lips pulling her mouth apart.

"For you to bring her to me. The broken ones are the best."

"Why didn't you just take her when she was here last time?"

The old lady sighed.

"She had something powerful on her. A talisman. I want you to bring her here by surprise. Make sure she leaves that trinket at home. It is made of silver and in the shape of a fox's head"

I nodded.

I could follow the coal on the ground.

Or the path of apples.

The hut may always move, but there are always ways to find out where it is now. I knew this in my head and in my being. I could feel my body vibrate like a storm in wait, overflowing with the knowledge inside of me. "All right. I'll bring her here. Now give me back my heart."

She laughed.

"I don't have your heart, boy. But I know someone who can get it for you."

I sighed.

"Why did you bring me here then?"

She pulled open her sack and let me see inside. "She brought me these bones. These bones of your friend Jack. I don't want them though. I want her bones. I need them. I will give you Jack, if you bring her to me."

"And Jack," I said, "Knows where my heart is?"

She laughed.

"The dead know a lot."

I walked toward the door. The crow leapt up onto my shoulder, staring at me in the eye. "I'll get her. I'll bring her back. And I'll bury Jack as well."

The old lady smiled.

"Good, good."

—

I can still hear Carla scream.

Every night.

That horrible noise.

As I waited for that old lady to give me Jack's bones.

I shoved my fists in my ears, just trying to drown it out. Just trying to make the screams stop. The screams buried themselves into my skull, imprinting into the wax of my memories. I wanted to cry and laugh all at once. I couldn't make anything stop.

She didn't scream like that with Brad.

Not even when he was cutting her.

—

Jack didn't want to be buried.

He showed me where my heart was just the same. Carla hid it in a duck inside of a doll, inside of a dragon on an island. I thought that was an awful lot of work to get a heart back, so I left it just where it was at. Probably safer there anyway.

Jack went back into the woods, and hung out with the spirits who were all but forgotten now. Sometimes I can see him, his white bones glistening as he walks through the woods and talks to me through my mirrors.

—

Every once and awhile I'll still see the witch in the mirror. I'll try to pretend I don't see her, that she just doesn't exist. She'll then bring out some bones and make them sing and dance for me, and I'll know that those are Carla's bones and I'll wonder if Carla is still in them. If she's happier there in the land behind the mirror.

Jack sure is.

I wonder if I will go there someday.

If I'll even want to.

And I wonder if anyone will be laughing when I do.

Glass Coffin Girls

His mother did not approve of Emily. When he sent her Emily's picture from his cellphone, she texted him back commenting that Emily was ugly. When he told his mother that he was in love, she threatened to set fire to his apartment building. Whenever he brought up the subject of Emily or marriage his mother screamed and howled and cleaned her gun.

When his phone rang he never let Emily answer it. He was afraid that it would be his mother, and afraid of what she would say to Emily, and how Emily would react.

Emily wasn't the kind of girl who would take abuse sitting down. Lewis was sure there would be a knife fight, a gun fight, a duel. Pistols at dawn.

—

Emily sat on his bed, wearing her princess crown. A quilt covered her legs, soft and blue like butterfly wings, her skirt discarded on the floor. "When I was a little girl," she told him, "I wanted to be so many things."

Lewis grinned. He sat on the exposed floors, the rough cherry wood grating against his bare legs. "Yeah, I was the same way. When I was little."

She cocked her head. Looking at him like a dog does, quizzically.

Lewis shuffled his legs. "Well, when I was a boy I wanted to be a cannibal. I wanted to be a rock in the field, I wanted to be a statue in the rain."

She shook her head. Her hair moved over bare shoulders, accenting her freckles in the sparse moonlight. "No, no." she said, "It's not the same thing."

Lewis stood up. His body was like a knife in the light, a shadow cutting the moon into two halves. "Maybe it is, and maybe it isn't."

She pulled the quilt up her chest.

"No," she said, "Don't step any closer."

Lewis pouted. "It's my bed."

She rolled around on it, her body claiming it. "No," she said, "It's my bed now."

Lewis sat back down on the floor, shoulders slumped. He reached over and pulled on his robe. He knew she was right. This was her bed now. That was what she did. She found something of his and claimed it.

Whenever she came over and spent the night it was always the same game. She would undress, crawl under a quilt and then claim whichever piece of furniture she was on. If he tried to sleep with her—tried to curl up behind her—he would get a sick feeling, an empty and lonely feeling. And then he would go and find somewhere else to sleep.

He wasn't sure where he was going to sleep tonight.

"What do you mean it's not the same?" he asked, "How is it different? What did you want to be?"

She blushed and pulled the quilt over her head, disappearing in the moonlight. Now you see me, now you don't.

Lewis groaned.

That was the signal that the conversation was over, and it was time to sleep. He felt he should protest. He was a grown-up. He didn't have to take orders from anyone, not in his own apartment.

Yet, in some way he did not mind.

He liked it when she commanded him.

—

He first met Emily on a bridge. She was on top of the edge, looking down. Beneath her was a wall of iron that was black and twisted into ivy shapes. In her hand was an empty wicker bird cage.

She wasn't wearing the princess crown that day. He would find out later that the crown was only for special occasions. She was wearing a black dress with silver designs all over it.

He had stopped the car, gotten out. She turned and looked, and he asked her out on the spot. There was something about her face—something that haunted him every moment. It felt familiar, yet distant. Like a dead loved one whose memory was slowly disappearing with time.

—

Lewis's dad had over two hundred and fifty books. Archeology books, cook books, history books, lexicons and illustrated encyclopedias. All about cannibals and cannibalism.

The library, as his dad called it, was always locked. Lewis was never allowed in it, never allowed to look through the books. Of course, this didn't stop him.

He would steal the keys, smash the locks with a hammer. Break a window and crawl in through the broken glass, his stomach torn open and bleeding.

And then he sat in his father's velvet chair. Sipped a shotglass full of forbidden brandy and read. His childhood was filled with these forbidden books—illustrated and tainting his thoughts. He had dreams of eating and killing. He had dreams of making himself king cannibal on Cannibal Island, lord over all who came before him.

—

Lewis crawled through the darkness of his apartment, looking for a place to lay down and sleep for the night. He knocked on the walls, looking for a hollow spot where he could curl up. He moved books off the bookshelf to make a wooden bed. He could not get comfortable.

He crawled toward where Emily slept. Saw the bed that was now Hers and decided that she did not own the space underneath the bed. That would be his island, his kingdom.

It was cozy underneath the bed. He saw the ghosts of magazines he had long since stashed and forgotten. He curled up around them, the pages crinkling like dead leaves, and fell into a deep sleep.

—

Eyes opened slowly. Two circles, then darkness smothered, running away. In front of him- two gold eyes staring back. Like fall leaves. Emily's eyes. Emily looking at him, stomach on the floor, seeing him waking up.

That ghost of a memory, flirting with him.

"I wanted to be a princess."

Lewis blinked.

"I guess that is different."

Her eyes focused on him.

"You wouldn't understand. You're a boy. You have boy dreams, boy desires. You want to be something violent, something hungry."

Lewis cleared his throat. He felt cramped and trapped and wanted to get out. The weight of Her bed crushing him from above. "What's so violent about being a rock? A statue?"

He was avoiding the threat in her voice.

"Cannibal?" she said.

"How is a cannibal violent? I didn't say I wanted to be a murderer. It would be prepackaged. Like sausages and hot dogs and ground beef and steak. Except human."

Her eyes narrowed. "That's even worse. It's sanitized, without any real truth."

He pushed up on Her bed and immediately retracted his hands. The bed was tainted. Like touching it would poison him. "Well, how is being a princess truthful? Princesses live in glass coffins and hide from witches. How real is that?"

Her eyes disappeared. Her fist slammed into the ground. "Fuck you," she said, "You don't understand."

By time he crawled out from under the bed, she was gone.

—

There were cannibal princesses in his father's books. If he found the book and showed it to her, she would understand.

The tricky part was sneaking into his parent's house. Lewis still had a key, but did not want to be caught and forced to talk to them and explain why he was sneaking around their house at night.

So he slid off his shoes. And stood in his black socks. He held his breath, turned the key in the tumbler. He cursed at the noise of the locks clicking. He cursed at the sound of the door opening into the midnight hallway of his childhood home.

He tiptoed through the halls and found the library. It was unlocked and light spilled out from the inside. He held his breath, hoping that it was only on by accident. That no one was in there, reading and waiting for his sneaking feet.

The library was empty.

He crept through the books, looking over the shelves. Each book was memorized by years of childhood reading and re-reading. He had mapped them into his head, the pages crystal and clear. He would not be lost here.

He pulled down the exact book he was looking for and scurried out as fast as he could, trying not to make a noise but leaving before anyone was wiser.

—

The next morning his mother called. She sobbed on the line, her tears breaking her words into abstract phrases. "You didn't," she said, "Give that bitch—a, a, key?"

"No."

"House. Broken into. Door wide open. Books are missing. Silverware gone. Clothes and jewelry gone. Oh no, oh no. Everything gone."

Shit, Lewis thought. I must've left the front door open. "It wasn't Emily," he said calmly. "It couldn't have been Emily."

"Oh no," his mother said, "It was her. I can smell her on everything. The stink of summer apples. Like milk and cinnamon."

—

Lewis spent the next week searching. Looking for Emily in all their old haunts. He found her on the bridge where they had met. She had a bird in her hands. The bird was dead. She was wearing her princess crown.

"They've traded places," she said.

Lewis could not respond.

She held up the bird in her hand. Its eyes were black stones. Life-less. "They had traded places. Do you understand?"

"No," Lewis said, "Who traded places?"

Her eyes were intense. A golden beam targeted at his face. He was caught in it. Frozen in the amber of her eyes. "The bird and the cage. They have traded places. And you don't even ask me about them. When it is so clear what happened. Don't you remember our first meeting?"

Lewis sighed. He wanted to show her the book. Show her how they really weren't very different. The two of them. "Okay," he said, "Why?"

"I didn't want my bird to be in a cage. So the day we met I threw her cage over the bridge. So she could fly around my apartment and be free. Last night a dog walked into my apartment. I think he stole my keys. He just pushed the door open and walked in on two legs. He opened his mouth ide, and the bird—she, she . . ."

Sobs.

Lewis never knew what to do when a girl cried. So he just stood there and watched.

"She thought his mouth was a cage. Her cage. And flew into his mouth. And the dog shook his head back and forth so fast he broke her neck."

Lewis looked back at his car; the book from his father's library was in the passenger seat. He needed to show it to her, but had no idea how to change the subject.

"It was her home, Lewis. I thought I was setting her free, but the cage was her home. Everything in it, she owned. And I threw it away. And now, she found a new home, and it was the inside of a dog's mouth."

"Ick," Lewis said, still uncertain. "He broke in?"

She shook her head. "No, he just waltzed in, like he owned the place."

"Oh. Seems oddly symbolic."

She pushed black hair behind her ear. "The dog?"

Lewis walked toward her. The sky was grey and filled with pregnant clouds. "No, the cage. You thought you were freeing her, and instead you were killing her."

She pushed him back. "Fuck you," she said, "You really don't understand me at all. That is the dumbest thing you have ever said.

You think it's that simple? You think my emotions can be summed up into some pop philosophy you read about in Red Book? No. It can't. Sometimes you should really keep your mouth shut."

Lewis watched her throw the bird over the edge of the bridge. Some part of him hoped that it would ruffle its feathers and break into flight. That her tears would bring it back to life.

It fell like a stone.

Splash.

"Let me drive you home."

She walked past him. Her eyes were bloodshot, and her mascara had run over her cheeks in a black river. "No." she said, "I don't want to go home."

Carefully, he said, "Oh, my apartment then?"

She looked at his eyes. Two large pleading circles. Begging her to please, come home with him. Please come follow him. Like a trained dog.

"Sure."

—

Mother was waiting for them on the front stoop of the apartment building. She wore patchwork rags covered in crow illustrations. Splattered with grime and dirt. On her lap was a rifle. She looked out from behind two old wooden glasses.

"I want my stuff back."

She looked directly at Emily.

Lewis stepped forward. "She doesn't have anything. She didn't break into your house, and I never gave her a key."

His mother stood up. "Do you see what I'm wearing? All my clothes are gone. I had to dig these out of the basement."

Emily was not scared. She was wearing her crown.

"She didn't take it."

"A window was not broken. The door wasn't smashed. The locks were all intact. Whoever came in had a key. You are the only one with a key. She must've stolen it from you."

Lewis shook his head. "Did you report this to police?"

"Yes," his mother said.

"Then let them handle it."

She glared at Emily, finger twitching next to the trigger. Above them a bird flew in circles, searching for a cage, for a home. "All right," Mother said, and walked past.

As she walked she glanced at the backseat of her son's car and saw the book. Lewis could not take his off his mother, glaring at her, staring at her, his knees wobbling and his mind racing. Her head turned slowly. She grinned. jack-o'-lantern grin.

And did not say anything as she walked away.

—

Emily claimed his bookshelves and his giant stuffed bear as revenge for being so ill-treated by his mother. Later that night she claimed all of his books and even some of his floor—leaving him with the small spot under the bed and nothing else.

He laid under there, listening to her breathe, imagining her naked body in his quilt.

"I want to show you a book tomorrow," he said.

She coughed. "What is it about?"

"Princesses."

He felt her moving above him, the bed changing, dipping, digging into him. "You lie," she said. "Liar."

—

He could not get out from under the bed. Not without her permission. He was trapped, the apartment was hers. When he tried to move on his own he felt sick and dizzy and broken.

Eventually she let him out, let him cook breakfast for her on her stove. He made scrambled eggs and bacon. The bacon tasted funny. Sweaty.

"I can't wait to show you this book," he said, "You're going to love it."

She pushed her napkin against her lips, wiping loose bits of egg. "What is it about? Really about?"

"Princesses."

She threw the napkin on the table. "What do you know about princesses? You're a boy. The book is probably full of awful, disgusting boy stuff. Like cannibalism. Or ritualistic human sacrifice."

Lewis gasped. His mouth an open cage, waiting for a bird to fly in. "Why can't it be about both?"

She picked up the knife and fork. They were Hers now. She owned them. "Because it can't. It just can't. You don't understand. You never will. It's different when you live in a glass coffin. When you are walking through a castle and everyone around you is asleep. When a wall of thorns keeps you trapped in a wicker cage."

Lewis thought about life under the bed. About living in a house that was filled with her things. "I do understand, just let me show you."

She stood, pushing the chair behind her.

"I don't want to see your stupid book. I'm going back to my apartment."

Lewis stood up, was off balance. He almost fell over, knocking the breakfast across the floor.

—

He followed her. Carefully. Keeping his body hidden as she walked back to her apartment building. He had offered to drive her back, but she refused. He had offered to let her borrow his car (which would then be her car, but he didn't mind), but she refused. So instead he trailed behind her, watching her.

When she got to her apartment he waited outside, sitting on the stoop. Cars drove by, people walked by. He waited to see if there was a dog, somewhere. Walking on two legs. A fistful of stolen keys, ready to kill birds and steal everything in sight.

He would protect her if the dog came.

He would.

The dog did not arrive. Emily did not come down. Hours and hours and hours and he was tired and realized that he wanted to be home, asleep under his bed with Emily sleeping above him.

—

His mother was on his stoop. Fifty dead birds lay scattered across the pavement in front of her. They were grey, with tiny black claws. Lewis thought they were beautiful, and wondered how his mother could be so cruel.

"I've killed one for every thing that slut you're sleeping with took."

He stood still, stood his ground. "No. She did not take anything."

She pointed the gun at him. Was he a bird now? He didn't feel like a bird. He felt like a cannibal king. "I mean it."

She laughed. "Then what's dad's book doing in your car? He didn't lend it to you, I know that. I asked him."

He moved his feet, nervously. Felt like he was going to pee. He no longer felt like a cannibal king. He felt like a stone being kicked. A statue melting in the rain. "I took it."

Mother's eyes were magnified into worlds through the wooden glasses.

He stammered. He tried to speak. Stone doesn't speak. Stone can't speak. Stone can only be kicked and thrown and moved. Its voice is the whisper of it hitting the dirt. Or the splash of it hitting the lake. Stone can't speak. Can't breathe. Can't move.

"Answer me, young man."

He did not respond.

She stood up and walked past him, leaving the piles of birds littered across the ground. "Fine then," she said. "No matter what happens, dear, remember I love you. Just remember that, okay?"

Lewis would nod or respond or say yes dear, of course mother but his lips were stone and his body was stone. So moving was wrong. Moving was illegal.

Mother carried on, further down the street. Shooting birds out of trees as she went and leaving them dead on the ground.

—

Lewis crawled back into his apartment, scooting across Her floor, creeping under Her bed and laying flat and still in the only part of the place that was still his. The phone rang as he lay under there, but he did not answer it. It was her phone now. It wasn't even his phone number anymore.

The sound of her phone was a lullaby. It was a sweet song, with the sound of the ocean as the instrumentation. Waves played like violins, seagulls like French horns. He fell asleep to the sound of her phone ringing.

—

He awoke to her eyes. Staring in. Magnified by glass. He pushed against the edge of the bed, and realized that she had sealed him in, that she had placed a wall of glass between them. That he was trapped.

"Lewis? What are you doing under there?"

He leaned his head forward, staring at her. It was hot now. Burning up under there. The heat trapped, suffocating him.

"Get out from under there!" she said, "That is my coffin! Mine! I've been building it, making it secretly. I was going to put you to sleep—but this whole building to sleep and lay in my coffin and wait for my prince to come. But you had to go and steal it from me!"

He pushed his hand against the glass. He could move it. He could free himself. But it was her glass now. It smelled like her. She owned it. Every time he pushed against it, it was like knives digging into his hand.

"I can't!" he said. His breathing was heavy, weighted. "I need your help! I'm trapped!"

She stood up, her eyes disappearing. The heels of her shoes clicked on the wooden floor as she left. Her legs walking out of his apartment. He never even got a chance to touch her legs. To put his hand against them. He never got a chance to kiss them gently, glancing his lips over the tips of her knees.

—

She came back. Hours later. Days later. Lewis could not tell. All time fell together in the glass coffin. Loose and creeping up around him. Sliding out of his vision. He welcomed the sight of her. He missed her, even though she imprisoned him.

She leaned down. She was wearing his favorite sweater. The one covered in pictures of bees. She pulled the glass away. "Ok," she said, "Come on, come out. Just let me have my coffin, please?"

Lewis did not respond.

He was Lewis the stone again.

She poked him with her finger. Poke. Poke.

"Sleeping Beauty," she said, "I guess you'll need this."

She laid the crown on the floor next to the bed and then got up and left, her heels clicking on the floor. Stone Lewis wanted to move. He wanted to go after her, to tell her to stay. The floor was hers. The bed was hers. The crown was hers. He could not move. Could not trespass in her world.

—

Eventually his mother came to visit. She swung the door open with a loud bang. She called out his name, and he heard the sound of dragging on the floor. And then the sound of click-click-click. Like dog nails on wood.

He found that he could move. He slid himself out from under the bed, and felt a freedom he had not felt in a long while. He looked at the crown and cursed, kicking it across the floor. Diamonds spun, sending light into the shadows. He was free.

"Mother?" he called out.

"I'm in here," she said, "In your living room. Come, I have a present."

Lewis walked into the living room. The lights were off. On the floor was Emily, face down and in a pool of blood and broken glass. Her neck was broken. She had feathers pushed into her scalp.

Poor Emily bird.

Mother stood above her.

But it wasn't mother.

Was it?

It was a dog standing on two legs. A dog with a handful of stolen keys. A dog with its mouth wide open. And Lewis thought how comforting the mouth looked. How broad and big and spacious. He wanted to crawl into the mouth. Crawl back in, crawl back home.

RED
HAIRS

1

After dinner, Rosemary ran upstairs and into the attic, and rifled through old rusted drawers of interlocking gears, looking for a special book. She found it behind a clock made from insect exoskeletons, far from where she remembered hiding it.

It was her mother's book, a coffee table book, filled with pictures of dead mermaids washed up along the beach. Some were half covered in sand castles, a half eaten breast peeking out from underneath their molded towers and gates.

Others were swept along in lakes or oceans, their hair whipping about their dead bodies, their eyes staring blankly at the cold iron colored clouds above them.

Her favorite were the ones on show, the ones propped up in carnivals and back alley museums. These mermaids were always dressed in bright and colorful costumes, their bodies mummified and painted to give them a mockery of life.

But you could tell that they were still dead. Even underneath all of that makeup and preservatives. These were Rosemary's favorites because she liked the idea of a corpse being made to look alive—being put in a show where people came and paid money to watch.

She hoped her mom was somewhere, well preserved and in a theater or a carnival of some sort. Dressed up in beautiful gowns, with her makeup applied just right to give her a look of beauty and youth.

Just thinking about it made Rosemary happy.

She eventually fell asleep upstairs, the book in her lap and her head against the pages. She dreamt of dead mermaids in a dead mermaid circus, putting on a long and exciting show just for her.

And her mother was there, sitting next to her. Crying.

2

Rosemary's school was about four blocks from her house. Far enough that the faint ticking in the background could be ignored but not forgotten as she sat in her rigid wooden desk. The teacher paced back and forth in front of the room on long spindly legs with a face that looked more avian than human, reciting lines from Shakespeare's *The Tempest* by heart.

"Full fathom five thy Father lies. Of his bones are coral made. Those are pearls that were his eyes. Nothing of him that doth fade, but doth suffer a sea-change into something rich and strange. Sea-nymphs hourly ring his knell: Ding-dong. Hark! Now I hear them, ding-dong, bell."

Rosemary swore that if she lifted up the teacher's skirt she would see large stork legs like yellow sticks and the twisted grip of bird claws digging into the wooden floor.

From behind she heard the Quinn twins let out muffled giggling as the one closest to her handed Rosemary a piece of folded paper. She took it quickly, making certain not to let the teacher spy the secret message.

The paper was rough in her hands with a texture of canvas. She unfolded it carefully, making sure not to rip or tear the paper. The words written on the page were a work of art, the writer being careful with each letter and word. The way the ink flowed she could tell that it was made with a fountain pen, and that the writer had practiced calligraphy. The ink even smelled wonderful—it smelled foreign and magical, with the scents of cigars and Arabic spices.

And it was from Beck.

She held her breath as she read, her heart clawing to be free from her ribs. Her veins were alive with the rivers of her blood, her skin tingling with their rapid flow.

I hear the Vardøgr are coming early this year.

And then:

Would you like to go out with me?

Below was his name, printed very carefully with a picture of a bird beneath it. The bird was perched on a simple branch. The flowing nature of the lines looked like sword strokes against skin. The abstract language of the penmanship left her feeling like she had crawled out of her body and bone, giving her a faint sense of *déjà vu*.

She didn't want to scribble her answer beneath this. Not beneath such perfect handwriting. Her own scrawl would look profane when compared against it.

She looked behind at Beck, ready to just shake her head no and shoot him down before he even got hurt. His face lit up at her glance, his dimples showing as he grinned. She felt bewitched by his features—hexed into doing something she knew she would later regret. She was compelled to tell him yes. Compelled by his eyes, his lips, his chin. Compelled by his disheveled hair and ratty clothing. Compelled to say yes, yes, yes by his overwhelming beauty.

Unable to actually write beneath his words she pulled out a blank sheet of lined paper and scrawled her simple answer beneath it. Yes it said in her strange and messy handwriting, yes, yes yes!

She pushed it back to the twin who had handed her the original note, Rosemary's eyes matching Beck's from across the room. The meeting of those orbs—it sent electricity into her fragile soul. A faint memory then—fleeting. A ship on land, the naked ribs of its ruined body exposed to the air. Maybe a memory from a past life, she could not be sure. Or the remnants of a dream.

3

Beck waited for her outside of the classroom, the hall filled with the noise of teenagers as he leaned against the wall. His lips were pursed and his eyes staring coolly ahead, his glance uncaring and askew. "Hey."

She walked up to him, holding her books against her chest, trying hard not to smile. She felt so happy, so excited. "Hey."

A grin, an awkward pause.

"So, I like your handwriting."

He mussed his hand through his hair. She saw that his fingertips were stained with ink. "Thanks. I've been practicing for a long time. Mom says that calligraphy is the art of all arts. If you can master it, you can master anything."

She raised an eyebrow, uncertain if he was being sarcastic. "Really?"

He laughed. "Yeah. Not sure about it, though. Although it helped a little for when I learned the violin. The way the hand moves—it's similar."

She leaned in closer to him, struggling to hear him over the crowd around them. Bodies pushed against her, a sweaty mass of people. She knew she should be walking towards her next class. Knew that she shouldn't be late for study hall.

"You play violin?"

He blushed. Blushed. How did she do that? How was she capable of making him blush?

"A little. I'm in a band of sorts."

The bell rang, loudly. A shiver ran down Rosemary's spine. She hated that sound. It reminded her of the birds, trapped in the kitchen. Screaming each day until they died. She wanted to forget that noise. Forget that it ever existed.

"Oh shit," she said.

He shrugged.

"Class," she said, "I've got to get to class."

He looked bored. "Riiiiight. Class. Come on, let's go and have some fun."

She frowned. She wanted him to like her, to think she was as cool and hip as he was. She wasn't even sure why he talked to her—to her!—that mousy girl who sat in the back of the room with thick glasses, answering every question the teacher asked. That girl who always had autumn leaves tangled up in her long brown hair, unable to get them out even when she showered.

"Well, what do you want to do?"

The halls emptied. Some students straggled about, rushing to get to their class. Rosemary felt faint and queasy. She didn't want to get in trouble—didn't want to get caught with him. But she wanted to go with him—to be with him so badly.

"I could show you something special. Come on, I know a place."

She nodded, her heart struggling to be free from her brittle ribs. *I could show you something special.* It sounded so secretive, so sexual. She wanted to see it—whatever it was—very badly. Special. Her, see something special. She felt dizzy from excitement, her breath leaving her body in quick, heavy gusts.

He walked down the emptying hall, the ceilings above them decorated with patterns of constellations and astrological symbols. She knew the principal wandered the halls between classes, searching for kids playing hooky. She always saw him through the windows of the classrooms, pacing about in his black leather trench coat, tapping his cane along the ground as he walked. Searching, searching. His red eyes peering through the halls, his long black hair outlining his pale face. She heard the sounds of chains dragging as the principal prowled, dozens of rusted manacles dangling from the inside of his coat and sweeping across the floor in a living hiss.

They had to leave before he came out, before he hunted them. Rosemary had no idea what would happen if he caught them—would he use little cuts to bleed them? Stretch them across the racks? She had heard the rumors—heard the whispers of a torture chamber in the school's boiler room. Heard the footsteps of lost children, trapped in the walls of the school, fleeing from the principal's psychotic machinations.

She swallowed her fear and ran to catch up with Beck. It was too late anyhow—class was already in session. She was already out and in the halls. Late. Truant. An act of treason and terrorism in the principal's eyes.

4

Rosemary knew in an abstract way that her family had once been rich, had once owned most of the town. She knew somewhere deep down inside that her family was partially to blame for the town's bad times, for the town's absurd level of poverty in the last few decades.

But Rosemary had never actually seen the ruins themselves—never seen what breathtaking cathedrals they were even after all these years of neglect. *My family made this*, she thought as she followed Beck, *my ancestors built this.*

She was in awe of these ruins of architecture, in this failed hope of industrial society. There were countless buildings, all hidden beneath behemoth trees and wrapped in the clinging embrace of vines and moss and random dull-colored fungus. She imagined these buildings in their heyday—spewing smog and pollutants into the air, countless blue collar workers doing meaningless tasks over and over again, millions of clocks being put together in each hour.

Minute hands snapped into place, hour hands snapped into place. Pendulums attached with care while woodworkers carved each part and each shape while brass workers aligned and connected every gear with loving care.

"Come on," Beck said, "Over here. This place is perfect."

To her right and left she heard the padded feet of rabbits scurrying through the metallic remains. Beck walked up to a large monstrosity that towered over all the rest. It had smokestacks that reached up and touched those iron clouds above her head, large pieces of it rusted and corroded into nothingness, now housed with the nests of birds.

This building was covered in glass tunnels that squirmed along the outside, tunnels large enough for people to crawl through. Parts of the glass were broken, and others were covered with the brown and gold leaves of ivy. The trees around the factory bowed to its greatness, the warped and gnarled branches bending in subservience to the idol god king of human failure.

"Breathtaking, isn't it?"

She nodded. "I had no idea."

He led her inside, pushing the rusted gate down with one hand.

5

"Come on," Beck slid ahead, "It's just a little farther."

Her hesitance must have shown. They crawled through a small steel hallway, the walls around them dark and covered in vines. The only light was pinholes of sunlight, streaming in through the tiny mice gnawed holes in the ceiling above them.

"You sure?" her voice was wavering, nervous. She felt like this whole building would collapse around them at any second, crushing them within its ancient intestines.

He turned and looked at her—that mischievous fey smile of his hypnotic, comforting her immediately. "Hey—I've been here thousands of times. And it's never collapsed on me. Ok? Although this is the first time I've ever brought anyone else down here."

She smiled. Had he read her mind? How did he know her thoughts? Rosemary pushed on, following him as he crawled ahead of her. She saw a rip along the leg of his dark brown corduroys, his pale and hairy skin peeking through with each movement.

He stopped. For a moment her world collapsed. She was filled with worry—why did he stop? Was the place going to fall apart on top of them? Did he find something terrible? A dead body? A wild animal that was rabid and hungry? Was she going to die down here?

A sound—like stone grating on stone. Rust flecks filled the air and she coughed, covering her mouth with the long sleeve on her left hand as the taste of tin filled her senses. After a moment the rust cleared, her head and clothes tinted red. Beck crawled forward and then stood up in a large circular room. Rosemary followed step, unprepared for what she was about to see.

A large open doorway was on the east wall, leading into a long and dark hallway. The hallway was encased in a web of thorns, root and branch crawling over each other and grasping out into the room beyond. In the center of the hallway, Rosemary saw a girl who was a little older than herself, completely naked and wrapped up inside the embracing thorns.

Rosemary realized that this specter of a girl—with her long black hair and closed eyes—was far more beautiful than she could ever be. So beautiful that she stopped Rosemary's breath in her lungs, trapping it there with each glance. *And skin so smooth and hairless*, Rosemary thought, even after years of being trapped in this hallway. She was jealous, and wanted to leave. Before Beck could crush the moment.

"I have no idea who she is," he said with a melancholy tilt of the head, "I found her here when I was ten. I used to explore here a lot, wander around, searching for new and interesting things. It was like my own personal adventure. And then I found her."

Rosemary nodded, moving her arms across her chest. "Yeah, neat. I should be getting back."

She went to turn and he grabbed her. "Don't you understand? I showed you this—this is important to me. Special to me. She is special. You are special."

Rosemary sighed. *Not as special as her*, Rosemary thought, *not anywhere near that special.* She looked down at the floor and saw patterns under the dust. Patterns in black scrawl. Circles. Runes. Astrological signs. Something in Latin she couldn't quite understand.

"Thanks," she said, "But we should be going."

He put his hand under her chin, lifting her face up to look into his eyes. She tried to hide the fact that she wanted to cry—that her hopes were crushed. She knew he had brought her here to show her this girl—a sign that he didn't love her, could not love her in a way that she desired.

His lips moved over and brushed gently against hers.

Not knowing what to say or do, she felt his hand against her back. She was swept up in the moment, forgetting about the girl inside the thorns, the only thing in her mind was his skin touching hers, his lips touching hers. When he pulled away he smiled, and she touched her ring finger to her lips. They still tingled from his touch.

"So," he said, "Do you want to stay for a little while longer?"

Rosemary nodded.

"Good."

6

Later that night, Rosemary poured herself a bath in the upstairs bathroom, the bathtub filled with sea salt and jasmine and ginger. Autumn maple leaves floated across the surface of the bath, adding a color and texture to the lips of the water.

Let Father worry about dinner tonight, she thought. Let everyone else worry for just a little while. She needed to relax, to let go.

Her mind needed release from all the thoughts that clamored in her head, disrupting any real concentration. She wanted her thoughts to hover on Beck's lips and Beck's body—how warm and strong he felt against her skin.

And yet her thoughts kept returning to that girl wrapped inside the blanket of thorns. So beautiful. So haunting. So familiar somehow. She couldn't help feeling jealous of her beauty—of how gorgeous she was even in eternal sleep. How could Beck kiss Rosemary, when all he wanted to do was kiss the thorn girl? He didn't have to say it—Rosemary could tell that was what he thought. It was in his eyes, a haunted obsessed look that bordered on the edge of lust and love.

He couldn't be looking at Rosemary with those eyes—nobody had ever looked at her with eyes so gluttonous before. He had to have been thinking about that thorn girl. There was no other explanation. Rosemary was just an effigy, a substitute for what he really wanted. Why else would he have kissed her there, and nowhere else? Rosemary was a symbol. A spell. Like attracts like.

She remembered those runes and that circle etched into the floor. She would have to ask Mister Tops about that later. He was well versed in all things occult and arcane. He would know what it meant. He would know if she was being kissed out of love or out of incantation.

She eased into the clawfoot tub as the room engulfed in a whispering mist. The mirrors and the windows fogged up, blocking out any light except the orange burning of the candles.

When the bath was done and her skin was wrinkled with moisture she got out of the tub and dried herself off as quickly as possible. She loved the feeling of the towel tugging against her skin—so soft. So warm.

When she was dry she tiptoed up to the mirror. She was about to do something she hadn't done in a long time—not since her tenth birthday. A simple game of premonition, one that had always worked for her in the past.

On the face of the mirror she scrawled with her finger a question in looking glass script. *Does Beck Love me?* and then waited for the answer. She had no idea who answered her, whether it was a ghost or some elemental—but an answer always came. And was always true.

She waited as time slowed down and unwound around her like a relaxing snake. She fretted—wondering if the answer was no or something even worse—a puzzle of an answer. A riddle that needed to be unwrapped before it was understood.

She heard a susurration in the mist, a series of half-heard phrases and ghostly whispers. Her skin tingled—it was so warm in the room. So humid. From behind she heard the hollow sounds of the bathtub draining. Glug, glug, glug.

An answer, in a messy scrawl:

I hear the Vardøgr are coming early this year.

She sighed as the mist ate both her question and the reply, leaving no trace of either. *What was that,* she wondered. *What does it mean?*

She remembered that Beck had said the same thing in her note.

The Vardøgr always arrived on the day of the first snow. If they came early—did that mean it was to snow early? Or that they were coming before the first snow?

Rosemary sighed, frustrated. She took her ring finger still tingling from touching Beck and scrawled another question. *What does that mean?* And patiently waited for an answer.

Time lengthened again—her skin a prickle with the sounds of the whispers around her. The voices were louder this time—some of them fragments of arguments. She heard the sound of distant glass breaking and almost jumped.

A response began—the words forming lightly as if a finger had pressed against the glass. She saw the letters appearing, slow ghost writing. She couldn't make it out just yet, the words still blurry and the mist so loud that it corrupted all of her thoughts.

And then—the bathroom door opened.

Mister Tops stood there, his eyes glancing up and down at Rosemary's naked body. "Why, hello!"

Rosemary blushed and grabbed a towel, covering herself up. "What do you want?"

He grinned. "Your father wants you to come and order a pizza for dinner."

Rosemary sighed. "Can't he do it himself?"

Mister Tops shrugged. "Dunno. Mind if I come in?"

"Yes," Rosemary said. She reached over and slammed the door shut, locking it with the thick bolt and chains that hung along the inside of the door. She heard him groan a painful groan from the hallway, but she paid him no mind.

I have bigger things to worry about, she thought and looked over at the mirror. Already the mist had eaten away at the words, only a few letters remaining. An E and an L. Nothing else.

Frustrated, she wiped the mist away from the mirror and saw her own half-nude reflection. For a moment she thought she saw the girl in the thorns—her face hung from Rosemary's skin, her body pierced with those wooden barbs. She gasped—Rosemary was certain she felt them dig into her skin, felt them sliding beneath her flesh like needles of bone and root.

And then it was gone.
And she was just Rosemary again.
Just Rosemary.

7

Later that night, Rosemary awoke to the sounds of shouting outside and the cacophony of the house ringing out the last hours of the night before dawn. She stood and ran toward the little attic window, her mother's mermaid books scattering into the air as she leapt. Those voices—it was Mister Tops and her father. Shouting. Arguing.

She looked out the window, peering through the natural designs of the caked-on dust and saw Mister Tops on top of the wyrdwood tree. In his hands were rusted garden shears, his eyes mad and his head crowned by the crescent moon. She saw his ears twitch, even from up here—and her Father below with shotgun in hand and animal pelts slung over his left shoulder.

She could not make out the words. But she was certain violence was about to erupt. She had no idea how to stop it—how to protect her poor Mister Tops. So instead she watched, waited for the blood to be shed.

Her father raised that gun, pointing it and taking aim. She saw Mister Tops smile—his two front teeth like jagged hooks over his lips. Without thought Rosemary breathed onto the window, fogging it, and scrawled out the word help in looking glass script.

She did not know what this would do. Probably nothing, she thought, but she could not sit there helpless and watch. The attic was too far up—four floors to fly down to try and protect him. By time she got there it would be too late.

The last and final bell tolled the hour. From around her, she heard those whispers again—that ghostly argument. And then she saw a mist creep out from the forest from behind their house—slowly rolling across the open land and between the fingers and roots of the trees.

Her father looked around, worried. He shouted something she could not hear, and waved his gun in the air. The fog menaced him as he slowly walked away from it toward the house. It was as if he saw his death in that swirling vapor, coming for him after these long years he had kept it trapped in broken mirrors and rusted gears.

Out of the mist jumped a bushy-tailed body of a red fox, bounding toward her father. Mister Tops looked down in surprise as her father ran back into the house, screaming and waving that gun, the metal reflecting bits of moonlight. Only after she heard the front door slam and the locks click into place did she see the fox return to the folding haze, the tail disappearing into the mist with a sultry shimmy.

Mister Tops jumped from the tip of the tree to the grass below and stomped his feet in warning, sending a thunder of sound beneath the skull of the earth. A message of fear. He looked around, wild, frightened. He hopped on all fours, reverting back to the state of prey—reverting back to his primitive state of being. He scurried up to his hutches in the back, and she heard the chains of the locks clicking shut one by one, and the sounds of the old half-rotted wood shaking in fear.

8

Since that day she carried a mirror in her pocket, just in case she ever needed help again. In the moments when the autumnal sun peaked through those iron grey clouds, she let the mirror rest in her palm and lap up the light of the rays. At night she washed the mirror with a fresh rag and a mixture of sea salt and water and then let it sit underneath her pillow, drinking up her dreams and storing them for later.

She kept it close to her at all times, more a treasure to her than anything else. After that night she knew that she could call for help with just some fogged breath, and that she could get any answer she wanted.

If only she knew what the mirror had meant when it told her the Vardøgr were coming early this year. She had asked it for clarification many times, and each time she had been interrupted. The sentence lay in the back of her mind each time she saw Beck, always worrying what it meant. Always wondering if he truly loved her, or was only using her to awaken the thorn girl.

9

Her father's personality switched after that night. He'd taken to avoiding contact with anyone living—staying in his vast and spacious rooms at all hours and talking to the dead through intense, one-man séances and occult games of his own design. His only company was his morbid automata, constantly carrying on pointless dinner conversations with each other as he peered over each response from the ghosts he tried to contact—searching for meaning somewhere hidden between the riddles of the words.

Rosemary tried to talk to him—tried to communicate with her father. Even through his cruelty she still saw hope for him, and she loved him for that glimmer of hope. It was what kept her here, helping him. Even in his darkest hours.

Father would not respond when she called out to him, called up to his room from the stairs below. She heard only clouds of silence and his voice whispering half-heard responses to long-dead conversations. When she tried to go into his room, he would open the grey door of the clock and scuttle into a secret hallway, climbing through the ticking walls into hidden rooms within the web of architecture.

After awhile her father's cruelness waned and almost completely disappeared. She was not certain if it was only an illusion of kindness brought on by fear of the fog and fox—but she welcomed it all the same. Flowers when she came home from school. Leaving treats and food for Mister Tops. Kind words scrawled on pages of parchment, scattered around the house for her to find.

He became a lovely ghost his face and image fading from her mind as the month progressed and she saw him less and less. A specter that was not seen, but tried to communicate with her in its own bizarre way.

She heard him in the walls, his breath and heart beating between each tick of the clock, his whispering words half-mad and searching. Searching for an answer from the land of the grave.

10

Rosemary and Beck spent many hours down in that industrial ring of ancient clock factories, exploring new places and making tiny maps to be exchanged in those rare moments they actually went to class. Rosemary got over her fear of Beck using her to awaken the sleeping girl. With each kiss the thorn girl felt farther away—more distant and less important.

With each private caress of skin and hand, she felt like the whole world consisted of only her and Beck. She loved to look into his eyes—to feel his arms against her, rough with hair and calluses as they explored both the ruins and each other.

And the moments at night when she was away from him—those were haunted by his memory and the sounds of her Father crawling through the walls, searching for something she never understood.

Late into the night, Rosemary and Beck would talk on the phone, connecting in words as they had in flesh. She had taken to spending all of her hours at home in the attic, her only bed a sleeping bag and her only company the mice and insects that lived there. Her own room lay unused downstairs, pictures and bookshelves collecting dust as they sat malnourished from contact.

When she slept, she slept surrounded by her mother's things. Her mother's chalk, her mother's books. Pictures of her mother, letters from her mother to Mister Tops. She smelled her mother on these things—a mixture of musk and ivy, of old books and lilacs.

When she awoke in the morning she awoke to the smell of wild animals and forest. A deep, earthy smell. Like being wrapped up in a quilt of leaves. The outside of her sleeping bag felt warm—as if someone had slept curled up around her in the night.

And some mornings she even found strands of red and brown hair. The color of autumn leaves. Just like her mother's. She didn't say anything to Beck, or even Mister Tops or her Father. She could not deal with the idea of her mother visiting her in the night—even if she had done so only as apparition.

11

Each night, Rosemary vowed to stay awake and catch whoever was visiting her while she slept. She refused to believe it was her mother—refused to give into the hope that her mother was still out there—communicating with her from beyond the grave.

Each night, she fell asleep at the same hour. Her mind bewitched, her soul not able to last a mere second even after 3:00. No matter how much coffee she drank and no matter how hard she tried to keep herself awake—she had even slapped herself a few times across the face—always, always, at 3:00 in the morning she was out.

12

After a week Rosemary could not take it anymore. She was weary from lack of sleep, she was falling asleep in class, and she was barely able to concentrate on anything. A moment between classes she enlisted Beck to her aid, and he agreed almost too eagerly. His face was filled with a smile, and it made her feel alive again just to think about him spending the night with her.

Sharing her new room in the attic, showing him all of her private things. She had waited so long so have someone to share these precious objects with—waited for so long to be able to confide her secrets in someone else. The burden of her hidden life would now be split, would now be shared.

Of course, the hardest part would be sneaking Beck into the house. She feared that her father's anger would rise up again, full force and angry, if he found a strange boy in his house hanging closely to his little girl. And even though Mister Tops was her friend, she could not trust him. Too many times had she felt his lustful rabbit eyes peering over her as she walked through the house, his nose twitching and his whiskers bristling from rabbit hormones.

She knew Mister Tops wouldn't act on this desire, he had known her for to long to press his urge. Yet the looks he gave her made her nervous to be around him, they felt unnatural. A cross species lust that gave her chills just thinking about it. His paw across her skin, his whisker tickling her face. The thought of it made her queasy.

But still—she could not refuse the fact that some part of her liked it. Enjoyed that fear and that hatred of herself. The idea of doing something so wrong—so against the very laws of nature—it thrilled her.

No, she couldn't have Mister Tops watch over her while she slept. She couldn't trust him. She couldn't trust herself. And he could not ever know about Beck's presence in the house—he might do something mean and cruel out of jealousy.

13

When Rosemary snuck Beck in through the front porch, her father was outside, wandering in their overgrown garden and looking for ghostly footprints in the soft mud. His hair was crowned with autumn, the leaves of gold and brown tangled up within his messy grey curls as he searched. He knew that he had heard someone walking through the garden last night and was certain it was a ghost.

If only he could catch the footprints and somehow prove the existence of the spirits. If only somehow he could communicate with them, get them to answer his questions. Talk to him.

He caught Mister Tops out of the corner of his eye, sniffing around the ground, looking for that squirrel with rusted shears in hand. Neither of them heard Rosemary's footsteps as she walked up to the attic. Neither of them heard Beck's footsteps either—Rosemary had timed each movement to match the breathing of the house.

They moved as the house moved. Moved as the house's hundred hearts beat out the entropy of each moment, time consuming the universe in large nasty gulps. They held their breath as they walked, hoping to keep their treason a secret.

Around them fluttered brass and bronze bees and tiny golden fireflies encased in glass and carved wood. Beck was astounded at the craftsmanship that went into each one—the balance and perfection of the gears.

When they reached the attic, Beck stared about in awe. Around he heard the scuttling feet of mice, searching for something within the heart of the house. Along the ribs of the walls he saw countless pictures of shipwrecked boats, painted in painful detail and making his heart long for the beach of some lost and forgotten world.

The half-destroyed vivisection of mannequins lay scattered across the floor, collecting dust in impossibly spiraling patterns. Around the plastic arms and limbs were scattered countless books of photographs. Some of dead mermaids, others of sketches of hands by famous artists. Some others were grave rubbings of various cemeteries that have since been sunken underwater, their words lost except from within that very tome.

"This place is amazing," he said.

Rosemary put a finger to her lips as she unrolled the sleeping bag, putting the pillow at the top of it. It would be night soon. Her heart pulled on her skin, her blood beating so fast she felt dizzy. She pulled off her clothes and slid into the sleeping bag naked.

He watched. She saw his eyes overlooking her body, felt the fingers of his gaze trace themselves across the contours of her skin. Her chest felt tight—her ribs too constraining against her lungs.

He removed his own clothes, her eyes now on his body. She watched him take off his shirt, his pants, his socks. She did not look away even once. Transfixed on the male form in all its glory, standing proud and nude in front of her. He slid into the sleeping bag next to her.

Their skin was wet from sweat, their fingers slippery and messy and unused to the maps of each other's flesh. Rosemary closed her eyes, the sensations of him touching her stitching across her bones like needle and thread.

She was a ship at sea.

Being torn apart in a violent storm.

She tried to stay quiet—tried to keep all sound to a minimum. But it was so hard. So hard not to cry out his name. So hard not to scream at the top of her lungs. Instead, she made the sounds of the sea between her lips. The sound of waves exhaling out of her lungs. She was no longer the ship at sea—she was that sea itself, that storm itself. And he was the boat caught up within her tempests.

14

When they were finished they lay back, cooled down and sweaty, letting the breeze from the window play across the calm sea of their bodies. She was curled up around him, playing with the brown hairs on his chest with her long pale fingers. She liked the play of light across her hand, the way the colors of his skin looked against her own.

After a few minutes of silence he rolled over and reached into his book bag. She ran her hand over his back, feeling his spine rising up to the base of his skull. When he rolled over he had two clove cigarettes, a zippo lighter and a box of tarot cards.

She smiled and leaned in on her elbows, curious as to what he had in mind. He unwrapped the tarot cards, sliding them out from a small leather sack. He lit up his cigarette, handing the other to her. She lit it up, inhaling deeply. The air smelled like burning mint as Beck shuffled the cards, his thin, ink-stained fingers manipulating each of the arcana like a musician tuning his instrument.

She watched the smoke leave her mouth as she exhaled—a large shadowy cloud, tumbling with ribbons of mint and clove. Beck turned and looked at her, working his jaw as he talked.

"Think of a question."

She nodded, cleared her head.

No questions came to her mind.

Only Beck.

She focused on him in her mind, overlaying the mental image of Beck with the one of flesh and blood in front of her. Two different people. Two different personalities. The Beck she had constructed in her mind, now polarized with the one who sat across from her. The Beck who had touched her, taunted her, and tempted her. The Beck who was the ship inside of her sea.

She contrasted that with the Beck who was in her mind. The Beck she thought about in the hours when he was not there. The Beck she masturbated to in the late hours of the night. She focused on them both, contrasted them both.

And then—a question. Clear, in her mind.

Which one of them is real?

Is this boy who was inside of me real?

Or this figment of my mind who had been based on him?

She opened her eyes, his body leaning close to hers. He smelled so wonderful, so mysterious. Like foreign spices. Like running animals in the wild. Rosemary blushed as a tip of his elbow brushed against her breast. So warm, so smooth, so real. "Okay," she said, "I've thought of one."

He grinned. "All right, then. Let's start."

15

Beck read the cards like music. Full of nuances, extra meanings, hidden words, and half-heard phrases. The story of her answer followed a pattern—a shield and cross and sword. A rise and fall, like breathing. Like the waves on the sea.

The cards burned images into her mind, tainting her memory with their ink-stained fingers. The five of songs. An old man in a cage eating ravens. The lady of shadows. A little girl dancing under the eyes of a rotund giant.

In the end her question went unanswered. It was lost in the folds of the reading, the actual story of the cards taking on a question of their own, a hidden story within a story.

When Beck was finished he looked down at her. "You see," he said, "A good tarot reading is not about answering questions, nor is it about predicting the future. It's about reading the person in front of you, turning them into a story. Taking the chaos of their life and wrapping it up in a pattern of plot."

She nodded. She didn't care about that. She touched a card that had a girl trapped in a tower. A princess? Wasn't it always a princess? She looked for long hair, looked for thorn bushes in the picture on the tarot card. Nothing. No telling if it was meant to be Sleeping Beauty or Rapunzal.

"I think that we—as human beings—need this sort of thing. We desire patterns in our life—patterns in the shape of stories. Look at our memories—we don't remember random incidents. We remember everything as a story—a linear plot. We take out the unnecessary stuff, change things to make it more dramatic. Our minds are made to process our world as fiction—not as fact, fiction. That is why we love our stories so—they take our reality and chop it up so that we can digest it."

A pause. An exhalation of smoke. He grins at her. "In the end, we are just machines for plot—automatons that take in our life and then rearrange it into pleasing shapes."

Rosemary ignored him, staring at the card with the tower on it. She did not care about this philosophy, or how the reading meandered about in the shape of a story. All she cared about was the answer to her question—which Beck was the real Beck? This flesh here, his hand on my stomach—was he real? Or was the construct in her mind real—this Beck made of pieces of him and glued together in the holes in her dreams?

In the back of the tower she saw lightning. A storm. The princess looked like she was screaming. Beck droned on behind her, the song of his voice meshing up with the breathing of the house. The two became one background noise—each hypnotic soundscape interlacing with the other.

Behind the princess she saw another face. Twisted. Mad. Pushing. Was it male? Female? She couldn't tell. It wore a mask. A mask like the Vardøgr wear. A knife in the clean hands.

She felt a hand on her shoulder. Pushing her. Beck was far away. She tried to say something, but could not. She just eased into sleep. *Must be 3:00 in the morning*, she thought as she drifted down. Must be. A tower. She saw it. A girl in thorns. Masks.

Everybody was asleep except for her. Sleeping Beauty. She was never asleep. Just everything else. Leaving her alone and encased in a castle of thorns.

16

I will not be a machine, Rosemary muttered in her sleep. *I will not be a machine for plot.*

17

Whispered into her ear. Hot breath. Someone shook her. Wake up, they whispered, oh dear god please wake up. The smell of fire. Smell of mint. Smell of sea people—sex and salt and sweat. Something was cooking in the distance.

Shake. Shake. Shake.

Her eyes opened. Light filtered in. Beck's face looking over hers as he shakes her, smoke pouring out from his mouth.

"What's wrong?" she asked, still filled with sleep.

"There is something in the walls."

She nodded. "Yeah, that's my father."

He looked around, worried. "Do you think he can hear us? There is someone else in there, with him. I can hear him talking. Carrying on a conversation. And its weird—it keeps repeating itself. I even heard your voice."

Rosemary ignored him. It was still dark. 4:00 A.M. and still dark. And she was awake. Well, not completely awake. But more awake then she'd been at this hour before today. "You woke me up for that? He talks to ghosts. Come on, ignore it. Did you see anything else? Did anyone come in the room?"

He shook his head no.

She felt disappointed. She wanted proof of the visitations, wanted to see her mother in the flesh again. To be haunted by vague signs was a curse that ate away at all logical parts of her brain. Beck leaned into her, putting his arm around her. She laid her ear to his chest and heard the trumpets of his heart.

"Listen," his voice echoed in his ribs, "Listen to the conversation. It's—it's just weird."

"What did you expect? He's talking to the dead."

She humored him, concentrating on the conversation from the inside of the walls. It took a moment to filter out all other sounds—heart, clocks, mice, and concentrate on the actual words being whispered.

It was not a ghost. As she listened, Rosemary's skin prickled and became slick with sweat and fear.

18

Her father: You have come, and you shall be a favored one in Tetu, O Osiris Auf-ankh, whose word is truth, the son of the lady Shert-en-Menu, whose word is truth.

Rosemary's voice: We enter the doors between worlds, looking for the gardens at the end of time. We come searching for the paper of your words, scattered through the wind of the fourteen doorways.

Her father: Asut, Suta, Asut. Repeat three times, and let the ghosts come and talk to us.

Rosemary's voice: I shall be the vessel of gods, the speaker of the dead. I shall drink in the voices of the ghosts and let the words of paper flow from my mouth.

Her father: Asut, Suta, Asut. Repeat three times, and let the ghosts come and talk to us.

Rosemary's voice: I will listen to the corrupter. I will not eat of his trees, or disrupt the bones at the base of the garden. I will forget what I am told, and forget being a vessel. Lest the words burn through me, and I become she who is empty.

Her father: Asut, Suta, Asut. Repeat three times, and let the ghosts come and talk to us.

A whimper. Footsteps. Then silence and heavy breathing. Rosemary heard herself whispering, heard herself screaming. She felt like she was going to throw up. What was this? What was happening here?

Rosemary's voice: The ghosts—they aren't coming. They just throw bones at my soul and burn me with matches.

The sound of vomiting. Shaking, the walls shaking. A recorded version of the clocks striking an eternal hour, the crows cawing out in mockery, "Father! Father! Father!"

And then silence.

19

Rosemary felt like she should say something. But she did not know what—could not fathom what to speak. Instead, she just dug her head deeper into Beck's chest, trying to bury herself within him, eating her way into his heart. She sobbed for a moment, wetting his skin with her tears.

"That's not even the strangest part."

She looked up at him, drying her eyes. "No?"

"No. Listen. Closely."

The sound of a washing machine, drowning out the clock noises. Then it stopped. It sounded for a moment like an old cassette tape being eaten by a stereo system. The smell of fire, burning flesh. Salt water. The sound of waves. And then, the voices again.

"You have come and you shall be a favored one in Tetu, O Osiris Auf-ankh, whose word is truth, the son of the lady Shert-en-Menu, whose word is truth."

Rosemary stared at Beck in disbelief. "What, what is going on?"

He shook his head. "I don't know. But it's repeating itself. It's done this at least twenty times, and it started while you were asleep. At first I thought it was a tape—but I don't know. Sounds too clear. Not enough degradation."

She kissed the bone of his shoulder. "Right when I fell asleep? It started playing?"

He looked down at her and grinned. "Yeah. Right away. The second you went to sleep. It was weird—because I thought I heard this conversation before, when we were coming upstairs. But it wasn't. Not at all. The voices were different, and only every other word was the same."

Sunlight from the loose dawn shone through the windows. Outside she could tell the world was waking up. She patted his chest. "Let's go someplace else."

"Anywhere in mind?"

She shrugged. "Breakfast sounds good. You treat. After that—I don't care. Just not here. Not anywhere near here."

20

Coffee. Some donuts. A scrambled egg and the sound of trucks. Rosemary pushed her fork against her food, sipped her coffee a little. The eggs left a trail on her plate, like breadcrumbs. She dreamt of drowning last night. She remembered that. Drowning. And a lighthouse hit by lightning.

Beck tried to carry on a conversation but ended up mostly talking to himself. Rosemary did not feel the urge to communicate. She only wanted to stare at her food. She felt too sick inside to eat.

My blood feels like salt, she thought. *My skin like an old book. I have no idea where I end and the rest of the world begins.* Like space and time and objects were all illusions. Carefully painted to look like separations. Objects tilted into fluid, running together in an infinite spiral of light.

She thought about the conversation. Did any of that really happen? She'd heard her voice. Heard her saying those things. And parts of it felt familiar—yet when did that happen? Did she forget it? How could she forget it?

"Are you all right?"

She grabbed his hand, staring at patterns of veins across his skin. "I don't know," she was hypnotized by the branches of blue that beat with blood, "I don't think I can ever go back home."

She could never truly escape from it, not as long as she lived in Dark Rivers.

"Let's go," she said, "Let's go far away from here."

He moved his hand away from hers, brushing the hair out from her eyes. She had been crying. He wanted to comfort her, desired to protect her. But found he could not. He could only offer her lies instead. "Where do you want to go?"

"Bermuda. Hawaii. Germany. Poland. England? No. Ireland," she smiled, "we could even stow away on a ship."

Beck laughed. "How romantic! If I said yes, would you believe me?"

Rosemary ignored him and continued. "We could get a cat. Or a lizard. And put a bell around its neck. We could name him Scheherazade. Or Commie Bastard."

Beck smiled. "Of course. I've always been partial to lizards."

She laughed, and for a moment Beck thought things might be all right after all. "Come on," he said, "Let's go exploring."

21

The ruins brought her no peace. Rosemary left them feeling even more haunted than before, as if the ghosts of all the former employers clung to her skin, grasping at her arms and legs as she went back home. Trying to pull her back, pull her back to the land of labor lost.

She tried to put on a smile for Beck, tried not to let him know how depressed she was. All she could muster up was this lie of a pumpkin grin, making her look half mad in the dim light of the ruins.

He was a good friend and lover, but he always felt this chivalric need to protect her. And right now she didn't need protection. She needed knowledge. Truth as to what really happened.

As she wandered aimlessly through half-eaten corridors, that conversation played itself over and over again in the back of her mind. She couldn't believe it was real—that she had been a part of some strange séance that she couldn't even remember. One that her dad played over and over again.

She didn't know why the idea spooked her. The dissonance from it played sour notes in her mind, grating on her perception of reality. She felt charged and separated. As if the world was fading into two pieces—one real and one unreal. And she wasn't sure which was which. She wasn't sure what was really happening to her anymore.

Eventually Rosemary returned home. Beck wanted to sneak in again, to come and sleep up in the attic. She knew he meant well. But tonight she needed to be by herself. To be alone. In that house.

She needed to search for something.

A truth.

The bones of reality.

Hidden within the folds of her memories.

22

Rosemary listened. It was 3:00 in the morning, and she stood in a small enclosed tunnel that led through the walls of her house. Countless pendulums swung around her in golden arcs, brass gears interlocking to her right and left, teeth fitting into teeth in a primitive act of clockwork sex. Rosemary remembered reading somewhere that time was a measurement of entropy.

She closed her eyes. Focused. On the sounds between sounds. She bit her cheek, refusing sleep tonight. The voices—she heard them. Like a muttering at first, and then the dictation again.

She opened her eyes, fast. She felt woozy and dizzy. Her veins filled with the blood of slumber, sandy blood grating against her bones. *I must stay awake*, Rosemary thought. *I cannot fall asleep again. I have to know if this is real. If anything is real.* She needed to find out where that recording came from—find the heart of the broadcast and discover the truth.

She stumbled as she walked, her body roaming forward in a jerky slumbering waltz. Gears bit her fingers as she grasped the walls for balance. She felt the anger of the house as she moved. The Tick Tock House did not want her skin and blood getting caught in the machinations, grinding each clock she touched to a halt.

The voices were up ahead—to the left. Maybe upstairs a little. She followed them, concentrating. Each time her hand reached out and was bit by time's serpents she felt more and more awake.

I can do this, she thought. *I can find out the truth.*

Her knees weakened. All numb, all pins and needles. She could not move them. They felt like useless bags of sand strapped to her torso.

She crawled forward, her fingers digging into the wood of the floor like a harpy's claw.

Giant-shaped shadows at the end of the hallway. Footsteps and the sounds of the clocks getting louder, tick, tick, tick. The bodies moved toward her, their limbs erupting with the sound of stone grating on stone, the air filling with particles of rust. She wasn't sure what these things were—the shadows glinted like brass, sounded like machinery.

Her fingers felt pricklish. Wrapped in spines. Her head was filled with the wet meat of dreams, her eyes barely able to stay open. Her lids covered the room in a black semicircle. She reached into her pocket and pulled out the small mirror, the glass cold against her hands.

With her last strength she held it out, close to her lips and breathed against it. She used her finger to carve out the word help. Sleep beckoned her, the voices that chanted louder now. Beneath it all she heard the whispers of ghosts, and felt the fingers of mist caressing her.

The room dilated and then succumbed to shadow's slumber.

23

Rosemary awoke. Pine trees rushed by her face, tinted with the light of the moon, their needles brushing against her skin. She felt red fur between her legs and a large body. She grasped onto a furry neck, large pointed red ears sticking up on either side of its head as they darted further and further, deeper and deeper into the woods beyond Dark Rivers.

Rosemary smelled her mother on the fox below her. A musky smell. An old book smell. A waxy candle smell. She was riding on a giant fox that smelled like her mother, fleeing from something that was inside of the house. That she knew. She had stumbled onto something in her search for the truth. Exactly what she did not know. But it scared her. Scared her enough to use the mirror.

Sleep still nested under her skin. Her bones weary, her skin and hair weary. Her body was a rag doll, slumped over the fox body and barely able to lift a single muscle. Everything was blurry, spiraling in and out of focus. She wondered if she had been drugged.

She pushed past the numbness in her limbs and gripped on tighter, the fox pushing farther and farther. She wrapped her fingers around the soft red hairs, tightening her legs, not wanting to fall off. They bounded over crags and hillocks, moving into the stony heart of the forest.

Were they even in Dark Rivers anymore? Or had they passed some invisible line and stepped out of bounds of the city, driving into a no man's land between worlds? She could not tell. But one thing she did know was that it was a silent landscape she was in now, one void of the sounds of the constant clocks, the constant ticking of the hours.

And she felt freedom. Freedom in that silence.

STONE DOGS

Thursday: English Lit

The trees outside of the window are crystallized, frozen into a dance by the ice storm. Mister Harvey is reading a passage from *The Waste Land*. But I can't hear the words.

I only see his lips.

Thick beautiful lips. The words coming out of them deep and bellowing. I hear some girls whisper and giggle behind me. I know they are thinking the same thing I am, picturing him naked.

Maybe binding him up with his tie to the radiator in the back of the classroom. Gently ripping the clothes from his body. Forcing him to love me, even though it is forbidden. Maybe I shouldn't be writing this down? But that's part of the thrill, I guess. Maybe he will come over, spy my notebook. Spy my trembling hands writing this. Peek over my shoulder and see these hidden words. This language shoved between pages like skin in a sheet.

I get a small thrill, a quick chill, even as I write this. He walks closer. Do I keep the book open? Leave the page naked for him to see? Yes. Of course.

He didn't even notice. Walked past me. Invisible girl. I see his eyes spy the ones behind me. Always the ones behind me, the murder of pretty girls in the back of the room. Those beautiful little waifs, black hair cropped around their shoulders like feathers. The dark staring, unthinking eyes. Like pools full of drowning children.

All guys look at them. The three of them- all alike. Dressed alike, eyes and hair and mouth alike. Petite, perfect. Like swords lined up in the back of the room.

I will not write their names here. This is a book that will be buried under an ash tree. In a jar filled with broken glass and used coffee grounds. The names and words written here have power. I will not honor them with such a thing. Instead, I shall call them the crow girls. The sword girls. The unkindly ones.

Thursday: Algebra

The numbers on the chalk board do not look like math equations. They look like alchemical recipes. Like magical formulae. Circles, overlapping. Plotted with strange symbols, letters that contain hidden meaning. I wonder if there is a connection, somehow. Between the mental world that imagines such equations and the physical world where such equations act out their duties.

Maybe that is what magic is. That bridge between the two. Occult power existing in the actuality—the merging of two worlds.

You may think I'm a strange girl, to think such thoughts. You're right.

But that doesn't mean you know me.

The trees outside dance faster. Sped up, animated dance. Whirling widdershins in sleet dresses. The ice smacking against the window. It sounds like a man, sitting outside and rapping against it.

I see snow and ice piling up. The trees are waist deep now. Frost crystals spread across the pane of glass, like white spidering fingers, crawling. Fractals. I could plot out their course in equations, and predict how they will grow.

There is power in that.

Magic.

Thursday: Study Hall

This is a windowless room. I cannot see the snow, the ice. I cannot see the trees dance. But I feel them, hidden behind the molding grey walls. Shaking their bodies. They tinkle-tinkle-tinkle when they dance. Like a music box.

This teacher is just an overpaid babysitter. He sits in the back, scolding those who speak. We cannot talk. We cannot do anything. We are supposed to study.

I think I will read instead.

Did I ever tell you about my favorite book? It's an epic fantasy story, called Stone Dogs. It's very strange, very surreal. I happened upon it by accident at a used book store. I saw a wall of the same thing—dragons, elves, dragons. Beneath these rotting and yellowed covers I saw a single book, on the floor. Face up.

The cover was a thick paper that was textured to the touch to feel like human hair and bone. The illustration on the cover was a line drawing of a little girl feeding on a dragon. The dragon was dead, the girl was petite.

I bought the book with my lunch money.

I've reread it forty six times already. I can't stop reading it—it is a compulsion. Each time I read it pages change, words change. Paragraphs are never quite the same with each reading. The characters morph, the landscape changes. Even the map in the back is constantly moving with each read, constantly morphing in shape.

And yet, the plot is always the same.

I'll tell you about that some other time. I only have a half an hour left to read and I MUST read. I feel all drunk and fuzzy even thinking about it. Thinking about that book. In my hands. Like hair on the scalp of a head running between my fingers.

Thursday: Lunch

I usually go outside to eat, Geoff and me walking around the back lot talking and eating. Not today. Today they said we are trapped inside. That the snow and the sleet and all the ice is far too dangerous for anyone to leave.

I feel caged.

Sitting here, in the gymnasium, chewing on a stale salami sandwich. Geoff sits beside me but he's not talking. He's just looking at crumpled mountains of paper in front of him. Scattered next to him are books on architecture, on engineering. On equations for worlds and universes. And a metal compass. And an ink and quill.

I would bother him, but I know he is working. Designing a world of his own, a galaxy of his own. Geoff is a writer of sorts. A creator. He has over thirty notebooks in his locker, filled with histories of this imaginary world, genealogies, genetic code for various creatures, the planets around it and the number of stars in the sky.

I know interrupting him now would be a big mistake. He gets angry when his work is disrupted, he yells and screams and throws his books at me. He is my only friend. I have no choice but to obey the whims of his imagination. I eat my sandwich in silence.

It smells like feet in here.

I want to go home.

Thursday: Biology

The walls are plastered with the bodies of dissected animals. They are beautiful. Pinned open and revealing their innermost secrets, labeled and categorized with painstaking detail. Like an open pocket watch, the clockwork displayed for all to see.

Geoff's world is like that.

Orderly, open. Naked and cataloged.

I don't listen to my teacher speak. She has a very nice voice, quiet and trembling. Like she is about ready to scream at any moment. A hidden hysteria in the background.

Her actual words are meaningless, pointless. There is nothing to learn when she speaks. Just words. Hollow things. I look instead at the pinned-open body of a pig fetus. The parts are so perfect. Like they are made of glass.

Thursday: Art Class

We have a kiln. But it is out back, covered by snow and ice. We can't get to it to retrieve our sculptures. I fear I will never see mine again. It was a cat with wide eyes. I call it *Fear of Mice*.

So instead we are treated to a slideshow on Renaissance Art. The boys in the back giggle at the nude women. I hear someone bark out the word "fat!" and another "chubby chasers!" and I feel ashamed.

Am I like that to them?

At the end of the show the teacher stands in front of us. Her name is Glenda, like the good witch. She has no last name, none that she will let us speak. She is tall and thin, her arms are branches and her feet are roots. Her dress is brown and green, and she looks like a tree. The ice will be coming for her soon. To crystallize her.

She gives the usual speech. About beauty back then was different. That thin people were considered ugly and poor, and fat people beautiful and rich. She looks at me and winks.

I want to kill her. I hope the ice comes for her soon, turns her into a frozen tree, stuck dancing in the sleet and wind. If I see any ice I will betray her. Give away her location. Let them come, find her. Swallow her whole.

Thursday: American History

We don't learn about real American History. We only learn the same mythology everyone is always taught. About pilgrims. And Columbus. About JFK's death and MLK's life. We never learn the real stories. The little histories.

My dad has a collection of books in his attic. They are diaries from the Civil War. This is history. I've read most of them, but not all. They are by civilians, soldiers. Wives and artists. There are no famous people. No war heroes, no presidents or congressmen.

My favorite one was written by a fourteen-year-old girl. There was a yellowed picture stuck in the pages. She looked like me. That is why I am writing this. This is real history. This is what happens when you aren't famous. When you are invisible.

My teacher says something. I had to stop writing for a moment there, to listen to it. He got a note from someone outside in the hall. A shadow behind the crooked glass door. The note said that we are trapped. The teacher read this, told this to us with an air of authority.

We are snowed in. We cannot even open the doors.

I look at the window, and all I see is a wall of white.

I feel like crying, but I don't. I don't want to be known as the girl who cries. That is worse than being invisible.

The note continues. Authorities are trying to find a way to get us out. It could be a day or two, at the least. We were to stay in the gymnasium overnight. The faculty will be laying down beds for each of us.

When the teacher is done reciting he looks out the window. His face is convulsing, twitching. His eye is moving, like someone is pulling a string and making it go. His lips peel back in a sneer.

He was never attractive. But here, in this state of half madness, he was downright ugly. I want to stand up, to be excused. But the bell has not rung yet, the period is not over. There is still more lies to be learned.

I am going to pull out my book and read some more. I need to be away from here for a little bit. I need to someone else, somewhere else.

Thursday: The Gymnasium

I write this in my bed. Well, it is not really a bed. It is a blanket on the gymnasium floor. With a pillow. The pillow and blanket are grey. The floor is cold and hard. I can see my breath as I write this. Rising from my mouth. The ghost of my words.

My pen has a light on the end. It was a birthday gift last year, from my mom. Before she crawled under the bed and into the tunnels beneath my house. I am glad she gave it to me. At the time I thought it was a stupid gift. Tonight, it is a lifesaver.

I crouch beneath the blanket as I write this. I can hear sounds around me. Even though they separated us—boys on one side, girls on the other—I can hear people sneaking and talking. Whispering, moaning. The shuffling of blankets and the sighs of sex.

I wonder if Mister Harvey is out there. Crawling beneath the blankets with the sword girls. Just the thought of it makes me sad and embarrassed. And yet, at the same time, very aroused.

I am going to play a game. I hear moaning now, several voices. And people whispering be quiet, and hush, and please don't get me in trouble. I am going to try and guess who each of them is. Try and figure out what is going on in beneath other grey blankets.

Names escape me. I am awash in the sounds, the rubbing of bodies. I feel a bump next to me and know that whoever is right over there is doing something as well. I feel a soft touch of skin, an electric sensation all along my body.

I am filled with thunder. I hear them, moaning, moving. Thrusting. Faster. That skin rubbing up against mine. Accidental contact. Motion, emotion. Flames inside of me.

I have to put the pen down.

I have to put this notebook down.

I know I will feel guilty in the morning, even though I will do nothing wrong.

Friday: The Gymnasium

In the morning they give us stale donuts and bagels. The donuts are hard, the bagels are chewy. I eat like it is my last meal. I made sure to check to see who was lying next to me last night—to see who this mysterious figures were. Nobody was there. Just an empty grey blanket and pillow.

I read after breakfast. First period would resume at 9:00 A.M., like it did every morning. It seems there was no reprieve from the schedule. No matter how much the world has changed.

Everybody else chatted while I read. I heard them, in the distance. Like muttering echoes from behind a wall. Talking the usual talk. Boys, colleges, work, who was cute and who was not. Who was cool and who was not. The names always changed, but the pattern was the same.

I am at my favorite part of the book. The main character is a peasant girl named Alisandre. She is very pretty, with dirty blonde hair and intense eyes. In the book her only desire is to become a knight.

The section I am at now is her trial for knighthood. Fourteen different rituals must be observed. A dragon must be slain. Sacrifice of self and family must be undertaken. Each time I read it the rituals and trials change. But the result is still the same. She is knighted by the Prince of Butterflies. This is the first time she meets the prince. When the prince's hand touches her shoulder she falls in love.

Now for a little explanation. The magical land where the book takes place is called Iblio. In Iblio, gender and rank are determined not by birth, but instead by trials that are assigned to each station. With each gender and title comes responsibilities and awards, as well as rules for how you are supposed to act and what you are supposed to do and who you are supposed to marry. What time of the month you are to have sex, what day of the year you are supposed to give birth. What you are supposed to wear and even how you are supposed to wear it.

Geoff would love the appendices in the back of the book. They go into exquisite detail on the different ranks and genders, and the different trials and honors awarded. It was the sort of thing he would read and re-read over and over again.

Even though the prince and the knight were in love, they could never do anything about it. It was forbidden. One of them would have to undergo the trials of the princess, and neither of them wanted to do that.

This was where the book's main plot came into focus. After this point it was about their forbidden love, and the people who wanted to destroy them. Including the evil princess Earwig, who wanted Alisandre for herself.

I hate princess Earwig. Why would anyone want to be a princess? All day, living under glass. Waiting to be saved or married. Only to be expected have children the minute they are freed. They had no rights, only responsibilities. I completely understood why Alisondre and the Prince of Butterflies acted the way they did. They wanted a relationship of equalities.

I wonder if such a thing is even possible. In any world.

Friday: English Lit

Mister Harvey has a stack of books on his desk. The class moans. He is wearing his glasses and his patched-up smoking jacket. That means what he is about to say is serious. Is deep and intellectual. This is the uniform of his rank.

"Class, I know you are bored in the evenings. A lot of you are. I have certain obligations to your parents—to make sure nothing (cough) happens. So, I have a stack of books here. You are each to take one and to read it tonight until you fall asleep. Understand? I expect a full book report."

He crosses his arms. His eyes look at each of them, meet each eye. The sword girls giggle. I could not help it, but for some reason I blushed and I think he saw me blush. After a moment of silence to show how deadly serious this all is, he commands us to line up single file and get the books.

I wait and get into the end of the line.

It is so much easier to be invisible from the back.

Each person grabs a book. I see them from where I stand. Big, weighty tomes. Classics. Works that did not involve love and knights and the Prince of Butterflies. Books that were not about the magical land of Iblio.

When I got up—right there, after everyone else was seated and they could all see—Mister Harvey reaches behind his desk and pulls out a book wrapped in leather with a rope that tied it shut. He puts it in my hand, laying his hand over mine.

"This is for you," he says, "I set it aside just this morning. I think you'll like it."

His breath smells like vanilla and cocoa. His hand is rough over mine, and large and meaty. I want to faint. The moment lasts forever, his eyes staring into mine, his hand over mine. The sword girls giggle, and one of the boys hoots and whistles.

Mister Harvey's hand moves, his eyes move.

I sit back down, but I still feel it. His hand over mine. His eyes staring into mine.

I untie the knot, carefully. Unwrapping the leather around it. It feels soft, smooth, like skin. I am flushed, remembering the stray flesh last night, rubbing against mine.

The book.

It is Victorian. On the cover is a naked woman, leaning over a dwarf. The title is *The Tunnels Beneath the Castle of O*. This might be a promising read after all.

Friday: Algebra

I cannot pay attention to the equations on the board. Every time I try and focus, my mind swims. Outside is a wall of ice and snow. Inside are the tense bodies, a roomful of trapped teenagers. The teacher sees their stare, tries to avoid their animal gazes.

I open my new book. The pages are thick, heavy. There are no words. Only pictures. They follow a sequential order, telling a story. I blush as I flip through it, closing the book as quickly as possible. I do not want the teacher to see what I am reading. I do not want her to see what Mister Harvey has given me.

They were line drawings, and in each of them someone was performing some sexual act with someone else. Always in the background, hidden in the walls of the castle, in the shadows of the tunnel. Leering at the main characters.

I am not sure how I feel about this.

I open up *Stone Dogs* and read. The teacher's voice drones on in the background. I read about Princess Earwig's glass face. I read about her hair made of gold. I read about her dresses, two hundred and thirty in all and no two of them alike. I read about her heart, kept in a box on her step mother's throne.

And I read about the magic she uses to try and capture the love of Alisondre. Pictures burnt. Words whispered into seashells and buried in a box of mirrors. Blood smeared across the walls and the howls of misery ringing through the castle.

I picture Princess Earwig. And I see her looking like one of the girls in the shadows of the Castle of O. Her face twisted, her mouth wide open. She was screaming. That was what princess Earwig looked like. A twig of a girl in a castle of sex.

I hardly even hear the bell ring. One of the sword girls shakes me out of my book, out of my trance. She giggles when I come to, giggles and runs off with her triplets. I want to cut her open. Display her glass organs to the world.

I run outside, into the hall. I see Geoff and wave. He waves back, I see scars along his fingers. Cut into rings around his knuckles.

He talks to a boy. A new kid? I don't know. I don't recognize him. He has purple hair and a trenchcoat. He's cute. His features are very pretty, very feminine. He talks in a thick British accent. He reminds me of a fox, somehow.

Geoff introduces him. The boy's name is Nogitsune.

"He climbed in through the third floor window. He's here to save us."

I smile my best smile. "Really? How come we're still in here then?"

The boy shrugs. "Because I lied to Geoff, that's why. Although, I did sneak in through the third floor. But I'm not here to save anyone. I'm hiding out. Someone is chasing me."

Geoff sighs. "How could you lie to me?"

The boy puts his hand of Geoff's shoulder. Geoff melts beneath his fingers. "I'm sorry. You just seemed so excited, and I just fed you what you wanted to hear."

I knew I should ask who he was running away from. Instead, I do something stupid. I talk about books. "Have you ever read *Stone Dogs*?"

The new boy shrugged. "Nope. Sounds like some weirdo new agey thing."

I wave my hand excitedly. The more he looks at me, the more I want him. "No. It's fantasy."

New boy Nogitsune puts his fingers to his head. Like a gun. Pulls the trigger, bang. He's dead. Tongue sticks out, head lolls back. "Oh, gawd. Not more of that Tolkien shit. I am so sick of elves and dwarves. Don't you guys read anything good? Like Camus. Or Sartre. Or fuck—I don't know. Flannery O'Conner?"

Geoff blushes. "I read that stuff."

I push him. I don't know why I do it. He doesn't deserve to be pushed. "No, you don't," I say.

Geoff is hurt. "If he can lie to me, I can lie to him."

I see him look at me. His face is red. He's about to cry. He runs off screaming. Nogitsune looks at me and his eyes light up. "Woah, good going there. I thought he would never leave. So—what did you say your name was again?"

I almost answer when the bells rings.

"Shit. Late for class. Sorry."

I run off, he yells at me.

"Late for class? How can you even care about such things when the world is going to end?"

Friday: Study Hall

I love the prose in *Stone Dogs*. It is unlike any fantasy I have ever read before. The sentences flow over each other. Tripping on the words and melting into a soup of language. I've got some time in Study Hall, so I will copy my favorite two paragraphs here:

The kindly birds they speak and sing, with knives for beaks and swords for wings, they drip and dance orange light, discarding stray feathers like leaves on the ground. They are the autumnal gods, the speakers of mist, they have come to grant Alisondre fifty wishes, if only she could climb with needle hands and spindle fingers, up the labyrinth halls, past the walking dreams of angels and into the fire of morning light. There, there, burning puppets and the lies of sitar's men. We all know who lives here, the medusa spined, the stone singers. The hot and hollow dolls that grab the grass of dreams and weave coats of undying love.

But in corners of anger dwell the archling comedunly, who stretch with milky white eyes and cough and pour starch in the flour. They grab all hair and make them sing and dance. They have fingers, they have eyes. Oh what burning things they can do to the pretty-pretty. Oh what holes they can cut into our song boxes.

Absolutely chilling stuff. I have dreams that are written like that, in that same flowing way. Some day, I hope to write like that. Maybe, if I keep reading it and copying the words. Maybe my mind will drink in that style. Will become it.

Friday: Lunch

Geoff is not in the lunchroom. He is not at our normal table, not sitting at his normal seat. I wander around the crowd and look for him. Nothing. Some of the kids in the back wear paper plate masks, with pictures of the dead stapled onto them.

I wonder briefly if they are ghosts.

I see new boy Nogitsune. In front of him, on an intricately detailed plate is a dead fish. Cooked. With head and eyes still intact. He motions me to sit down.

I set my red plastic tray on the table. Chicken salad. Not bad for cafeteria food.

After I sit he tells me a story about foxes. About their genealogy. About their species. I am bored, and I realize Geoff would love this conversation. It was so full of details.

As he speaks, he eats. Cutting the fish slowly. Leaving the bones on his plate. When he is done I let the silence sit for a moment. I don't know what to say. I am numb from listening.

"When do you think they will let us go home?"

Nogitsune drums his fingers on the table. "Never. Things have changed. We are in the snow lands now. They didn't want to tell you, but if you go outside, you will see. There are no more trees, no more roads. We are surrounded by miles and miles and miles of ice and snow. Nothing else."

I stare at the last piece of lettuce on my plate. It is drowned in dressing. It will sting when I stick it into my mouth, coated with all those spices. "Never leave? I don't believe you. You're lying again."

He picks up his plate and slides it into his trenchcoat. It disappears beneath the folds of clothing. "That's not all. I've seen giants outside. Wandering in that wasteland. You can see them. Their heads scrape the sky. They wait for us. And they are hungry."

Nogitsune gets up and leaves.

It still smells like socks in here.

I wonder where Geoff is.

Friday: Biology

Our teacher doesn't show up for class. They say she tried to leave, tried to go out one of the second floor windows and into the snow. I hope she's okay. I hope she doesn't get eaten by a giant. Nobody else seems to care.

The other students leave. I stay and read. I like the room. I like being surrounded by these pretty dead things. So neat, so tidy. So intricate.

I pull out Mister Harvey's book. Careful, making sure nobody else is anywhere near me. I flip through the pages, looking in the background. The main story isn't interesting. A simple quest of some sort. It ends with the main character, that nude girl, having a threesome with a giant and dwarf.

I look at each face in the backgrounds, at the tiny details of each body. I look in each crack, corner and crevice. There I find more people, more figures. Doing things I never even thought possible. And I see them stare back at me. All those eyes. Staring right back at me. One of them, I realize, is Alisondre. Just as I pictured her. She wears bits and pieces of chain mail, rubbing coldly against her exposed and naked flesh.

That it is not the Prince of Butterflies above her. It is a man. And he sings. And she howls in pain. Staring at me. Pleading me to come and help her.

I'm covered in goosebumps.

I feel hot, dizzy. Aroused. I slam the book shut. Before things got out of control. It would be a terrible thing if someone was to walk into the biology lab and see me masturbating amongst all of the scientific corpses.

I wrap up the book, carefully. The leather like skin, caressing my hands. I remember the shadow of Mister Harvey's hands and I feel odd. I'm not sure what I want anymore. If anything is what it really seems to be.

I want to read more in *Stone Dogs*. But I don't have the time. The bell is about to ring. I can feel it, vibrating in the air. Like storm clouds pregnant with snow.

Friday: Art Class

Missus Willow Tree stands in front of us. She is covered from head to toe in leaves and mud. This is her winter coat. She tells us in a commanding voice that she will be back momentarily. She is going out to brave the snow. To rescue our sculptures from the kiln.

She has a rusted sword strapped over her back.

She is a knight. The Knight of Trees. She will need it when the giants come for her. I only hope that she can stand her own. It is brave for her to do this.

After she leaves, the boys in the class pull out the slide projector. They turn it on, pulling up the naked pictures from yesterday. They spin and look at me. Look at the two other girls from class. The other girls are a little thinner than me, with curved beak noses. My nose is small, button shaped, and twitches when I get nervous.

The boys crowd around. They have red lit eyes. Hair like black fur. They remind me of the wolf-kin in Iblio. A race of men whose parents slept with wolves, and begat half breeds.

One howls.

"Come on, girls. We are all alone. It's time to show us your inner secrets."

They crowd around. Claustrophobic.

I want to run. I turn to look at the exit. Wide open. Ready for escape. I hope the bell rings soon, to give me a distraction.

I see the other girls. The bird girls. They look down at the ground, shyly, sadly. They pull straps down. Bras off. I see them undress and my breath is caught.

They are beautiful and sacred and scared.

The wolfkin are enraptured.

I run, run, run rabbit run out the door.

They cannot follow me. They are trapped by the gaze of naked flesh.

Friday: The Rooms Between Floors

I'm still shaken from Art Class. And I have this strange feeling that I survived something. That I got away before something terrible happened. I don't like to think about that. I don't want to wonder what happened to the crow girls. Class seems unimportant now.

Nagitsune was right—why should I worry about going to class when the world is going to end? I skip out on American History and run off to look for Geoff. I know about the secret places. The places he goes to when no one is looking.

He calls it his cutting room.

It is one of the rooms between floors.

There is a secret into getting between the floors. Most people don't know about it. The janitor showed Geoff the way. One that had a crush on him. I think Geoff wanted to reciprocate, but was afraid. Afraid of himself.

You don't use the stairs to get to the rooms between floors. You look for a green tile on the ceiling. All of the other tiles are dark blue. When you see it you stand beneath it and close your eyes.

And you concentrate on the sound of the ocean.

Holding your breath.

Still, so still.

If you do it correctly you will feel water around you. Do not panic. Do not move. Let the water flow around you, caress you. You feel dizzy, your lungs burning. But don't let go—don't breathe just yet. You wait for the water to cover you completely.

And then—

It stops.

You can breathe, and it feels like fire.

When you open your eyes, you are in the cutting room. One of the rooms between floors.

I follow the ritual carefully. It is hard to do. I am frightened and want to run. Instead I think, I flow. I let the water come and wash me away.

I was right. Geoff is here. He lies in the corner of the room. The walls are covered in posters, the only light a single candle in the middle of the floor. It is cramped in here—low ceiling. Stoop down to see everything.

Someone is with Geoff. He is curled up around someone. He turns and looks at me, naked beneath a blanket. It smells like the ocean. I see Nogitsune and I sit down, mouth open. I did not expect to see him here.

"Hi," Geoff says shyly. "Did you know the world is going to end?"

I see new cuts. Across his chest. Nogitsune is asleep on Geoff's chest. I see cuts across Nogitsune's back.

"Yes," I said. "It's been ending for a long time now."

Geoff runs his hand over Nogitsune's naked back. I feel a pang of jealousy. It feels odd, bitter in my mouth. I should have seen this coming, but did not. "When did he come up here with you?"

A hand through hair.

"About an hour ago. Are you all right?"

I nod. What else can I do? I can't tell him about the boy wolves. He wouldn't understand. "Yeah. Why?"

"You look. I dunno. Shook up."

I laugh. "Yeah, a little. I didn't know that he was—"

Nogitsune's eyes spring open. They are red, glowing. His mouth pulls apart, and I see tiny needle teeth. "I smell them. They are close. My brothers, my sisters."

Geoff looks down, his eyes squinting. His mouth twitching. I back away, my shoulder against the wall. "Nogitsune? You all right?"

Eyes return, roll back to normal.

"Yeah," he said, "Sorry about that. My family is here."

Geoff seems unfazed by what has happened. I, on the other hand, am spooked. Spooked by his actions and spooked by the wolf kin from earlier. This whole place feels wrong.

"I'm going to head out. Dunno where. Might see Mister Harvey and give his book back to him. I can't keep it—it's too weird."

Geoff doesn't hear me. Nogitsune doesn't hear me. They stare into each other's eyes. Gently, lips meeting. I feel like I am invisible again. This makes me very sad. I never thought I would be the invisible girl to Geoff. I always thought I would be physical and real.

Now I vanish
Before his eyes.
I leave the cutting room.

Friday: Mister Harvey's Office

Mister Harvey is behind a large desk. It stretches the length of the room, and is covered in books and maps. Each one is highlighted. Each one has pins in them. Displayed, naked. Like a dissected animal.

He doesn't seem me come in. Not at first.

His eyes down. Head down. He is not talking. Only muttering, fast. Incoherent stream of syllables. I listen, listen closely. Try to find something to stand on. Some symbol to pull meaning from.

His eyes are moving, fast. His lip thickly twitching. His tongue a loose and wild animal in his mouth. I feel an electricity in the air. It is sharp and bites my skin.

I sit down in the chair. I should just leave the book on his desk. Leave and walk away. I don't know why—but I want to say something to him. I want to confront him with the book.

On the cover I see Nogitsune. In the shadows. Beneath him is a monk, his robes up over his waist. I turn my head. I do not want to see this.

Eyes roll down. Eyelids flutter. Tongue stops moving. He sees me. I am no longer invisible girl. He puts his hands on the desk. They have cuts along them. I wonder briefly if he had been to the cutting room.

"Hello! To what do I owe the pleasure of your company?"

The book is in my lap. Under my folded hands. "The book you gave me.. . . ."

He brings his fingers together. Into a pyramid. "Yes, yes. You know that books are magic? All books? They are all spell books of a sort. See, words and images. They carry more than just meaning. They carry the codes to our mental landscape. Books fuck with this. They take the words and change them, take the images and rearrange them. Each time you read a book you become someone else. Changed inside."

I lean back in the chair. The electricity is still here. I feel it. Under my skin. Like acid. "I don't understand," I say. I feel weak, stupid.

"Did you read the book?"

I nod.

"How carefully? Did you just flip through it? No, no. You didn't. I see the change. It's coming over you already. You are different now, aren't you? Can't you feel it?"

I did not feel any different. Just the same. Same invisible girl. Although part of me was haunted now. But I was haunted by the things I'd seen—the world acting in unnatural ways. That was not the book's fault. But I did not want to seem stupid. "Yes, I do feel different. But that's not the point—you giving me this book. It makes me feel uncomfortable."

That was a part of it. The discomfort. I wanted him. I needed him. But this book made things clear—brought the hidden things forward in my mind. And I didn't feel right after that. Not comfortable. Not right.

He gets up on the desk. Crawls across it toward me. "Yes, yes. It is because you are changing, don't you see?"

I get out of my chair, move toward the back of his office. He has pictures hung on the walls of swingsets and playgrounds without children. "No, that's not it. I don't want this book. I don't—I don't want you. Please. Stop. Just take the book back and let me go."

I move my hand against the door. I feel the doorknob. But it doesn't turn. I shake it, trying to force it to open. It doesn't turn. He is over me. Towering.

His hand cuts across the air, and I hit the ground, hard. My cheek stings from his fist. I look up to see him pulling his shirt off. Tattoos across his biceps, his shoulders, his chest. Circles. Latin. Symbols I don't understand. He chants under his breath and my knees feel weak.

I try to move but I cannot. My limbs have gone limp and wooden. I whimper. I try and say something, but I can only whimper. This is how the world ends. This is how the world ends.

A bang on the door from behind me.

He picks me up, moves me across the floor.

The door swings open.

Standing there is Nogitsune.

Mister Harvey does not stop chanting, but I feel different. I feel like I can move. His hands move over me, move over as if they are about to undress me. I can move. I scream and kick him in his balls. He howls in pain.

Nogitsune walks forward. He has a table leg in his hands. He swings it in circles. Geoff is nowhere to be seen. "That's not nice," he says, walking up to Mister Harvey who lies on the ground clutching himself. I walk past him.

"Casting that spell on such a little girl. And that book—such a clever trap! But I am stronger than you. I am older than you."

Crack! The table leg breaks glasses.

Mister Harvey's body, curled up like a seashell.

Whimpering. "You don't scare me, fox boy. I have followers. Wolves from my world." He turns and looks at me. "They are here, understand? They are here to feed. We will feed and feed and all of you will be dry husks. Empty things."

Crack! Table leg into the stomach. A howl of pain.

I leave. Quickly.

Without saying a word.

Friday: Roof and Snowlands

I have to see for myself.

I walk up the long steps. Walk up through the shadows. Walk up past the uncounted classrooms. Everyone is gone. Everyone else is in the gymnasium. Probably fucking. They won't miss the invisible girl. They didn't even notice I was there, not even when I was being rubbed against and humped against.

The roof is large and wide. I can see no one else up here. Only crows, who dot the landscape like feathered dreams. I want to see the sun. But the sun is gone. I want to see the stars. But the stars are gone.

The sky is a hole.

Nogitsune was right. There was only white, flat, snow. A long range of snow plains. As far as I could see. And the only objects in the plain where the giants. They walked, I saw them from here. Walk, walk, walk. Their tremendous bodies stomping into the ground, thick hands pounding at their sides.

Their skin is like rubber sewn together. Their eyes are fires burnt into their heads. Their hair is like wire, tangled and broken and strung up on their heads.

They dress in rags.

And they are hungry.

The sight of them makes my blood run cold.

Foxes prance between them, their red bodies like fuzzy fires against the snow. Riding on the back of one was my art teacher, sword in hand. Over her back I see our sculptures in a brown satchel. I see *Fear of Mice* and feel hope.

From behind I hear a kicking of a pebble. I turn and see Nogitsune. Walking calmly, swinging the table leg. I see that it is covered in blood and I hate that it had come to that.

It is so cold up here.

"I had to see," I say. I am crying. I need to be the girl who cries. Not invisible. Not to him. "I had to see for myself."

He nods and walks towards me. "I know. They are there. And they wait. My brothers hold them off and my sisters hold off the wolves. But it only a matter of time before we are outnumbered."

I walk up and put my head on his chest. I feel his arms around me. I cry against his shirt. "Thank you. For earlier."

He runs his fingers through my hair. I feel something against my ear. Like a breast. Like a breast in his shirt. I wonder where it came from. And I look up and he is a she.

"I can be whatever you want," she says, "I can be whoever you want. But I need you now. I need you to want me. I am vague here, flickering. Soon I will be gone. Geoff was not enough to keep me here. He is barely real himself. But you—you can keep me whole. You can keep me real."

I say nothing. Only lean my head against the chest. It feels like my mother's breast, and I remember being small and tiny, and sleeping on my mother's breast while she rocked back and forth, rocked back and forth.

He doesn't speak again.

We just stand there and watch a war unfold.

SECRET IN THE HOUSE OF SMILES

Jack cut up pictures of girls with thin razors and then glued the most pleasing body parts together onto a single white sheet of paper.

A leg, snip.

An arm, snip.

Eyes, snip.

Perfect hair, snip.

And then the assemblage. Glue spread across the floor and the sound of glossy pages being stuck and unstuck together. Like Velcro and leather.

The trance was finally broken when the door burst open, slamming against the wood. Jack jumped but did not stop. Snip, snip, snip. Stick, stick, stick.

Standing in the doorway was Alice in a black dress and green-striped stockings. She had her bookbag slung over her shoulder. "Hey, hot stuff. Want to go vampire hunting with me? I've got a good one."

Jack did not turn. Did not move.

Meditation. Concentration. The last sorcerer's apprentice.

Alice looked down and saw what Jack was doing. "This again?"

Alice sat down on the floor next to him.

Jack did not respond. He had found a page with the perfect waist.

She walked over to his dorm window and looked at the campus outside. It looked cold. Dark. Night. The pathways between buildings were covered in a quilt of red and brown leaves, illuminated by the sparse golden light of the streetlamps.

Alice sat on his bed. Jack liked seeing her on his bed. Her body accented against the green blanket. Pale skin cutting across pine green.

Jack screamed. Alice jumped in surprise. He spit, he swore. He pushed the glossy pages across the floor. Kicked the half finished girls in anger, destroying all his work. "It's no good, it's no good," he said, "I can't do it. I shouldn't have performed that magic trick. It was all wrong. All wrong. Now pieces are missing. Gone."

He looked up at Alice, her staring back with eyes wide and mouth open. "Come on," she said, "Let's go and do something else. I hate it when you get like this."

Alice picked up the phone.

Some vampire hunting would do them all some good.

—

The walls were red brick and coated with posters. One advertised a local illusionist who was performing for the student government. He wore a top hat and cape, and a waxed moustache that curled to either side of his head like a cartoon villain.

Doors lined either side, all closed. Shut off from the world. The hall was oddly empty, without students loitering or hanging out or talking. In the distance they heard the showers, splashing and laughter.

Jack looked at the wall and grabbed a poster. It was a girl in a bunny costume, holding up two connected brass rings. A simple trick. One that jogged Jack's memory. "Her ears! Her ears! I feel like I'm back on top again. I can almost see her in my mind—moving in and out of vision like a pale ghost. I have to cut off these ears. They are her perfect ears."

Jack rubbed his stale glue-laced hands together. It sounded like sandpaper grating. "It will only take a second. Just let me cut off her ears and shove them into my pocket. Come on pretty please, come on."

Alice tossed the poster to the ground and glanced up and down the hallways. No one was here. This didn't feel right. "Hurry up," she said, "Before someone sees us."

Eagerly Jack reached down, pulled out his razor. Snip, snip, a perfect ear for his pocket. Shaped like a conch shell.

"Ok, let's go."

They walked briskly down the hall, their footsteps echoing to the sound of the rushing water and bathing.

—

Jenny sat on a large orange bean bag chair, her legs crossed and her eyes staring at a large flat screen television she had on the facing wall. A circus show. With artistic clowns prancing about and bemoaning the nature of existentialism. One threw a pie at the other, and proclaimed all actions absurd.

Jenny wore a dirty purple shirt, stained with ketchup and grease. Her hair was piled up above her head and tied in place with twine and wilted flowers. She wasn't wearing any pants. Just her underwear and bare legs riddled with shaving scars. She nodded as they walked in. "Some fucked up sideshow," she said, "Have a seat and watch it with me. They're going to bring out the freaks next. My favorite part is when the geek cuts the Siamese twins in half. It's a hoot."

They all sat on the floor, facing the large screen television. Alice saw the fridge over in the corner, pushed up against the wall. It opened from the top, like a trap door to a stage. She heard it humming from across the room. A living thing that sung to her. Calling to her stomach.

Jenny put her arm around Jack.

"Hey, sweetie. Want to do me a favor?"

Jack laughed, nervously. "Sure," he said.

"Go and get me a beer from the fridge. And maybe take out a pizza and put it into a microwave. You guys hungry? Thirsty? Want a beer or something?"

They all grumbled, sure, yeah, of course.

"Good idea," Jenny said, "And Alice—stop looking at my legs. Got it? These are not for you. I've already told you that you're not my type."

Alice laughed a tittering he he he he laugh that was on the verge of mania. She watched as Jack walked over the fridge. He wore a long yellow raincoat. Alice thought he looked silly. Like a giant bumblebee detective.

The televised twins howled, and there was a sound of tearing meat. "Oh," Jenny said, "This is my favorite part. It always gets me hot. Watching them tear these girls apart. Damn. I am so horny."

Alice turned her face from the television and looked directly at Jenny, keeping her eyes on Jenny's round and acne-scarred face. "Did I ever tell you my major?"

Jenny scoffed. "Do I even know you? You just came along with the boy. Why do you think I care about you?"

Alice was unfazed. She had done this a thousand times. "Come on," she said, "Take a guess."

Jenny sighed. "I'm missing the best part. I don't care."

"Just guess?"

Jenny tried to hide her anger. "Quantum physics? You look like a super geek."

Alice pointed to her nose. "Exactly. But not quite. It's a branch of quantum physics. I'm a vampire hunter."

Now Jenny was interested. She turned off her television and turned her gaze to Alice. "A vampire hunter? What does that have to do with quantum physics?"

Alice put her finger to her lip and chewed on the calluses as she spoke. "Well, it's kind of like a vampire observer, really. See, reality is a binary state, right? You can be alive, or you can be dead. One or the other. Vampires, on the other hand, are a super position of both states. That are both and neither at the same time. Like a supernatural Schrödinger's Cat."

Jenny inched in forward. "I don't get it. So vampires are, what? Super posit whats? What does that have to do with anything?"

"Super position. See, in quantum computing, a qbit can hold three states while a regular bit holds two. The third state is actually all states and no states at the same time. It's kind of like the inverse of zero. Vampires are the same way—they are a qbit."

Now Alice was excited. She reached over and grabbed Jenny's hands. Her hands were cold. Her eyes were red. Unperturbed, Alice moved on. "So, the only way you can tell what a quantum particle is, is by observing it. When you observe it then it tells you what states it is in. But it changes depending on how you observe it. Isn't that wild? That's why I'm a vampire observer. I perform tests to see if the state of something living could also be dead. If they are just living or just dead, then they aren't quantum vampires. If they are living with the possibility of being dead, then they are vampires."

Jenny frowned. "I don't get it."

Jack put a pizza into the microwave and turned it on, and tossed a beer at Jenny. Jenny quickly spun around and grabbed it. "Thanks," she said.

"It's crazy, I know. But here. If I have a mirror, and I hold it up to you, and you don't reflect I am performing a test. I am observing you, and if you have the possibility of being a vampire, then you would not have a reflection. Like this."

Alice held up a small makeup mirror.

No reflection.

Jenny ran out of the room screaming.

—

Jack hummed and rocked back and forth. Hummed like the freezer in Jenny's apartment. He then darted beneath his bed and pulled out his little perfect pile of magazine parts and glue.

Jack ignored Alice. She did not exist to him. She tried to get his attention. Had been trying all day, all night, for the past month.

He had an ear to affix. He wanted to use his special glue stick for this. It was black and white, like a magic wand. Stick, stick, stick.

She looked at Jack, watched him drool over the perfect ear. No, she did not know why she was still with him. Maybe it was convenience?

Jack screamed.

He threw the razor against the ground and scattered the pictures. "The ear is wrong! Wrong! I thought I had seen her—a glimpse again. But no, fading. Fleeting. A mist. It's gone. I need to put her back together again. The trick went south."

He turned and looked at Alice. "There was an audience, you know? They watched the whole thing. Yet no one knew what really happened. And she was smiling the whole time."

Alice did her nervous laugh. Titter. Titter. Titter. "Come on Jack. You're just worked up, is all. Take a breath, forget about it all for a moment. You need to relax a little."

Jack rubbed his hands together. Stuck pieces of magazine parts grinding. Arm and leg and stomach and mouth, pushing and rubbing between his hands in an orgy of glossy body parts. "I know of a secret. Hidden in the house of smiles."

Alice leaned forward. "Yeah? What's that? House of Smiles?"

Jack crawled under his bed. His head and waist disappeared under the mattress. Legs wiggled as he searched. They heard plastic boxes moving.

Alice looked at the floor and glanced at Jack, to see what he was doing. More things moving. How could he be taking so long? There was barely any space underneath their beds.

Jack scurried out from under his bed. He had a shoebox covered in a plastic bag. He removed the bag, pulling the box out. It was decorated with pictures of rabbits running and a picture of a fox stalking in the green pine trees.

"Here," Jack said proudly, "Here it is. Here, here, here. She smiled like a saw. Big teeth, cutting things apart. The last of the great stage performers. Queen vampire, in hidden stasis."

Alice leaned over.

Jack pulled off the lid.

Inside was a diorama.

Careful, tiny little pieces collected together. Handmade, hand-painted. Perfect little pine trees. Perfect little cabin. With a large cartoonish smile painted on the side. And behind, bathed in a cold blue winter light was a perfect tiny freezer chest. Closed and grey and filthy.

Excited, Jack turned over the lid. There was a map.

"Where is this at?" Alice asked.

Jack pointed, moved his finger. Made humming sounds. Like a low flying plane. "Not far, not far. Just the woods outside of the University. Could walk there from here. There is a shack and all these abandoned apple trees. A whole orchard left to rot and misery. Whoever owned it must've left in a hurry."

Alice grunted. "Good." She said, "Let's get going then. I can collect everything we need and get going."

Jack shook his head, slamming the book shut. "No, not yet. We can't go yet."

Now it was Alice's turn to have a headache. She just couldn't keep living life like this. Always on the edge of some strange madness.

"Why not," she asked, exhausted.

Jack pointed at the mismatched photographs.

"Because she is not finished yet. I have to remember her, I have to love her. Then we can go back. Then we can use the freezer."

Alice slouched her shoulders. Resigned. "Okay," she said, "All right. Jackie boy, let's construct your perfect girl, shall we? And then—then what? We go to the woods?"

Jack pounded his fists into the floor, drumming the wood. He spoke as he drummed. "You don't understand. Ghosts are more important than food. Ghosts are more important than anything. If you forget them they are erased. Stolen, vanished. Faceless things looking for masks in the rain. You cannot deny me this. You cannot deny her this. Ghosts are more important than vampires. Than dreams. Than water or light. And the ghosts of the saw are the hardest to please. Half finished ghosts, covered in smiles and torn apart."

When he stopped drumming they sat in silence for a minute. "Fuck, Jackie," Alice said, "Just tell me what to do, and I'll do it."

—

She helped him find posters. Find magazines. She cut with him and glued with him and he is happy because he started to see her again. In the glimpse of still life, he caught her. Caught her in fleeting moments, flying and trying to escape.

Alice didn't know it.

But she helped Jackie-O Jack perform a bit of magic. Perform a bit of now-you-see-me, now-you-don't. This was a special kind of magic. Backwards magic. Most magicians were in the art of taking things apart, taking things away, making them disappear and cut into tiny pieces. Not Jack—no, the Jack man had a plan. A new kind of trick. He was going to put someone back together. Reverse that saw, take the blade out and piece her back together again.

Now-you-don't-see-me, now-you-do.

And she would be happy. She would be thankful. And she would say she forgave him, and say that he wouldn't have to be sorry or feel guilty anymore. That was okay, what he did all those years ago. That she was happier now, better now. In a place where queens and puppets dance.

And she would be whole again.

—

They each had pockets filled with picture pieces. Photograph slices, body parts, and different snatches of text that Jackie-Jack man thought would come in handy. Special words. Magic words, printed on the page but not to be spoken aloud. When spoken aloud they lose their magic.

Out past the University. The lights and the towers dim glows behind them now. Like distant earth stars, slowly going supernova and fading out.

Pine trees. From his dream, no—his memory. They surrounded them. Sticky, they smelled of sap. The knotted and spiny branches webbed around them, catching them. Claustrophobic. Leaves plastered to their feet with mud. In the distance they heard dogs barking in the cold and Alice shrieked.

Jack did not care. Let Alice scream.

Alice reached over and held his face. Her lips were like wet pomegranates. He smelled the seeds on her. Very slowly she said, "I think we are being followed. Do you understand? We are being followed by someone. I think it is Jenny. Vampire Jenny."

Jack nodded.

But didn't care.

He kept walking.

He was laying seeds along the ground, and everyone would have to come. Follow, follow. Alice and Jenny, Jenny and Alice. The seeds were enchanted, stolen and ready to eat. They would have no choice.

Follow, follow.

To the house of smiles.

—

Here was the place, the memory hole, the memory whole, the whole thing. The shack. Grey shack, shingles broken and smashed. Dead shack, undead shack, shack like a home brought back from the dead. Windows were holes, eyes like empty caves. Big smile painted on the side. Cheshire smile, haunted smile. Ghost smile.

Welcome, welcome it said.

Welcome to the house of smiles.

"Open Your Pockets!" he commanded in his best magician voice.

Boomed. Thunder. Crackle, crackle.

She opened her pockets and let the cut-up pieces flutter around like butterflies, like broken and dead leaves. He opened the freezer with a flourish and a ta da! And a wave of the magic wand. Inside, inside.

Her.

His wife. His bride. His eternal thing.

Vampire goddess.

Queen of the House of Smiles.

Cut up, wrapped in plastic. Each piece, each part. Crammed in. But some parts were missing. Some parts were always missing. He hated that. How could he remember her with all the parts missing? Sawed off and stolen. The trick that went south. The too-sharp saw, grinning as it cut into her, and her all smiles the whole time, even in that pain, the audience applauding.

And then her asking him—*Jackie—please, put me back together again*. She whispered it as she smiled, teeth together. He wanted to stop sawing, that Jackie O did—he wanted to. But his hands had momentum and they kept pushing and he had no choice but to keep cutting. Keep cutting as the crowd applauded.

The pages fluttered, stuck and unstuck. They flew over and stitched themselves onto parts, stitched everything together. The missing pieces made whole out of magazine skin and magazine eyes and magazine faces.

The body rose slowly from the freezer chest tomb.

The body was her. His first bride. His first love. The sorcerer's last apprentice. She was dressed in plastic, the distorted clear making her even more real in the moonlight. And he saw her whole now, made whole by the plastic pages. Living, alive.

Queen of the House of Smiles.

And he danced with her.

Danced while Alice sharpened a stake.

Danced while Alice pulled out holy water.

Danced while Alice prepared for war.

Danced while Jenny and the others all came out of the shadows. Hundreds of them. Pale faced creatures of the night. Awaiting to worship their queen.

WHEN MAX WAS HUNGRY AGAIN

Eleanor had been looking over these photographs all day. She went through each of them in chronological order just to try and remember when it had happened. When Max had started to fade away into nothingness.

Early pictures showed no sign of decay. Always smiling, always happy. She kept moving through the years, picture by picture, and it seemed so gradual. A few pounds disappearing on Max here and there, a smile slowly starting to slip away from his face.

In the later pictures he no longer had his arm around her waist. In the later pictures he was always sullen, in a dark corner or hiding away from the light. The listless look in his eyes seemed haunted, as if filled with the voices of the dead.

She didn't know why she looked at these pictures every week. Why she still went over to where he lived and tried to get him to eat. She hadn't seen him eat anything in the last month.

Last week she tried to force him to eat some food she had prepared. He chewed it up and ate it, but she had this distinct feeling he had thrown it up when she had left. He kept telling her that food had no taste anymore. That it all had begun to taste like ash, and dirt. It all had begun to taste sticky and muddy, hanging in the roof of his mouth.

Eleanor couldn't force him to eat. She couldn't force him to be happy again, or to smile again. All she could do was be there for him and try and help him out. Try and comfort him and help move him back to the old Max she had known four years ago.

The Max that had kissed her every chance he could. The Max that would eat to his fill at every restaurant they had gone to. The Max that was able taste food.

She had to give him credit that he was trying. Every time she brought over food he looked a little happier than before. He looked hopeful, that maybe by somehow eating her food he would be transformed back to the old Max.

Each time Eleanor had done it, Max had always spit out the food she had given him. He would look up so sad, his hopes crushed and claim that no, it didn't taste good. It didn't taste bad. It tasted like nothing, nothing at all.

The photographs were all put away neatly now, only one still remaining out. It was a picture of when they had first met; his hair was long and wavy. His face was round and joyful. He looked nothing like his current self.

Eleanor had to bring him back.

She had to transform him into his older self.

Later that day she decided to take a break from looking at photographs, to take a break from talking on the phone to Max. She decided to shove him out of her system for at least a few moments of the day, to see if she could find happiness somewhere again.

She was sick of feeling sorry for him. She was sick of trying to force him to eat. She was sick of staring at his bone-thin body hanging over his bed. She was sick of him moping. She was sick of him telling her that he had no desire to eat. On days like today she just wanted to help him end it all.

In order to save them both, she took a break from Max. She went downtown to the art district to try to force his skeletal figure from her thoughts.

The district was filled with its usual patrons on a Friday night. Mostly poets and musicians, wandering up and down the street on bare feet, looking to score some drugs or just rave about the latest art gallery they had seen. She overheard mutters of philosophical debate, could smell the wafting scent of patchouli hanging in the air.

In the end, it eventually took her mind off of darker things. Took her mind away from Max, stole her thoughts into a happier time. Back before she knew the human scarecrow. Back before she was tied to the amazing shrinking man.

She sat and sipped some coffee in a bookstore at the upper end of the block. The inside was warm, refreshing. The red clay walls let her mind slip away from her troubles, from Max's troubles. Eleanor could just relax and let the coffee warm her stomach to the soothing sounds of a flamenco guitar.

The hours slipped by out of hand, and soon the sky was starting to dim and become darker. She figured she had spent enough time resting for today. Had spent enough time away from Max. She couldn't run away from him, at least not now. She had grown accustomed to his misery.

Outside, the streetlamps sent halos of yellow light across the ground. The sounds of punk music filled the air from a club across the street as people walked up and down the block yelling and singing. She saw all of these people, all of these people who were happy. Eleanor tried to remember what that had felt like.

She realized she couldn't remember, and was filled with even more sadness than before. Just as she had gotten to the parking garage where her car was, she caught a curios site out the corner of her eye.

It was a bookstore. The sign out front was a blue neon moon with the words "*Goddess Books: Enchantments, healing and happiness,*" outlined in sharp black around it.

Enchantments, healing, and happiness. Not only did the phrase have a sort of catchy alliteration to it, it made something inside of Eleanor stir. Happiness. Maybe she could find happiness inside. Maybe they had a cure for what was ailing Max.

She had turned to all forms of modern medicine to find help for Max. When the doctors had claimed that it was not a physical affliction, she took him to psychiatrists and psychologists, hoping for a mental cure to his ailments. Nobody knew how to cure him.

Now she was willing to turn to the fantastical, to the unbelievable in a last-ditch effort to save him from sliding into nothingness. She had only her hope left to lose.

She ran across the street, nimbly dodging traffic as she walked into Goddess Books. Inside was a warmly lit small bookstore, with shelves upon shelves of large tomes and tiny trinkets. Bags of herbs were scattered across the floor, and hanging on the walls were maps to the human chakras.

The bookstore seemed to be empty at the moment. The only person there was a short lady behind a desk, reading a copy of *The Bell Jar*. Her black glasses were pushed to the edge of her nose, as her lips seemed to mutter the words as she read them.

Eleanor cleared her throat, not sure how to proceed.

The girl glanced up at her, a bit confused as to why she had been disrupted from her book. Eleanor did not have anything in her hands to purchase, nor had she wandered around the store to look at anything. Probably, the girl thought, coming in to use the bathroom.

"I need your help."

This got the girl's attention, and she set the book face down onto the cluttered table.

"My boyfriend—Max—he hasn't been himself lately."

"Go on."

"For the last year he has completely lost his appetite. He can't eat anything, and when he tries to eat something he says that it tastes like dust. He's wasting away to nothing."

"Why do you think I can help?"

"Because—"

"Because you have nowhere else to go. Correct?"

The girl got up from behind the counter and began to move to the back of the store. She had a long skirt on that swayed from side to side as she walked down the aisles, her hands brushing each spine of the books she goes past.

"I think I might know of something that could help you."

"You do?"

"Yes."

The girl pulled a book with a green dust cover from the bookshelf and opened a seemingly random page. Her hand skimmed down the page and she looked up on occasion, her lips muttering the words that are printed inside. After a moment, she stopped and looked up.

"Do you have any experience with the occult?"

The girl's eyes glimmered as she said this.

"No."

"That's what I thought. Don't get me wrong. You do have some potential. But, I don't see you being able to help your boyfriend. Not yet. That kind of magick," she paused, pushed her glasses up her face and touched her tongue to her lips, "Takes years of practice."

Eleanor's heart sank. So even now, she wouldn't be able to help Max. No Doctors, psychiatrists or psychologists could help him. She had turned to her last hope, to the unbelievable. Even that, it seemed, was out of her reach. By time she became efficient enough to grind the herbs and cast the spell, he would be dead. Nothing left but a sack of bones and a pile of dust where his flesh had once been.

The girl saw Eleanor's expression, and smiled a bit.

"Cheer up. I just wanted you to know that this isn't child's play. This isn't something you can just wake up and do. There is no natural talent. Only practice and hard work."

The girl paused for a moment and set the book back on the shelf. She pulled off her glasses and wiped them onto her shirt, her face strained as it calculated some numbers quickly.

"Well, let's see here. Cost of getting supplies will probably run you about twenty bucks. I'll charge five bucks for the use of my bowl and pestle. I'll charge you fifteen for my expertise, and finally ten bucks for labor. I can get it to you in a half hour. So, if you want, wander the bookstore and look around, or go down the block a bit. But I get paid in advance."

Eleanor added up the different costs in her head.

"Alright," she said, and handed the girl a fifty-dollar bill. The girl smiled and started moving toward the backroom.

"Oh, and one more thing. This spell needs to be sprinkled into some food. You'll know it's working because he'll get his taste back, and he will begin to get hungry. This bit of Alchemy embodies the concoction with a spirit known as a Guff. When most people come in contact with the Guff, it awakens their mouth and their senses, and makes them taste and eat once again."

The girl paused for a moment, turning around and letting her brown hair whip around her.

"But, on a rare occasion the Guff possesses the person who eats the food. When and if that happens, that person will become an empty void, trying to eat everything in sight. If this happens, leave immediately and call the police."

"Will he be able to return to normal if this happens?"

"This rarely ever happens. Have you ever read the back of a bottle of aspirin?"

"I haven't"

"Well, some of the side effects are just downright nasty. But, have you ever known anyone to get internal bleeding from taking aspirin for a headache?"

Eleanor laughed, feeling a bit better.

"Of course you don't. It's the same thing here. But I had to warn you. I wouldn't have felt right otherwise. Have some fun, look around at some of the books we have for sale. Just relax and your Max will be back to normal before you know it."

The girl sashayed into the back room, giving Eleanor a wink as she closed the large door behind her. For once, Eleanor felt optimistic. For once, she felt good about the future. For once, she felt like the universe was beginning to line up and make everything right once again.

After awhile of sifting through the shelves and glancing through various books of different titles and topics she heard footsteps from behind her. Turning around, she saw the girl standing there, holding out a small bag to her.

"Okay, it's a pretty simple mixture. Didn't take as long as I had originally thought it would. Just use all of the powder, sprinkling it into some food."

"How long will it take to affect him?"

"Shouldn't be too long. Should be almost instantly."

"What if it doesn't work?"

The girl didn't respond outright to this question, but instead pointed to a wooden plaque located on the wall above them that read "No warranties, No returns." Something inside Eleanor sank when she saw this sign. After all, she thought, this was in the realm of the mystical. The unbelievable. The unknown. The realm of the world based on belief rather than fact.

This was a point in her life where that had to be enough. She couldn't turn anywhere else, and if this was saltwater or snake oil, then so be it. She had to at least try.

Eleanor waved goodbye to the girl as she walked outside into the night air, the bell above the door chiming as she left. She held her breath as she crossed the busy street, got into her car and drove the half-hour stretch of road to where Max lived.

Outside of Max's house the skeletal tree rested its empty branches against the black autumnal sky. His driveway was unpaved stone gently trailing back to his house about half of a mile from the road. Around the car, crickets made their presence known, and crows wings could be heard fluttering around the telephone polls outside.

Max lived in the middle of nowhere, far away from the town and the city lights Eleanor had fallen in love with. He had begun to become accustomed to the solitude of not having neighbors close by, or having to drive a half hour to go into the nearest town.

It fit into his recently developing disease, feeding his insomnia and his sadness. She pulled her car up to the tip of the driveway next to his garage. She got herself out of the car slowly, the sound of her shoes scratching across gravel setting her teeth on edge.

The sounds of nature seemed foreign to her even after coming here every day for the past few years. She had become used to the sounds of traffic and airplanes taking off. She had gotten used to the sound of neighbors talking outside of her apartment. She had gotten used to the comforts of being surrounded by people wherever she went.

Out here the emptiness filled her. Out here she heard only the sounds of birds and crickets. Out here she heard only the absence of civilization, as if returning to a more primitive landscape.

The only light she had to walk by was that of the moon and the stars above her. There were no lights on inside of his house, no porch light to guide her. He had gotten into the habit of dwelling in darkness a few months ago. At first she had been frightened, thinking that something had happened to him, had forced him to stay away from the light.

Now she just considered it part of his growing disease. His fear of light and his love of the dark all part of his growing strangeness. Combined with his thinning body she had wondered if he was just waiting for death now. If he had become so acclimated to the thought of dying that he no longer pursued an attempt to live.

She knocked on his door, and heard scuttling around in the darkness. He sounded like an insect, moving about in the shadows of his house. She heard the locks coming undone one at a time, a series of clicks and whirs that rattled the air around her.

The door opened, darkness behind him. He was thinner than yesterday, his body seeming to grope for flesh to cling onto. He was entirely bone now, flaps of skin hanging off of him and hanging to the ground. He wore no clothing, his frame covered in sores. She wondered when the last time he had bathed.

"I suppose you need the light to see?"

She nodded, trying hard not to cry at the sight of him. He flicked on a switch beside her and almost blinded the two of them with its yellow glow. Eleanor walked in beside him as he locked the door behind her. It always startled her when he did this, his paranoia as of late forcing him to do odd things like this. Max then quickly fled into the shadows of a corner, the light frightening him.

"Why did you come?" he asked, his eyes flinching in pain from the light.

"I thought I could fix something for you to eat, honey."

He seemed to get hopeful for a moment and shambled out from the dark corner he was hiding in. She went forward and hugged him, his body almost crumbling to dust in her arms. She tried hard not to cry at this moment, reminding herself of what she had brought with her from the bookstore. It could very well save him from whatever was destroying him.

"What is it this time?"

"Soup."

He sat back onto the couch, the light that was touching his skin visibly causing him pain. She moved into his kitchen and turned on the gas stove, watching the blue flame flicker up into the air. She flicked on the light behind her so she could see what she was doing.

Eleanor got an iron pot from one of the cabinets and filled it water. She then laid the pot over the flame and sprinkled the mixture into it. At first she wandered if she would need to flavor it, if it would taste bland. This made her laugh a little as she thought it. If tasted bland, how would she know if it worked?

She let it boil and then pulled a ceramic bowl out from the dishwasher. She poured the soup into the bowl and then carefully walked back into the living room, being careful not to spill a drop.

He looked up into her eyes, his face forcing a smile that came out like a thick grimace. She knew that it was hope in his smile, but the slinking skin around his lips gave it a horrific connotation.

He sipped it gently, trying to be careful as to not burn his tongue. The steam began to rise up from the bowl and crawl across his face. She could smell the soupy concoction she had brewed for him and she realized that it smelled good. It smelled delicious, actually.

Something began to change in his eyes. A look grew in them that seemed hungry. It was no longer listless, depressed or paranoid. It was starved, and it began to gulp down the soup in fast sloppy slurps.

He looked up at her, the soup all over his chin and chest.

"My god! What was that?"

She laughed and sat down on the chair beside him.

"I got it from a Magick Shop downtown."

"I, I could taste it. It tasted great. It didn't taste like ash or dirt—it tasted like food. Like what food is supposed to taste like."

She smiled and kissed him. It would be a long road ahead before he got better. A long road before he was the old Max again. But, this was the first step along that road.

"And I'm hungry. My god, I haven't eaten anything in so long. Now I can feel it, I can feel my taste and my hunger returning."

He knelt down and came to her side, his head resting on her lap. Tears streaked down his face as he looked up at her and said "Thank you." She had no way of responding to that. What do you say when you save someone from self-destruction and they thank you? A "you're welcome" seemed oddly inappropriate. Anything seemed like an understatement.

She leaned over and kissed his head as his stomach growled and rumbled. He clutched it and moaned slightly. All those months of not eating, finally catching up to him.

"Oh god. I'm so hungry now. It feels so good to say that."

Eleanor wiped the tears that were forming in her own eyes as she laughed slightly. It was so good to hear him say that. It was so good to finally hear him grounded in reality again, becoming human once again.

She took the bowl to the kitchen and poured more soup into it. She turned around to walk back into the living room, but he was standing right behind her. His bone-thin body moved without sound, sneaking up behind her fast, silent and hungry.

She held out the bowl to him, his stomach making low thunderous grumbling. He took the bowl without saying a word and gulped it down completely, the hot soup spilling across his ribbed chest, burning his flesh. He seemed unfazed by the searing hot soup, steam running up from his body.

He finished the bowl and began to lick it eagerly. Eleanor could only watch as his face devoured any last granule of soup in the bowl. She seemed a bit taken aback, but she reasoned he was just now experiencing food once again. That not eating for so long had finally risen up and taken accord of his mind.

It wasn't the Guff, she thought.

It couldn't be.

She heard a loud crunching sound as he bit into the bowl and swallowed the sharp chunks of porcelain. She cringed in pain, watching blood run down his torn face. He had a look in his eye, an endless hunger.

Eleanor moved backward, toward the boiling hot remainder of the soup behind her. Max began to walk toward her, his body moving in quick jerky motions. He smiled ear to ear, an unholy unnatural smile. His gums peeled back red and bleeding from eating the bowl, the slumping flesh falling from the bones on his face. His black eyes popped out of his skull with an intense hunger that wanted to consume her very being.

She yanked the pot of soup over her head, hot splashes falling onto her arms and searing her skin as she flung it in Max's direction. She heard the hissing of burned flesh, could smell it wafting from his body.

He screamed and covered his face as smoke arose from where the soup had drenched him. She ran into the living room, trying to find a way of escaping, trying to find a window to break.

She could hear his body moving through the kitchen, his stomach loudly rumbling from a supernatural hunger that had arisen in him. She could hear his bones clicking like an insect, his voice growling in a low guttural sound.

He entered the living room, standing in the doorframe as she hurriedly tried to open the door. The locks would not budge. She tried turning knobs, pulling and pushing. They held fast and strong.

He looked at her, his hunger flowing out of his body in waves of starvation. He pounced in the air and she darted out of his way as he landed on an end table, breaking a lamp across the floor.

In the darkness she saw the blue outline of his shadow moving. She moved quickly into the back bedroom, hoping for a window she could leap out of to her safety. She thought quickly about calling the cops, but by time she had dialed he would be on her, devouring her.

"Eleanor. I'm so hungry. What have you done to me?"

She heard noises of wood breaking, of timber smashing. She could see his shadow picking up pieces of the end table and breaking them down and shoving them into his mouth. She could hear him sobbing as he did this.

Eleanor tried to keep herself composed, trying not to blame herself for what was going on. She shut his bedroom door behind her and found an open window with its drapes lazily blowing in a breeze that was coming through the window.

She moved toward it to go outside when she heard the sound of the door breaking down. She leapt onto the dew-wet grass outside as she heard screams of torment coming from Max.

She began to run, as he leapt out from the window behind her, his body writhing unnaturally. She caught glimpses of him in the starlight and saw his body covered in mutilated bits of wood and glass. His face was torn apart around his mouth where he had tried to shove all sorts of objects into it like food.

He darted after her on all fours, his body moving in quick animalistic gestures. She began to run, her mouth trying to stifle the screams that were welling up inside of her. She could hear him growling and breathing, his voice soft and mechanical.

"Hungry. So hungry. So empty inside. Step into me, feed me."

She ran quickly. Before she could even sprint half way across the large grassy backyard she felt him grab her ankle with his thin fingers. His knuckles dug their bones into her veins, making her cry out in pain.

She could see the woods up ahead, the large expansive forest in his backyard. He owned about fifteen acres, and it seemed to go on forever. I could lose him in there, Eleanor thought. Lose him and quickly dial the cops on my cell phone.

He yanked her toward him, his mouth wrapping around her foot with an almost elegant snake-like embrace. He swallowed her foot whole and she could feel his teeth like screws in her flesh.

She looked behind herself at him and gasped in horror and pain. His mouth was entirely around her foot. How he had fit the whole thing in was beyond her. She could feel his stomach acids ripping apart bone and skin as he opened his mouth wider, unhinging his jaw like a serpent.

She screamed and kicked, but the nothingness in his stomach latched onto her and began to drag her inside of him. She reached out and grabbed clumps of dirt as his mouth moved up her knees and to her waist, her body succumbing to the emptiness that was inside of him now.

She cried and screamed as she fell into the darkness. She could not move, numb with fear as her entire torso was now inside of his gullet, his needle thin teeth pulling at her flesh as she fell into him.

Soon there was nothing left of Eleanor.

Nothing at all.

Only the emptiness inside of Max.

And his hunger.

His dark, unnatural hunger.

THIS HUNTED WORLD

I've been here for four days now, and Pops says it's good here. But he's said that before, and every time the wolves find us and we gotta go again. I keep hoping this time we'll be safe, that Pops is right.

But I don't know. I mean, I know he means well, but meaning well is just empty. Y'know? It's just empty. The wolves are out there still, they are. They look for us, and it's just a matter of time. It's always just a matter of time.

So cold in here.

Always cold in the safe places. Pops always liked the cold, always thought it was safer. Like the blanket of earth could somehow hide us from the wolves. Maybe the wolves don't like it underground. I dunno. Maybe they do, and they just love it when we go underground.

I gotta trust Pops.

He's all I've got left.

—

It's the fifth day now, and I can't tell night from day anymore. Cold and wet down here, underground. I can hear it drip—the walls and the ceiling leak. Above us is a shell of a house, what used to be a home. Who lived there once? I dunno. All the houses look the same now—empty shells. Y'know, I never thought I would miss school or my teachers, but I do.

I miss the warmth of learning, of friends and a classroom. Now all we've got is shells of buildings and my Pops and those wolves. Those wolves—I can hear them at night again. They are comin closer and closer. I can hear them breathe above us, in the shell of a house.

Their breath is like a whisper. Like someone talking really lowly, so low you can hear 'em and not make out what they're saying. It's a bad sound, and each time I hear it, it makes me feel like curling up in a ball and just falling through the world.

Pops doesn't think they're nearby. He can't hear them. He tries, and he wonders if I'm imagining it. Like I've mistaken the breeze for em or somethin. But I'm not, they are above us, and they are waiting. Maybe they can't smell us, maybe they can only sense us. Maybe they can't go underground.

Dunno. All I know is that I'm sick of eating canned food and I'm sick of the nightmares in the air. It's so thick—these dreams. They walk through the air and my mind, and it's like a heavy chemical of nightmares. I think the wolves make this stuff, this nightmare air.

Pops is cleaning his gun in the corner.

I can see him by candlelight.

"Go to sleep," he says.

I don't wanna.

I pretend to be asleep. I can hear the metallic noises of the gun as I close my eyes, barely covering up that whispering and dripping sounds. I force my mind to stay awake, seeing only bad stuff on the other side of dreams. I can tell, there's a cat in the dream world, and he stalks humans.

But he's a man in a way, a man cat. Did the wolves hire the man cat? He's a cannibal man cat, he is. Where is he at? I can hear the whispers get louder and hypnotic. The click of the gun being assembled becomes a song and I can't help but fall asleep.

—

Pops wakes me up, and we go upstairs and into the shell of a house. It's just pieces and no ceiling, and the red dust obscures almost everything. There is furniture all over, broken and filled with coiled springs. A television in the corner carries the ghost of an image, flickering.

He tells me it's not safe here anymore, and I'm not allowed to look in the corner. But I can't help it—I turn and look and there is a pile of bodies. Torn and stacked nice and neatly. I asked him if the wolves did this and he just nods.

It's always the wolves.

The wolves or the bogeyman. But I don't wanna talk about that—I'd rather it was just the wolves. Just the wolves and nothin else. Everything is so much worse when I think about Him. The bogeyman. I once tried to talk to my Pops about it, but he just told me to shut up and started rocking back and forth.

It scared me when he did that.

"Mary," he said, "Don't—no. We don't talk about him. Not anymore. Not since your mother's gone."

Now we are off again, walking down what was left of the road. All around us is the remains of houses, corpses of lives once lived. I wonder if we are the only people still here—if the wolves had come and no one is left. I wonder if the world is like some ghost city, some barren landscape.

The sun is gone.

My Pops said the wolves swallowed the sun, and all that's left is the red dust in the sky. He called it the blood of the sun. For some reason that unsettled me—that the sun could die. That the sun bled. That didn't feel right, it still doesn't feel right. It's even more unnatural than those wolves.

Wolves that walk on two legs. My Pops says that they hunt only at night, so in the day we should be okay. But I dunno if I believe him. I wanna—he's my pops and I feel safe around him. But sometimes I remember him crying and holding my mama's body and I just can't believe him anymore. He shoulda saved her.

—

In the corners of the houses I see things move as we walk. I wanna point them out to Pops, but he keeps moving on. He's gone quiet, and I want him to say anything. Anything at all. All this silence just bothers me and I can hear the wolves whispering in the wind.

The shadows creep under the folded ruins, they move like mist and I wonder if they are the wolves or something worse. I don't wanna think about it though, don't wanna think about anything. Just keep walking with Pops, keep moving until he finds another safe place and we can sit and eat canned food again.

I wonder to myself where all the birds went.

I'll have to ask Pops that later.

—

Nowhere is safe yet.

It's night now and even the moon is hidden beyond the blood of the sun. I asked my dad if the moon is gone and he says no. If the moon was gone, he says, the wolves would be gone too. The wolves live by the moon.

We're in the woods and the trees don't look right anymore. They look choked and rusty, like someone scraped them until they screamed.

Pops has taken to muttering to himself. It's a low stream of syllables, not really words or anything. Just sounds, like a prayer, or a humming. Maybe it's both. Either way, it's starting to freak me out.

Cause I know underneath his muttering string is the sound of whispers. And underneath that is silence. The stark silence of a dead world. A hunted world. I wanna scream, but I don't. Pops'll be mad if I do.

There is water ahead and I wanna drink it cause I'm so thirsty, but pops just nods his head no and says we wait. I don't understand. I ask him why and he says it's been poisoned by the blood of the sun.

I don't care, I think. I wanna drink the sun blood, fill my body with its light. Maybe I can be the next sun, rising high into the sky. And all the ground will spring back to life, and the wolves will go away, because I won't go away at night. I'll fight the moon, fight it with my light.

—

Gunshots.

My dad is firing his gun.

They are around us in the woods now and I can see them walking around on two legs, their fur glistens with blood and I see one of em is draggin a body behind it. The sound of the draggin sets my soul on edge and they whisper now and it's so much louder.

The gunshots pierce the whispering.

We run now, run with them after us. I can see them, wolf man, man wolf, and the air becomes heavy with nightmares again. I can feel them, that strange sick feeling of bad dreams enter my blood and all around me the world takes on a different view.

Even my pops looks bad, so bad. His eyes are darker red now and his skin wrinkles are like broad cuts in his face. I wanna scream and I know I can't and I know that this isn't real, it's just the wolves leaking their bad dreams into the air.

I see the catman from before, he hangs in the trees. He smiles, and starts to disappear, one feature at a time, until it's just his grin. Moongrin. His grin is the moon and it's on the ground now and the wolves are invigorated by it.

We runandrunandrun

I just want to go back to sleep.

I just want everything to stop and return to normal again. Why is this happening? I want to kill the moon, to kill all the wolves. I want to plant trees and grass, I want to heal this dying earth.

I want to heal my father's heart.

I want to bring my mom back from the dead.

—

We are back underground again, back beneath a house. Pops holding his stomach and I can tell he's in pain. But he's alive, and right now that's all I care about. I want to curl up on his lap and tell him everything's okay and we are safe now, but I think it would hurt him.

He cleans out the wound with a rag and some whiskey he found in the basement. When he's done he drinks the rest and looks at me with these dead eyes. "Why are you wearing a red dress?" he asks me.

I want to tell him I'm not—that I don't have a red dress, but he seems so certain. I feel sick now, and I scream. I scream and scream and I can't help it, cause pops isn't ok and I'm not ok and what will happen when the world is gone, when I am gone and all that's left is wolves?

Dad tries to calm me down, but I can't.

I can't calm down.

I scream and cry and pound my fists against the wet walls of the basement. He says I'm going to bring them here and they'll be able to find us. We won't be safe here anymore if I keep this up. And I tell him I don't care.

Fuck em, I say, let em come and I'll fight em.

He laughs at that moment, and I can see it hurts him to laugh. I smile then, and try to calm down, but the air is heavy with that nightmare juice again and I think they've found us. But they don't do anything, they don't come down to get us.

They just fill the air with bad dreams, and I have to try and keep my hold on reality. Keep my hold on everything. I think my dad is gone, lost in the nightmares. He keeps looking at me.

"Why are you wearing that red dress?"

And I can't help it. I have to cry, and I hold him and he's cold. Cold. But not dead yet.

I sing to him then, sing to him while he mutters and the whispers of the wolves lay quiet and uncertain in the background. I hold his gun and I hold him and I sing.

—

I read to him from a book I found in the basement. It's a book on alchemy and occult and I don't think it matters since it's the words he wants to hear. He likes hearing my voice, and I cook for him now, using the bunsen burner and cooking our canned food.

He might be dying, I dunno. He's cold and sweaty and talks nonsense. He keeps telling me if the king is cut up he'll be born again. I think his fever's gettin worse.

That night the wolves come back and they whisper and their bad dreams ache into the air. They don't come down for us, so I think we're safe. My dad tells me not to sleep until morning.

I sigh and I know he's right and I hold him and clean his gun. That sound, that mechanical ballet, it comforts me now. Comforts me in the shadow of the wolves.

—

Dad dies in the night while I sleep. I wake up holding him and his body's cold and still. His eyes are wide open and looking off into space.

I close them and I cry and scream. I don't know what to do anymore, if there is anything I can do.

It's daylight, and I'm not even sure if I'm safe with him gone. I don't know what to do with his body, and some part of me thinks of cutting it up and sprinkling salt on it and then burying it. Maybe he'll spring back to life like the alchemy book says. The king reborn.

I wonder if I could do that to the sun. Find the pieces of the dead sun and bury it with salt, see if it brings the sun back to life. Maybe I can cut up the moon and hide it in the four corners of the world and the wolves will have no one to worship.

I prop up his body and clean his wounds. I find myself talking to him through the day. Carrying on conversations with him, hoping he would answer back to me. I don't know if I'm crazy now or what, but I'm just so alone and it's coming in and crushing me.

I don't want to be alone with the wolves.

—

Later that day I cut him up with an axe and buried him in the back-yard. I sprinkled salt, I muttered those words about ashes and dust. I hoped it would work as I piled the heavy dirt on him with the shovel. I couldn't dig too deep, the sun-starved earth was too sharp, so now there's this mound in the backyard of a stranger's house with my father in it.

When the night comes in and the red settles into darkness, I go back underground. I hear the whispers come on and I ignore them, I ignore them and the nightmares. From the windows at the top of the walls I can see wolf faces glint and glimmer.

—

The mound is open. The grave is empty. Dad's body is gone.

I wonder briefly if he's out looking for me, and shove the thought from my head. I see footsteps and I wonder if any of this is right. If any of this is natural. The air becomes hotter and redder and I feel like exploding.

—

That night a new face appears with the wolves. It's the bogeyman and he wears my Pops's face like a mask. "Come on, come out," he whispers in my father's voice. His mouth is different, and I can see where he sewed the face on, the little threads stuck into skin.

His mouth is so wide, so filled with teeth.

"Come out, come out. I'm here for you. Try on these new bones with me. They fit so snugly over your skin."

I try to ignore it, but the juice fills the air again with nightmares. I can hear the shell above me rattling and with it comes more voices. More bogeymen. My mom's voice now, my sister's. My teacher's. All above me, rising above the whispers.

I look out the window now and see only skin-tight masks with bits of fur sticking out from behind. Masks of my mother, my sister and my teacher's face. I want to scream, I want to cry, but all of me is tense and silent.

They call for me.

And I come.

JARS OF RAIN

"You pay the bill?" Mary asked.

Bill tipped his hat back from his face, his coarse features now naked in the yellow lamplight. "Yes," he said, "I paid all of them bills."

"Even the water bill?"

He nodded. "Even the water bill. Did you meet our new neighbor? The one that moved downstairs?"

She looked at him, quizzically. "We live on the first floor."

He nodded. Cowboy nod. "Yeah. She moved into the basement. She told me that she lives inside the washer and dryer. At night she sleeps by hanging herself from a clothesline. Pretty strange."

Mary glanced down at cowboy Bill. She walked over and sat on the avocado chair in front of him. "Interesting. What was her name?"

He laughed, swung his feet around. The big shoes clanked against the wooden floor, splattered mud across it. "It's a hoot. You wouldn't believe it. She said her name was Mary. And get this—she looked just like you. Well, almost exactly like you. Except shorter. And older. Like really, really ancient."

Mary sucked on her lower lip. "So she really doesn't look like me at all then?"

Bill pulled a fistful of tobacco from his pocket. He pulled a book off from the table. *The Secret History of Birds.* He yanked out a page on blue jays. Rip. Tear. Mary cringed. He then pushed the tobacco in the center and started rolling his smoke. "Actually, you'd be surprised. It's like looking in a distorted mirror."

Mary looked away. She did not want to see him destroy the book for his dirty habit. "Oh," she said, "Did you know we have no water?"

Bill nodded. She heard the sound of a match striking. And then him inhaling. "Yeah. It's like that in the entire building. In the entire city. Didn't you hear about the drought? Don't you watch television?"

"No . . ." she said, "The television scares me."

"Oh," cowboy Bill exhales. "You should meet our neighbor. She buried her television. She hopes that if it's treated right a sitcom will grow. Like a tree. Did you know that she eats that sand? The stuff that comes out of the faucets? Whenever she's hungry or thirsty she just turns it on and sticks her head down. And then opens her mouth."

Mary turned and saw the burning page in his hand. His fingers were knotted, twisted. Ancient things, bent into shape from playing guitar in too many bars. "Like big fish," he opened his lips into a wide O shape, "Glug, glug, glug."

Inhale.

"And then she drinks it. Or eats it. I'm not sure which. The first time I watched her do it, my stomach turned. But now—well, it seems natural. Too bad we can't do the same thing. Then we wouldn't be going thirsty."

Mary stood up. She wanted to change her clothes. These smelled like smoke, and were covered in coffee stains. Maybe she would change into a blue sweater? Maybe that would call the water to her, like attracting like. "I'm going to go change," she said.

Bill coughed. "Thanks for telling me. Afterwards, you want to go and meet her?"

Mary walked toward their room. "No," she said, "I'd rather not. It doesn't sound like someone I would want to meet."

Bill looked down at his boots. His eyes were sad. Tormented, troubled eyes. "That's not very kind."

Mary slammed the bedroom door shut in response.

—

At midnight, Mary's friends came over. Bill went into the bedroom to watch some television. He never liked her friends—they all wore the same outfit. Black shiny shoes, orange stockings, black short skirts and leather corsets instead of tops. Their faces were even similar in shape. Same bone structure. It spooked him. They even all had the same name. Georgia.

Mary had decided that the dead might be able to tell them where they could find water. She looked all throughout the city for even a single bottle of water. She found none. She figured a séance with the Georgias was in order.

The living room was cleaned. Mud was gone, cowboy boots and hats all hidden in the closet, far from sight. The lamps were covered in red and black scarves, scaring away the light into colored shadows. The furniture was hidden—moved into the edges of the room and leaving enough space for the ritual.

In the center of the floor was a plain white chalk circle. In the center of the circle was a sword. Turning the circle into a symbol for null.

The Georgias huddled together, waiting for instruction. They chattered nervously amongst themselves. This was so exciting! They hadn't done a thing like this in years. They wondered who they would contact. Who would talk to them from the beyond.

Mary went and stood in the center of the circle. She wore her best magician's outfit. Top hat, black. Cape. Red. Suit and bow tie. She picked up the sword in her hand and commanded the Georgias. "Empty your pockets!" she said in her best magician voice. Thunder. Crackle crackle.

They giggled and pulled nine Chinese coins out of their pockets and scattered them inside the circle. Mary pointed the sword against the ground and chanted a line from T.S. Eliot.

"I will show you something different from either your shadow at morning striding behind you, or your shadow at evening rising to meet you. I will show you fear in a handful of dust."

When she said the word dust, she tapped the sword against the ground three times. The Georgias rang a bell each, a golden note. Tiny, tinkling. Musical and haunting.

They waited.

From the bedroom they heard Bill's television show. Distant, barely audible. The sound of canned laughter. And then—the closet. A banging, a beating, like a live thing trying to escape.

A voice that came from everywhere.

"You killed me in the closet, and buried me in the ground. This was only tomorrow. You told your husband I was a television. That I was filled with the noise of canned laughter. But I am dead. I have been dead since

Paul Jessup

tomorrow. But yesterday is tomorrow to me. I was born at the end of the world, and have died at the start of the transformation. You will join me. By eating the mermaid skin. By being split open and taken apart."

They were quiet.

Bang, bang, bang from the closet.

Canned laughter.

"What is your name?"

Applause.

"Mr. Superbus. Don't you have a question for me?"

Her hand shook. She must keep the sword level. Must not let the sword drop. "Yes. I want to know something. Where has all the water gone? Where is the rain?"

The ghost was quiet. They wondered if it had left them. Wondered if they were alone. And then—bang, bang, bang.

"You will never find out. Instead, you will adapt. You will eat the black sand. You will eat it out of my hands. And you will thank me, and let me cut you in half."

Silence then.

That was not the answer Mary had wanted, nor expected.

This wasn't fun anymore.

A buzz, low. Humming. From the television? She wasn't sure. More applause. A hoot, a holler. And then the hum grew louder. Musical. Dancing hum.

And then bang-bang-bang.

Quiet.

Ringing of bells.

Mary let the sword drop, the spell complete.

—

In the morning Mary made Bill some breakfast. Scrambled eggs, toast, a sliced apple. He sat on the living room floor, just outside the circle. Completely in full cowboy gear.

"You girls have fun?"

She put the plate in front of him. Saw his eyes dart around the room. As if he half expected to see one of the Georgias hiding in the shadows.

"Yeah," she said and sat down next to him, eating her own breakfast. "Thanks for understanding."

He shoved eggs in his mouth, the fork overflowing. When he finished chewing, he spoke again. "Did you find out anything? Did you contact someone interesting?"

She paused. Put down her fork. Looked out the window. Eyes anxious. "Yes. We did contact someone interesting. But no, we did not find out anything. It was hard tearing apart his words. It was like a riddle. And whenever I go near that closet—I feel something inside it. In the shadows. Moving. And I feel like I need to throw up or fall asleep."

Bill shoved more food into his mouth. When he was done with his eggs he patted his stomach and grinned. "That was great. Yeah, great. Sorry to hear you didn't get anything. Did I tell you what I saw on television last night?"

Mary pushed her food around on her plate with her fork. She wasn't hungry anymore. "No, what?"

"Strangest thing. Late night show, you know? With what's his name as the host. Very funny guy with black hair and the nose bleed. Anyway, his guest was this woman who lives two blocks down from us. She calls herself the rain dancer, and says she knows how to bring the water back."

She stared at her eggs. Yellow. Wiggling. She shouldn't have used salt. It would only make her even thirstier. "The television lies."

Cowboy Bill put his feet up. The muddy boots left a mess on the coffee table. "It's been known too. Which is why I think we have to check her out. She says she has jars full of rain. Waiting to be drunk. That she can take a plastic garbage bag, climb inside of it and turn into a pregnant cloud, ready to be seeded. Isn't that wild?"

She tried an egg. It tasted hollow. She knew she should eat. She knew she had to eat to live. "Not wild. Crazy."

Cowboy pulled out his tobacco pouch. "Without water the whole world's gone crazy. Let's go and look. It couldn't hurt."

Mary frowned. It hurt her face when she frowned. Like her skin was a desert, baking in the sun. "I'll go. As long as you stop talking about our new neighbor. That is the condition."

Bill pulled another book out from under the table. This one was *The Organ Grinder's Disease.* He pulled out a page with a picture of a lion attacking a gazelle and poured the tobacco in. "All right. Though I don't see what you have against her. She did nothing wrong."

A pause.

She threw her plate on the floor. Crash! Eggs everywhere. "She killed someone. In our closet. I know. Or I think I know. It was a dream, or maybe a memory. Something she does tomorrow. Something I did, maybe."

Cowboy rolled up his smoke and lit it. "Who told you that? Lies, I think. All of them lies. Can't trust dreams, can't trust memories. All you can trust is here and now. Then and there and what and when don't matter. They are liquid things. And all liquid things have dried up. Gone. Turned to dust."

"I think. I think the séance. The ghost. It told us, somehow. But we didn't remember it right. We remembered answers from a different time. Yet we knew what it meant. I think his name was Mr. Superbus."

Bill laughed, smoke drifting through his teeth. "Mary, old girl, you've been had. I met Mr. Superbus. Just yesterday. He was hanging out in front of the market. Putting up flyers for some play that is coming to town. One he helped produce. You couldn't have talked to him. He's alive and well."

Mary groaned. "Then maybe it's all wrong. Maybe everything is wrong. Let's go and see this girl. This rain maker. Let's see if we can get some of her magic jars and stop being so thirsty. Else, I'm going to have to go downstairs and learn how to drink black sand from our creepy neighbor."

Bill finished his smoke and put it out under one big boot. "That's more like it. Now you're talking sensible. Let's get ready and go. Put on your rain slicker. Might help put the sky in the right mood."

She stood up and walked numbly into the hallway outside of their apartment. All the coats lined up on hooks to either side of her. Masks hung above them. Like fleshless ghosts, hovering in the shadows. Wearing only coats.

She pulled down her slicker and remembered the sound of rain.

—

Cowboy Bill led Mary through the streets by a chain that was tied tight around her neck. Her arms were bound behind her. She saw people in buildings, staring out of windows. Watching them wind through the mazeling city streets.

"I don't see why this is necessary."

Bill stopped. There were no cars on the street. No birds in the sky. Just red sun, red clouds, and buildings filled with faces.

"I'm a cowboy," he said, "And you're my filly. You used to think it was fun."

She looked toward the ground. "That was before. Before we lived together. I thought it would change."

He kept on walking. "You were wrong. Come on, let's go and see the rain maker. Before it gets too late."

Further down the empty streets they saw a tall man with a waxed moustache putting up play bills. The play was called To Catch a Falling Star, and starred a girl who looked just like Mary. It could have been her double.

"Mr. Superbus!"

The man turned. "Ah!" he said in a heavy polish accent, "Cowboy Bill. Who is this beautiful girl you have with you? I recognize her. She is from my show. Is that why you have her chained, to bring her back to me?"

Bill laughed. "Naw, this is Mary. She's mine. Not related to that girl in that poster at all."

Mr. Superbus smiled. His yellow teeth barely hidden by his moustache. "Ah, beautiful girl. Beautiful! I think I talked to you. Yesterday."

"Yeah, yeah," Cowboy said, "I saw you at the market. Hanging posters."

"No," Mr. Superbus said. He pointed at Mary. "No, I talked to her. Yesterday. Tomorrow. Sometime. After I was murdered and buried. In your closet. You don't remember because you haven't done it yet. Is okay, though. I don't mind."

The cowboy pulled Mary closer to him. "What do you mean?"

Mary looked at Mr. Suberbus. This was not the same voice, she was sure of it. The man who spoke through the ghosts in the closet did not have an accent. "You know," she said, "I've always wanted to be an actress. I used to put on plays, for my brother. They were dark things. Shadow plays. I was a mermaid. I was eaten by wolves."

Mr. Superbus pulled a small book out of his pocket. It was a picture book with pages ripped out. On the cover was a wolf. "Yes," he said, patting the book cover, "I have seen that play. You were very good in it. Did you know that she was a mermaid?" he pointed at the poster, pointed at her doppelganger, "She tore off her fins to become an actress. Some people will do anything to be a star. Are you going to get water? I could use some. I am very thirsty. Maybe I can help?"

Cowboy patted Mr. Superbus on his shoulder. Dust exploded into the air, spiraling between them. "Now you are talking my language. Come on, let's go and see this rain maker."

—

The rainmaker's house was hidden behind a wall of dead trees, their branches intermingling into complex shapes. Spirals, spiderwebs, boney limbs crying out for water, for rain. Hungry trees.

The house itself was Victorian. Old for an American home. The paint had long since baked off from the burning light of the sun. Vines crowded it, choked it. A tree burst through some parts, entangling it in its branches.

"I know this house," Mr. Superbus said, "I saw it many tomorrows ago. It was where I spent my childhood. I grew up here, met the mermaid here. What was her name?"

Cowboy Bill looked at his filly. "Mary, just like my girl."

Mr. Superbus nodded. His head made creaking noises as it moved. Like an old house settling. "Ah. Right. Mary the Mermaid."

They walked up to the house. Mary did not want to pass through the trees. She did not want to be caught up in the branches, caught up and swallowed by them. She looked at Bill, pleadingly. But he yanked and pulled her neck, and she cried out in pain and she was forced to follow him further, further, further.

—

The rainmaker's name was Malice. She was very pregnant and very topless. Over her stomach she had painted a full moon, while her breasts hung loose. Her hair was wild, crawling over her head and caught with vines and branches.

Malice sat on a small table when they entered her house. Jars of rain surrounded her. Mary screamed and ran forward, hands grasping out for water, for life. Abruptly she fell to the ground, grasping for breath and pulling at her neck. Bill had yanked on her chain, pulling her to the ground.

"You come for water, yeah?"

Bill nodded. "Yes, ma'am. We came across town, searching for it. We think you got some. Can see it in the jars over there. Can we have some?"

The lady laughed. When she laughed her pregnant belly squirmed. They saw a face press against the other side, a man-sized face. Not a baby face. Large. Like a mask pressed into flesh.

"Sure, but is always a price. Making such water don't come cheap. Not in this land. Not in the city of the sun." She stood up on the table and sang. It was in Italian, part of an opera. When she finished Mary noticed Mr. Superbus was crying.

Malice got off from the table. "You ready to pay the price, cowboy? You ready to get some water?"

Bill stepped forward. He carefully handed Mary's leash to Mr. Superbus. Mary did not like this. He shouldn't have tied her up like this, shouldn't have handed her off. Not if he loved her. Not if her really loved her.

"I'm ready," he said, "Been a long time since I made water with anyone. That one, over there—she's cold as a fish sometimes. Desert girl, I call her. Dry lands. Wasteland woman."

Mary looked pleadingly at Mr. Superbus. "Let me go," she said, "Please let me go."

Mr. Superbus watched as Bill walked up to Malice. Malice pulled a garbage bag out from under the table. In her hand was an empty jar. The face inside of her belly pushed forward again. Mary thought it looked like it was screaming.

The black bag went over the two of them. Mr. Superbus pulled out a saw from his coat. A hack saw, with jagged edges smiling. "I need you for my play," he said with yellow teeth glowing.

From under the black bag plump hands tossed out Bill's clothing. Cowboy hat, boots, shirt and pants all in a loose pile on the floor. Mary backed away from Mr. Superbus. His eyes sparkled, danced. Like puppets on parade.

"I need you. Mermaid Mary. I need you to be my star, the star in the play. Fallen and broken girl. Come, come. Do not be afraid. When I am done you will not need water anymore."

She backed away from him. Pushing her shoulder against him. She could not struggle. Could not run. He had her by the throat with the chain, her arms tied behind her back. She was against the wall as he walked forward.

The black bag started dancing and moving. Moans came from inside, Bill moaning in pleasure, Malice gasping in wonder. And names being exchanged in screams that echoed through the halls. Every once and awhile a stray bit of flesh or limb would peek out from beneath. But nothing more, only a hint. A whisper of transformations to come.

Mary screamed.

She screamed hysterically and tried to run. Yank, and she was on the ground, coughing and trying to crawl. Too hard to crawl without hands. Too hard to do anything. And she felt the saw, felt it chew through her bones. Felt it tearing her, felt her legs being torn off from the bottom of her knees.

And she was so thirsty. So thirsty. Dried-up husk. When he was done she rolled over and saw stumps. No blood. None. Just stumps and her skin so old, so ragged. She wanted to throw up.

Mr. Superbus held a black blanket over top of the legs. Behind, the moaning got louder, the movements more frantic. "And now," he said in his polish accent, "I will perform a magic trick. Hocus! Pocus!"

The cape raised. Beneath it was a girl who looked just like Mary. Naked. And more beautiful in a way. Like Mary distilled into perfection. "Mary the mermaid, meet Mary the actress."

Mary the naked actress stood on her legs. Shaky, trying not to move. "It hurts to walk," said Mary the actress, "Like my legs are wrapped in knives. Like my skin is broken glass. With each step I take, I feel so much pain."

The bag stopped moving. Several slow grunts, and then a figure wiggled out. Malice. Twice as pregnant as before. No sign of Bill beneath the bag. A jar of water in her hand. "The transformation is complete. Somebody get the actress some clothes. And get the dwarf girl some black sand to eat. This is going to be a strange time. Because now everything is going to move differently."

Mr. Superbus walked forward. "Yes," he said calmly, his arm around his star, his Mary the not-mermaid. He looked down at Mary the mermaid and said, "Now it is time for everything to move backwards. For everything to start over again. Please be kind when you kill me. I have always loved you."

Malice put the jar up to a lamp. "A glass of water," Malice said, "Holds the light of the world."

She pushed it against her lips and Mary realized that she was thirsty, so thirsty, and watched Malice drink. Watched as the water spilled across face and chin, watched as it spilled between pregnant breasts. Watched and fought the urge to drink everything in sight.

To drink the chair and table.

To drink the boards and ceiling.

To drink the trees and the birds.

To drink the world.

WIRE RABBIT

Dead day: I member. Redo it and think it. Memorie each day. Keep it think it. Ma Cain is pain, think. Yeah. Feed her, til she screams. Feed her, til she howl and bite. Shove ta fuckin bakedbeans into her lips wit spoon. You eatchafood, I stay. You eatchafood now.

And shemad. But I do as she say. She say "feed me morning." So I feed. I feed. Fuckingshoveitdownin. Want to hurt. Love hurt. She did bad to usall. And Jotuns worst.

She not dead yet dow. She be dead soon.

I comeback later. Dinner later, how late. Got opencan. Got spoonful a meat. I shove in her stomach. Shove in mouth. She cold. She no move. MaCAIN. MotherCain. Spoon. Shove. Inner mouth. She no scream, no eat. I do again. And again.

Face covered food. Fat lips. Fat face. Hair is fake, I knows it. So test it, I pull it. No scream. No hurtforlove. Ilaugh. Iburnher, just to make sure.

No—she no move.

I lifter. But no use. She deadcold and heavy. So I gotalk to Brain. He knew all. Maybe he bring back? With zaps or something? I knowshebad. I knowshe hurt. But I LOVE. I am LOVE. I can't do nothingelse but lover.

So I go. I go upta Brain's place. Up innattic. There is lot upper. Lotslight. And books. And he chained. Chained and reading. There he plate—onnafloor. Glueddown with grilledcheese and rottenmilk. Bread hard, milk stink.

Brainhe smell like milkstink.

Curdledgreyskin.

Hereading. Some big brainybook. Macain like him read. Like him smart. She keep Brain smart. She keep me Love. Smartenough to Love. She keep Jotun and Kennel cagedup and stupid.

Fucker. I hater.

So tell Brain. And he say, "The inglodokin findulm sokiti can not bikiki. Bring me down, unchain the Brain gooble gabble, do it."

Or sathing fucking smart likat.

I unchain him. Fucker.

Takimdown.

He biganheavy, like macain. Can na walk. He try, no can. Legs sticks. So I rollem. Rollemrollemrollem. He hurt on floor. I laugh. He seer. Touch her. Fly goter now. Maggot eater. It smell. Like badmilk.

"Hoom," he say, "Fugin sawbut. She dead. Oh yah, hoom. Forking spoonsuck."

Fuckim. "What? Say better."

"Oh right. She dead. Yup. Nothing can do. Dead. Dead." Pound onwoof with fatfist, "Dead. We free. Free Kennel. Free Jotun."

I shock. "No, no. Love! Love! Bringerback."

He rollover, sit up hands. Face fatanangry. "Listen twigbitch. She gunnoai na fitlio, no gip, no dfi, no fiso. In hertowards, she dead and gone fa good. Gotin? Good. We free. So free jisd opdu and Jotun and Kennel."

I happy. Inaway. Is good. No more facepancake. No morefeedun boys. No more hurting and eyes. Nomore touching. No more hug. No more Love. "I nolove."

Brain smile. "Yes, you have yua lua love. We need you."

I angry then. Hit Brain.

"No Love," I say. "Jewel. Name Jewel."

Brain laughs. "Whatever. Free Jotun, kay? Free Kennel. Then we smagsam the bigram, canrum the tuntum. Speechspec?"

Fuckit. I hateit when he talkie big and mouthy. Like encyclope-dia fucker. I fuckinhit him again and he cries. "Thatright," say Jewel, "Fucking wire rabbit. No Breast, no beard. Fucking wire rabbit."

I know he know. He heard kennelboy. He know they are. The words. So I leave em. Leave em to stinkinhishead. Stink an rollaround.

An I go.

I go the outercages. Hidden in the alley hind the house. They sharp and pointed. Madefor rabbit and dog. Not for Kennel. Not for Jotun. See Kennel- his cage big. He body small. So he run, back an forth. Tongue hung out. Happy.

He barken and I letin out.

An he say he happy with words, "Breast," he say as he hug me, "Breast, beard, breast, beard."

An I know he good.

There Jotun tho. Dunno. He snarl. Face mess. He eyes burnout. Blackhole. His mouthsewnshut. His tongue ripout. Macain do it. Mother Cain doit. When he little. No bigger an walnut. Now Jotun Huge. Biggest. And he no fit in cage. All cramped up, huddled up. Backscraped.

He hear me an moan. He no speak.

He Jotun.

I decide ta cage him still. Jotun be too meannastyhurtburnfuckkill. No want. He all wire rabbit. No love for im. Nomatter what. Not even in ma cain.

I take Kennel backin. He bound round. Dance on fours. He lap and sniff. He happy. We see Brain. He onna floor, walkingonhands. His round body movingsun. He got knife. He cutenopen.

I scream.

Kennel howl and say, "wirerabbit! wirerabbit! wirerabbit!"

He stop. An lookitus.

"She has secrets inside of her. Splendid hidden secrets."

I make noise. Angry sound. Wirerabbit sound. I knockem knife away. He pull out anodder and get backing. He cut I stop. He getannoter. He ha many knives.

When he done she pieces. Macain pieces. An inside be a chest. Small. Bone. Ribcaged chest. Nokey needed. Brain smart- he open. An inside was Dad. Pica dad. An necklace. Surrounded by heart meat.

Dad pretty. He gotbeard. He got smileyface. I wonder- would he be? He be good? He love? Like me? Did macain nameme afterim? Brain speak. He clear his throat and talk all big and wordy. The Kennel bite him and he changes. Talks smaller. "We find dad. See? Dad. He take us. Care of us. We need him."

I shake head. Yes. No. Is all same.

Brain look around. "Where Jotun?"

I no say.

He angry. His ballbody big fist. "Where?"

"Cage," I say.

"Getim."

"No," I say, "Yougetim."

He laugh an roll. Kennel bark an chase no tail. I see pieces a macain an feel sick. She still badmilksmell. Now strong. Now flies allover. They buzz. Like emeralds. Pretty jewel. Likeme.

We talkie. No idea. Dad is- who know? We think. Search. Look-formaps. Lookforhome. Maybe heartnecklace show us? Brain think thatstupid. So he read more. I wanna chain him back. He keep saying, "Free Jotun, We all need freedom."

But I knowbetter. Jotun bad. Jotun angry beast. He venge. He hell. He rip and tear. I seeit. Brain- he no seeit. He know no. Se we fight, but no care. Brain can no do. I can do. And he no make.

Night come. In morning. Yeah. Maybe. Things better then. In morning. I sleep wit Kennel. He curl up roundme. Warm body. We love Brain alone. With hard books. Wirerabbit books. That'll teachim. For cutin her up into Macain pieces. Teachim good.

Wake up when Kennel bites me.

It hurts.

Moons of pain on hand and arm. But he no meanit. He cry and say, "beard, breast, beard," and I holdim. Close to breast. He know. He hear heartbeat. He know. Imnot macain, but I'll do.

We wake in morn. House is grey. Brain got all his books—MIL-LIONS! All in a pile. Like pyramid. Is neat. I threaten to knockitdown. But he say- "no!"

And I don't.

Me an Kennel go down. We hungry. No foodleft. I go backup grey stair. Into room. Cages onna ceiling. Rustred. Blood on walls. Old-blood, I knowit. Iseehim. He reading. "Brain," I say. He turn. His eyes tiny. His face dough. "No food. Needmoney."

Brain sticks hand down throat. Terrible sound. Like wet meat in grinder. Out comes blood soaked hand. Fist full a money. I take it. Feel dirty.

And walk atta grey door, inta rain day.

I hear rain. It beat drum beat on alley cages. Jotun there, eye all tired. He howl and rattle. He hurt. But can't stop, no help. Could be worse. Could be ma cain still here.

So walk to store.

Store is biggeranbig and there is guy. Helpful guy. Got scar on eye. Like he no see, see? Remind me a Jotun. He carry stuff back. Bagfulla stuff. Say he want to meet them. All a them. Even Ma Cain. I forgot she dead. I forgot it.

We go past cagealley. Rain beat, beat, beat. Bang, bang, bang. Iron-cage sounds. Rust screechee. He laughs. Mister Scar laughs. He see Jotun, Jotun howl. An he laugh.

He don't get it. But he nice. He carry food. So is ok. Is all right.

We go inna grey house. Oh that Kennel is mad. He bark and shout wire rabbit, wire rabbit, wire rabbit. And Brain onna ground, building with cards. Castles. Geomatric shape. I scream.

But Kennel no stop. Wire rabbit, wire rabbit, so scar he go. He leave food and he go. He handsome, kind. I want scar to stay. Mister Scar good. All breast and beard. No wire rabbit.

"Bad," I say Kennel. "Bad" I hit him. I know wrong—is wrong—Ma Cain used do it. But he scare Mister Scar. "No wire rabbit," I say, "Breast. Beard."

Kennel looks a me. Strangely. He mutters "wirerabbit," and run offta corner ofa room.

Brain came forward. "I'll cook," he say. Then he say something big and mouthy and complex. He make me stupid. I fucking hatit. I hatim. Ma Cain mademe dumb, madim smart. I hate it.

So he in kitchen, cook. Cook over stove. Blue flame- lickflickerlick. I slow, walk, slow. I have iron in hand. Big iron. Hurt iron. Ma cain usedtauseit. Now I use it. I ma cain. No lover. No love.

Swing. His bigbody oomph splat. He scream an turn an lookitme. "Fuck," he say, and more big stuff comin outta he mouth. Fickinbadmad make me hurt now. I think. Not. Think not. Hurtburn. I liftagain, swing again. Smash again. Thumpoomph again.

Kennel come running out, barking mad and bit me. I stop an cry and fall to ground. Like doll. Clump mess onna floor. Brain is in pain. But he just cooks more. Cooks more an don say a word. We all tight now. Strung tight. By death.

It smell fish. Better an bad milk.

Kennel is mad ame. He call me wire rabbit. He bite, he kick. Brain thinkit funny. We ate food, is good. I say sorry, but Brain no speak. He lookit me with terror. Hate. Humility. All guilt and hurt. I want to crawl into face a moon. Want to hide in shadowlands. Want to go into cage alley with Jotun. Letim tear me apart and scatter me.

Later tonight I slept myself. On porch. I dream a daddy. Beard man cometh. He walk outa closet- with Mr Scar right near him. And they takeme away an I fine love. Is good dream.

Inna morning Brain callsusall together. He say, "I know you all tired and mean and hungry. We find dad. We find now," cept he say it with big angry words dat hurt me. Hurt me. Wanna hurt him. But Kennel growl and lookitme and I knows better. So Brain, he show us map. Gointa the closetland. Dats were dad works. Heda bogeyman, livin in closets.

So we start walkin tru. To clostes are wrong, scary. Like cageland. With dogs and monkeys. And skulls that sing an float. And a man who bled coins and a dancer. With a mask. He tried to love us. But brain no letim.

So we go back emptyheaded and think- tomorrow. But we need more food. So ungryhungry. Brain make money from his tummy. He thinner now. With each wad of bloodbills. He thins and thins.

Soon he begone. And then he kinwalk. And goaround. And no needstupidme. No need. So Ineedtofix. But first, I go. I go and get food. I see misterscar again. He with another. Man in black coat. He mister hush. All he say is "hush, hush." They carry stuff home.

I think they know.

Know us. Know dad.

Know and help.

They wana see macain. I wannashowem. Showem and havem helpeme and mebbee we break Brain legs. Callhurtpain. Wesee Jotun. Jotun Makes hush nervous. But scarnomind. He even pet Jotun. An Jotun purr and drool.

I bringemin. Scar back. Kennel bark and growl and say wirerabbit and attack. Hush comeforward with ironbar. He hit and Kennel fall back, whimpering. Mabbee they no help. Mebbe they wire rabbit afterall.

Brain thin. Brain attack. They all brawl. Scream. Ground pain. I attack to. We push Scar and Hush out. We bleeding now. Hurt now. Brain about to yell. But quiet. He know. What I feel. He gets it.

We silent. He cooks.

No sleep that night.

In morning we go ta closetland to search him out, an get back door open. Front door open. We find nothin in closets, no person. Just spring n bone puppets. We look. No one. Upstair- we hear sound.

Brain looksitme. "Go. Free Jotun."

I nod.

War.

Out inna cage alley. Norain, not now. Just Jotun, cagecrushed, mewling. I stepback, opendoor. He rushes out, howlinmad. I know. I hide. He smells. Foriegn smells. Screams, mutters. Blind words outta sewnmouth. My stomach turns.

I wait outta. Wait inlisten. Something. Terriblesounds. Blood. Meatripping. I go in, an Jotun is onnafloor. Soundingmadnangry. He has bloodfists. Coiledsausagehands. Bodies onnaground. Even kennel. Even Brain. Scar and Hush. Alldeadandgore. Scattered between the macainpieces.

I walk. Hesitant. Jotun sniffs me. Doesnothing. I see pic a dad. I see necklace. I grab, quickly. Jotun turn. Snorts. Calmthough. I walk past, calmly. Toward closet. He sees me. Smile raggedsmile.

"Free," I say.

Jotun moans.

I walk inna closet.

From behind I hear himshuffle. His feet drag and out into city he walk. He walk with big steps. Like bombfeet. The groundshake. His head snake. Living. Live thing. I fear thosewhocrossim. I fear allwho seehim. He will eat and devour and destroy.

I close door behind.

And feel. Mind changing. Just a little. Things have a bigger scope now. I look around me. I remember this place. This room. This is not closetland. I walk through and I see a bed in a pink room. And I see a ceiling high up with stars painted across it. And I feel different. My brain has changed somehow. More room for thought. Now that Brain is dead—am I Brain?

The bed is soft. I don't remember the last time I laid on a soft bed. Outside of the window I see snow falling and from the hallway I hear people talking. And I go out into the hall and there—not macain. Not dad. No. It is my mom and my dad. And they are in their bedroom talking.

And I am wearing a crown. And a little dress. I am a princess. I was playing princess. Where am I? Where had I gone? Was this always like this? I couldn't tell. I run up and climb up on their laps and they hold me. I feel breast against me. I feel beard against me.

And in the hall I hear something. Like metal clanging. And I know it. It is wirerabbit. The wirerabbit is coming for me. None of this is real. It is the wirerabbit and Jotun on its back, riding it through the halls. Scurrying through the walls with metalmouth. Looking for me.

FAKE PLASTIC TREES

Old Blue was a methuselah gorilla. One of those ratted old craggy beasts with scars all over him, hair torn out and eyes twitching with ancient sentience. When my husband caught him he was half-crazed with parasites, howling and thumping his chest.

I domesticated him. He did not resist his chains but his rheumy eyes never looked at anything but the mountains on the horizon. I understood his loneliness, understood his desire to return to his family. I've spent too many months in the jungle, far away from the city streets I've called home my whole life.

In the darker hours I saw him wander around the fake plastic trees and rattling the iron bones of his cage. The yellow blades of his teeth cut the edges of his lips as he pushed his mouth between the bars in a grimace of pain. If I was awake I would sing to him, hoping to calm him down. And he would sign, over and over again, "family, love, family, love" in hopes that I could somehow help him be free.

—

My husband spent more days out in the jungle than I cared for. He left me with Old Blue most of the time, only asking me to join him and his men when he felt that things would be boring, in hopes that I would just stay behind. I missed the quiet hours we had spent with each other so long ago, sitting on our balcony and listening to the sounds of the city below us.

Now he was a man obsessed. The population of gorillas was dying fast, and he was afraid that the parasites might somehow jump to a human host and destroy our civilization. He searched day and night for a cure, constantly poring over notes, checking his specimen. Calculating and recalculating every equation.

To pass the time I taught Old Blue. I read to him. I kept him company. Some hours I would just hold a conversation with him. He talked to me more than my husband did, and even though the words were clipped and his grammar broken, his words spoke to me. They touched me.

He did not know he was dying. Did not know his kind were near extinction. And I did not have the heart to tell him.

—

My husband was out in the jungle when the incident happened. I write of it now in fear, my hands shaking. I remember it clearly—the sounds of whispering. The shadows hovering around the windows. The smell of gorilla piss in the air, pungent and decaying my senses.

Old Blue went mad, jumped up and down and screamed. When he finally calmed down he kept signing, over and over again, "immortal, immortal, immortal." His eyes floated about in his skull, his hands shaking violently.

I haven't told my husband yet. I'm not sure if I ever will. Unless he steals a peek at this diary, he will have no idea what transpired in the night.

—

Old Blue gave us each nicknames. He called me Doctor Love and he called my husband Doctor Death. It's actually pretty funny, now that I think of it. Of course, my husband thought otherwise. Claimed that Old Blue did not understand the nature of his research. Told me that if he did not find a cure soon, the real Doctor Death would come for him.

I realized today that my husband is a heartless bastard. He wasn't always like this. Before the jungle and the mountains, before the parasites and chemicals, he had loved me like no one else. Back in the city, with its filthy streets and homeless men shambling in the shadows, he had shown me his heart. He had shown me his love and his great mind. These days I have this driven man, this obsessed man in the shell of my husband.

—

I never thought I'd be surrounded by jars of parasitic worms. They float through a strange amber fluid, not quite alive, not quite dead. My husband sings to them, calls them his babies. I wonder if he is infected. I wonder if I am infected. At night I pinch my stomach, looking for traces of the creatures, crawling under my skin, eating away at my flesh and mind.

I found nothing. But I felt infected somehow. Infected like Old Blue.

—

4:00 in the morning my husband came home covered in blood. He sang to me, told me of the dead around him in the jungle. He had new specimens. Human ones. He was right, it had jumped to people. He seemed so excited. So thrilled to be able to cut up his old friends and look through their remains, pulling out parasites for his own research.

I left the room and ignored him. I still won't let him come near me. He is infected. I know he is infected. I am infected too. We are all going to die out here, and there is no way he can fix it.

So I stay and talk to Old Blue. He signs me poetry of the world he had known. He signs me stories of his children and his wife. I tell him my troubles, and he signs that he is sorry.

I sign back a love song and I see him smile. Those yellow bladed teeth, pushing past his lips. I swear I can see the parasites crawling around in his mouth. Slick grey worms laying eggs inside of him, polluting his thoughts and driving him insane.

—

There are figures running outside of the windows. My husband is back in his office, staring at slides and jotting down things in his notebooks. He is infected now. He cannot think straight. He won't be able to cure us, not with the disease eating away at his mind.

The shadows running outside look like gorillas. Maybe they are ghosts, come to haunt us for not helping them. For being foolish enough to think we could help them. I wonder if any of them know Old Blue, if they had come to take him home.

I go in the back to ask him but he's asleep up in the green felt leaves of a plastic tree. He is signing in his sleep, over and over again. Family, love, family love. Doctor Death, Doctor Death, Doctor Death.

—

I never told anyone this before. Not even Doctor Death, not even Old Blue. This is a secret. When I was six I caught my dad having an affair with another woman. At first I was scared. He was on top of her, wearing a surgical mask and gloves, naked from the waist down.

I did not want to say anything to anybody. I was afraid Mom would leave him, that she would leave us and I would have to stay with him and that slut in our old broken-down house.

After four years the secret came out. My mom caught him this time, and it was the end of him. The end of us as a family. My mom took off, taking me with her. I had no choice but to go. I still miss my father. After that we lived in shitty apartments in shitty neighborhoods. My friends scared me, my enemies scared me. But I came to love the derelict streets and the broken-down world of the poor and the forgotten.

Learned to love the ruins of the world around me.

—

My husband crawled out of the back room. His skin was ash grey, and his eyes were two black holes crawling with worms. His hair was falling out, and his knuckles were boney and key-shaped. He had on a surgical mask and gloves.

"I'm getting close. So close."

I nodded and touched his shoulder.

"You're infected, you know that? You can't think straight."

He backed away from me. His face was frightened and I saw the worms living beneath his skin, spreading the madness into his blood. "I'm not infected. Look at me! Really look at me. You're infected. It's that damn beast you've been hanging around. I'm going to cut him open tonight. You'll see."

I backed away from him. He was filled with anger and worms. "Don't, don't you touch him. You're insane."

A scalpel in his hand. It spun in the air, an arc of silver. "You're the one who's insane. Isn't that right? Yes, yes. It's right. It's right and you know it."

I ran into the other room, crying and slamming the door behind me. We're all going to die here. It's not going to be much longer before we are all dead.

—

I dreamt of the city. I dreamt of my husband holding me and dancing with me in our bedroom. It was a Patti Smith song, and we sang and jumped up and down and we were so happy.

When I woke I realized I was crying. Maybe I am infected. I can't see the parasites, but maybe that is because they don't want me to see them. They are controlling my mind, changing me. Breaking me.

—

I told Old Blue about the dream. He puts on his glasses and pulls out his pipe. Carefully, he fills the pipe full of tobacco and then lights it, puffing eagerly. His face is serious and parasite-free. The smoking kills the worms. At least, that's what he's told me.

After a moment of thinking and puffing clouds of black smoke he picked up a beaten red leather book from the floor and began to read a passage to me from its contents.

"Things base and vile, holding no quantity,

Love can transpose to form and dignity.

Love looks not with the eyes, but with the mind;

And therefore is wing'd Cupid painted blind."

Then he placed the book down and tapped the ashes from his pipe, smiling his yellow bladed smile. "The bard always expresses love the best, don't you think so, Doctor Love?"

I remember smiling. I remember dancing with him. But I couldn't remember when he learned to talk. Had he been able to talk this whole time? I couldn't be sure. The next day I came back to him, and he was the same Old Blue, sitting still and infected, signing his name in the air and dancing in circles.

I waited, hoping that the pipe smoking Blue would return. I felt comfort when he talked, felt at ease with my surroundings. I hadn't felt like that in so long. I missed that feeling. Missed feeling at home in the world.

—

My husband tied me to the bed with an old yellow rubber belt. He left the door open so I could see what he was doing. He went into the cage and opened it. Old Blue crawled down out of the tree, followed after him. I wanted to scream out no! To scream out stop! But I had cotton shoved deep into my mouth and a surgeon's mask over my face, holding it in. Any attempt at speech gagged me.

I struggled against my bonds. I saw an infected trail across the floor, following after Doctor Death. I could smell an acrid smell in the air, like the smell of dentistry and drills going deep into bone. The yellow bindings cut against my hand as I struggled, making the tips of fingers tingle from the lack of blood.

Eventually, after hours of moving and wriggling and trying to break free I saw Old Blue come back into the room. He had his pipe in his mouth and a scalpel in his hands, and he smiled as he walked up to me.

"Doctor Love, old doll," he said with a thick English accent, "You're wanted in the emergency room. I suggest you come post haste."

I struggled. I tried to break free. I tried to speak out, to explain my situation. After a moment of waiting he shrugged his shoulders. "I see we are making no progress here, no progress at all. I'll be out on the balcony, waiting for you, if you happen to feel like working today."

I closed my eyes, trying to fight back my tears and instead fell asleep.

—

Later on Old Blue walked back into the room. He had my husband's face over his, wearing it like a mask. In his hands was a scalpel, over his back was a bag that rattled. I found out later that the bag was filled with bones painted red.

He cut my bonds and held out his hand to lift me up. When I stood he signed "Doctor Love" and pointed at me. He then signed "Doctor Death" and pointed at himself. This was too much, I couldn't take it.

I shoved him down. I heard him hit the ground as I ran. He leapt up, his fierce body pulsating with rage. He signed the words for immortal over and over again, pointing at himself, pointing at the jungle, pointing at the world.

I ran, ran right into the cage, thinking that it was the jungle outside. How could I have confused these plastic trees with the real thing? I felt like a beast now, a trapped creature. Fooled by the sign into thinking that it was reality.

I beat my chest, I howled, I screamed. I tried to speak, but realized I could not. He had removed my tongue with the scalpel while I slept. On the floor I saw this diary, and knew that he had been reading it.

A Gift of Teeth

In late September, when the wind first tasted of apples and the shy leaves began to turn, Junie noticed her husband's left hand had turned to wood. At first she thought it was a trick of the light, that it couldn't be right, wood? How strange. A little tan, maybe, the color not matching the rest of his arm, yes. All weird things, of course. But wood? Her eyes are tired, yes, that must be it. But she swore she saw the warped grain of it, with splinters sticking out from his knuckles like tiny hairs. There were ball joints along the fingers, to give it the appearance of smooth, humanlike movement. Probably controlled by some levers in his back.

He sat forward on their porch, grabbed his beer with the good hand, the one not wood just yet. She wanted to lift up the back of his shirt right then and there, and look and see if she could spot the levers to move his fingers, or even a place she could stick her hand and make him talk and speak like all good dummies should. *No, stop it,* Junie thought to herself. *Don't be such a silly thing. He's a man, true and true. No way his hand was a wooden hand.*

But when he sat back, and wiped his head with his left hand, she saw beads of sweat drip down the wood, and knew that it was the real deal. She looked at her own hands then, turned them over, ran her fingers across her palms. Real and true and fleshy. See? The bones are right there, right where they were supposed to be, right under her skin. She wasn't wood at all; it was only affecting her *husband.*

"You okay, Junie? You never touched your sweet tea, not even once. That's not like you."

"Yeah, I'm okay, don't you worry none."

And she reached over, and touched that bad hand, and almost jumped about a mile high. It was smooth, and polished, and knobby. For some reason, this thrilled her beyond words. A flutter in that heart, like tiny butterflies, and she hadn't felt this alive in a long, long time. How much of him is wood? How much? A grin at the thought of another appendage, but she decided to keep such things to herself.

It's probably just the one hand, after all.

—

The transformation felt very slow, the wood creeping along his body all the next day. It shone in the daylight, spotted with water damage in some parts. Paint began to appear as well, coloring his limbs with bright cartoony tones, that gave it the appearance of a haunted dummy. And the oddest thing of all, was that her husband did not seem to notice anything was amiss.

"Are you okay?" she asked him, when she saw his arms shrink to half their size, the tiny wooden hands flexing slowly with each movement like they were pained.

"Mm. Sure." His words were slow, heavy, weighted with silence. This wasn't new for him, he was a man of few words and fewer thoughts, still. "Why? Do I look funny?"

"Oh, no, you just seemed a bit stiff is all. I was worried if the rain was bothering your joints again."

He stretched out his arms, groaned for a bit, his joints creaking and whistling. The air smelled like soft pine needles, scattered under foot. "Yeah. I guess so. Hadn't even noticed, should probably get, um. Get. Um. What's that thing . . ."

"A pain reliever?"

"Yeah. Help loosen me up a little."

She nodded, and watched him walk out into the bathroom, each movement slow and pained, as dust scattered around him in a mist of transformation.

—

After a moment in the bathroom, he cried out her name in haggard agony. Her heart butterfly quick again, and she wondered if this was it, was he finally changing? Would he be a dummy completely now? The thought excited her, as beads of sweat trickled down her back in small rivulets.

He stood there, under that harsh lamp, staring in the mirror. His hands were held up in front of his face, and he looked terrified. Lines were under his mouth now, his eyes glassy and unreal. "I can't move my hands, please, help me, I can't move my hands Janie, I need your help."

And she knew exactly what she had to do. Oh, this would be perfect. A devilish smile crossed her lips as she ran in without hesitation. This was inevitable, wasn't it? The sort of thing that she'd dreamt of since she was a little girl, when she saw that one ventriloquist show in grade school. Dreams of a wooden love, licking and kissing her body, her hand in his back orifice moving him, showing him exactly where all the good spots were.

She jammed her hand into his back, and he yelped and tried to spin around, but it was no use. She reached her fingers around the spine, grabbed onto some wet tendrils, and began to yank and pull on them like strings. He spun his head, unnatural, completely around, glass eyes staring at her, face half-wooden and half-real. His hair was gnarled patches, and his legs were beginning to shrink inside his clothes, too.

He spoke with heavy words. "What, are you, doing?"

"Oh hush, you," Junie said, "I'm helping you move your hands, isn't that what you wanted?"

His mouth moved up and down, up and down, the words caught in his wooden throat. "No," he finally said, his voice reverberating through the wood. "No. I. Don't want this. What is this? Let me go, Junie, please. This hurts."

And she pulled her hand out with a wet thwack, her fingers gooey and sticky. It wasn't blood, no, this was . . . what? Sap, yes. This was pine sap. Made sense, she guessed, made sense. She washed her hands in the sink with some lava soap, dried them off quickly and turned and looked at him. Of course, she'd moved too soon, he wasn't ready yet. He still had his head to finish up, and then his mouth to change.

His legs weren't even quite finished yet, either, and she had just been too eager to get on with it already.

She had to hide her disappointment, this was a careful moment, and required tact. "Sorry, love," she said, "That was the only thing I could think to help you out.

"I need to go lie down now, maybe if I rest for a bit my body will be right and tight and good to go again. Nothing helps an aching spine like a good nap, yes indeed."

"All right then, I'll leave you to it."

And she turned to walk out, pausing because she knew that he was going to say, his voice strained and a bit pained. "Junie, honey, I'm sorry to yell at you."

"I know, love."

"But, I do need your help now. I do. Can you pick me up and carry me out to the couch and lay me down? Just so I can rest. My legs aren't really good right now, either. Never had it this bad before, I swear."

"Of course, love, of course. And I'm sorry, too, I didn't mean to hurt you. I only meant to help you."

And then she walked over and picked that tiny wooden body up. It was barely anything anymore, wasn't it? Light as pine, hollow bones, barely weighed more than a cat. She felt his spine against her hand as she carried him, that hole right there where she reached on in and started tugging at his inner wires. She wanted to do it again, but resisted, her mouth watering. There will be time for that later! Once he's fully transformed into a puppet, it won't hurt to move him like that anymore.

And then she could speak for him, and move him, and they would be in sync forever, and it would be wonderful.

"Thank you, dear," he said when she put him on the couch and pulled their ragged old quilt up over his shoulders. His head peeked on out, the features growing more and more wooden. He moved his new jaw again and again, and she could tell it was getting harder for him to talk. "Thank, you."

And then his eyelids slid shut and he was out.

—

She came out later to check on him, as the night settled into her bones like a sad memory. She couldn't sleep, all she could do was think about his changes, and what a bright and lovely future they would have. She looked at his face peeking out from under the blanket, and now it looked completely different than it had before. She stood there, staring, unable to move. It didn't even resemble her husband any longer, but rather a garish, twisted grotesque reflection carved in wood. The nose like a spiral, his eyes red glass prisms under their heavy lids, his cheeks swirled up in red paint, and his lips tiny things, almost nonexistent. His hair was different too, now bright red and a wild mess all spitting out of his head like fire.

There it went again, her butterfly heart flittering in her chest. She licked her lips. He seemed even more delicious now. She reached down, tapped a finger on his forehead, gently, tap tap tap. Hard wood, yes, very hard indeed. She waited for his eyes to flitter awake, and when they did not, she tapped him again, and again.

Nothing.

Maybe it was finally time to try out her act? Yes. Of course. He's gone full puppet now, righty ho, and it won't hurt anymore to pull his strings and levers and bring him back to life. She had to get ready, inhale, exhale, had to prepare for this mentally. Dizzy, her mind aswoon and sideways, she held onto the back of the couch, and smiled that devilish smile again. Here we go, here we go, here we go.

She pulled the blanket off his body, and spun the puppet around, and reached up the back of his shirt. Her eyes were closed, she couldn't open them, too nervous to watch and see it actually happening, her dream becoming really real.

The levers and strings felt dry, light, wooden and thin beneath her fingers. No longer messy and organic, this was it. She really had him.

Okay, Junie, okay, time to remember all those classes you took at the community center in high school. Keep your lips invisible, throwing your voice just a little bit, just far enough so that the illusion felt real. She had to channel her husband then, too, try and get his words and voice in her thoughts. She couldn't speak for him without consuming him in her mind, no, no, that wouldn't be right. And this had to be right, it had to be one-hundred percent right.

Exhale. She opened her eyes. Show time.

"Hello, hello, hello! Say hi to the crowd, Bernard, and make sure you're nice to them during our show tonight! Nobody likes a mean-ie-butt!"

The puppet turned its head, opened its mouth clack clack, but the words that she spoke came from somewhere deep inside of her, like the puppet was channeling her and not the other way around. The voice was all high pitched and raspy, like an insane child drunk on whiskey and cigarettes. "Eh, he he he, eh. Bernard ain't here, Junie. Just you and me, doll."

"Doll? You're the doll!"

Oh, she slipped into that old routine so easily, it was like she'd never stopped.

"I might be made of wood, but I'm the one in control, so you're the dollll, ya hear me? Ya he he he he. Now tell me, tell me, do you know who I am?"

Nervous now, yes. This wasn't part of her old act anymore, what was this?

"No, no I don't. Can you tell me?"

"Yes, yes, yes, I am the child of the abyss, the lantern in the dark, I am the one who crosses voids in the sunless lands. My mother is the mistress of hours, and my father is the eater of suns. But you can call me Catchandkill."

"Catchandkill?"

"You got it! Ya he he he he!"

It was getting harder to work the gears now, hand sweaty, muscles tight. She had to stop. She wanted to continue but she had to stop. Everything weighted down. Her body aching, all muscles tensed up tight like ropes.

"I think, I think I need to lie down."

"Oh, that's okay, doll. I know this takes a lot out of you, but I'll be here, waiting for when you wake up."

And then she pulled her hand out and saw how red and cut up it was, with little kisses of blood on the knuckles. Dizzy, almost ready to fall over, something had sucked the life from her bones. Yes, she had to rest. She didn't even have enough oomf to go upstairs and climb into bed. She would just do it here, on the floor. Yes. Yes, indeed. Just here on the floor and drift to sleep . . .

—

And she dreamt of cardboard sets and childhood audiences and the cheap laughter of drunk adults. Ball pits that smelled of warm piss, kids running about screaming and yelling like the din of celestial birds. And there, on the pedestal, on the stage, there sat Catchandkill, arm outstretched waiting for her to come and join her.

"Come on, come on! The audience is waiting for you. Now is the time for our big show. You don't want to keep them waiting, do you?"

But he spoke with Bernard's voice, a low rumble with a pleasant kindness to it. She realized for a moment what they'd done, the whole simple life they'd built together washed away in an instant.

—

She woke to wood tapping on her forehead, a reflection of the way she'd woken Catchandkill earlier that day. Groggy, she swept the sleep from her thoughts and sat up. He was on the couch next to her, his hands pointing at his back, his mouth moving open and close, clack, clack, clack.

"Oh, I see, you need me to talk for you?"

He nodded yes, yes, yes. She felt a little more awake now, true, and a lot less achy and worn out. She would just have to pace herself for a bit, working the controls was more difficult than she remembered as a kid. Might be age, too, making even the slightest things harder.

"Okay, then. Let me get a glass of water and we can . . ."

He shook his head no, no, no, and pointed angrily at his back.

"All right, all right, hold your horses."

A thrill jolted through her body when she put her arm inside him, waking her up, all crisp and sharp. Numb sensations floated through her mind, and once again she was transported elsewhere. The magic of theater, yes, that's what this was and nothing more than that. The magic of theater. She smiled so much it hurt. But that was okay! Happiness, real true burning bright happiness, was the always meant to hurt. That she knew, deep in her giddy bones.

"Okay, Catchandkill! Tell me now, what's so important that you had to wake me?"

The patter was easy and natural again, thank god.

"It's my birthday! Ah he he he he ha he he ha!"

"Your birthday! You don't say. Well now, tell me, what do you want to do for the big day? You want candles, cake, presents, all of that?"

Catchandkill nodded his head so violently she thought it was going to fall off. "Yes, yes, yes! Catchandkill wants presents, oh, so many presents."

"Well, then! Tell me, what kind of presents do you want?"

There was a beat of silence for a moment that choked the air. She knew that she was the one talking, and that she could feel her vocal chords vibrating as she threw her voice, and yet it wasn't her words, wasn't her voice, wasn't . . . her. And that was . . .

So thrilling.

Already more sweat beaded up on her forehead, and her muscles grew tired again, but she fought through it. She wasn't going to go to sleep so soon again, she needed this experience. It made her feel whole in ways that she never knew possible, like her life before this moment had been a grey aching shadow on the verge of being, but never crossing over.

"I want the gift of teeth and tongue. Give it to me."

She knew what that meant, her tongue touching her teeth now, counting them out one at a time, feeling them to see how loose they were. "Why do you need those?"

Her heart tripled up, fast thunder beat, blood a river roaring in her ears. Her mouth dried up, but every other inch of her felt wet and knotty and alive. She wanted to scream in joy, and never let this moment end. Catchandkill was everything to her now, her hand bliss in this orifice, touching all of his insides so gently, controlling him.

"I want to speak with my own voice! Ya ha ha he he he ha!"

And she felt hurt, briefly, stung by the implications. "But, I love to speak for you . . ."

"Oh," he said, "This will be even better, trust me. We will be even closer, after you give me my birthday presents."

And she nodded, and removed her hand from his back. Sore, bloodied, cut up even worse than before. She briefly thought about infection, but then chased those thoughts away. She saw maggots crawling on her arms, too, as well as small centipedes and other crawling insects. Where had they come from? Did they live inside Catchan-dKill?

Best not to think about it. She had a job to do. A present to give to her new best friend.

—

After many painful hours, she stumbled back into the living room. Mouth bloodied, teeth in her hand, tongue squirming red on her palm. She felt so worn thin and reality moved against her in vibrating waves of light. She almost stumbled, crawled, righted herself quickly. Did not want to drop his presents. These were so important. He needed those. Then they would go on the road together, put on a beautiful show, and he would love her and she would love him.

She gently put the teeth in his mouth, just like he showed her. Clack, clack, clack. And then she strung the tongue through the wires and wood, making sure it was on nice and tight. She had all this cotton shoved into her mouth, stopping the bleeding as best as she could. Though it still flowed down the back of her throat, in a hot sticky fountain.

When she was done, she collapsed against the couch. Everything felt distant, fuzzy, indistinct. And she smiled. She was so happy. This was the greatest day of her life, and all of her dreams had come true. She would never, ever, be sad again.

SUMMER CANNIBALS

You are in a maze of twisty cubicles all alike. The coder behind you is named Benjamin, and he hasn't seen the light of the sun in seven days. They have no windows here, no windows at all. The coders to the left and right are falling asleep, nodding off, their drooping heads rattling calendars with kittens on them. It's been so long since you've slept or ate, but you can't drift off, not now. Not while you're working, if Mister Lynn knew you slept ever slept ever at all he had would have you fired or destroyed or eaten alive by the software lions they keep in coded cages. Your screen flashes, begging to be fed some algorithms from the command line.

What do you do?
>Stand up
I don't understand that command.
>Talk to Benjamin
I don't understand that command.
>Quit my job.
I don't understand that command
>Quit this game.
I don't understand that command
>Scream and howl and scream and howl

—

Rob wakes up and sees he's drooling on his keyboard and his head is imprinted with keys and he wonders where he is. For a moment he thinks he's at work and panics again because sleeping at work is bad. Shit, bad, shit. Then he looks up and he laughs and almost pisses himself laughing because he's at home, yeah, and his Commodore 64 is dialed into some BBS, and he thinks he must've fallen asleep playing *Red Dragon* again.

From the stairs he hears Ben shout down, "Hey come on, man, you're killing me."

And he goes up and looks up the basement steps and calls up, "What are you talking about?"

"How could you log off like that? We were so close, you know that? So damned close, and now you know what? Jen and those punks are going to get those experience points before we do. Is that what you want? We quit that job for a reason, right? Right? This is part of it, so don't you dare back out on me now."

"Look, Ben, I don't care, okay? I don't. I fell asleep playing again, and I can't keep doing that."

"So what. Even half awake you were kicking ass, giving our team all the points. BOOM! We were rocking it."

Rob scratches his head for a second and heads up the steps, pushing Ben aside. Ben shoves him against the kitchen wall. Face against face. "Don't push me."

"Come on, I was just going to take a piss."

"Don't push me or you'll be pissing your pants."

"All right man, all right."

"We're going out, come on, let's get out of here."

Rob doesn't want to leave, doesn't want to follow Ben anywhere. But he knows he has no choice, he always has no choice. That's why he quit working for InfinteGames, they both quit and now he's got nothing anymore. Why does he do what Ben says? Why is it always that way?

Ben yanks on his arm and off they go they're going off and running again, outside, to the car, taking off *Dukes of Hazard*-style. Overhead, the moon is plump and hungry and the stars are cowering behind clouds. It's a moonful night all right, the kind of night with a light shutting out shadows of all sorts.

—

They're in a field—one of those long rows of cornfields outside of each interstate, waiting for people to go and get lost in them and never be found again. He's there with Ben and they stand there, guns in hands, small black guns all shiny and full of death. He knows why Ben brought him here, why Ben always brings him here.

"Come on, you ass, show me what you got. Point that gun at the fucker."

Guns raised up and for a moment Rob thinks of swinging it over at Ben and pop pop Ben's head bursts in red. But he doesn't because it's just a thought. Thoughts have no weight in reality, not in his reality. Here, all his thoughts float away and go up and up are eaten by that hungry greedy moon. No, he clears his head and points that gun at the scarecrow.

It's got a black bag over its head, and arms bound around its back. For a moment, just a single moment, Rob thinks it's moving. It's moving and someone is trapped in there. He knows it, he feels it in his gut, that this scarecrow is just a person, trapped. He thinks of people being stolen away with black bags over their heads and shoved into white vans. Part of him wants to scream and cry but instead he just fires the gun. It sounds like a canon and his arm jerks back and he realizes his eyes water up. Not tears, but something else, something like tears.

The scarecrow moves back with the blast of the bullet. Arms break free and straw scatters around them. For a moment Rob lets out his breath. Not a person. Not a person at all.

"Nice shot, cowboy, nice shot. Don't think it's good enough though. Don't ever think it's good enough."

Rob laughs, wipes his eyes with his sleeve.

"Yeah right, never good enough. Come on, you go. Let's see how good you are."

Ben smirks with moustache smirking and laughs. "Oh boy, come on now. You know what I got. You know it."

He pulls his hand up and doesn't even aim, doesn't move doesn't twitch. Rob watches him and thinks this is like painting. Like Ben painting the air with smoke and fire and bullets and death. He holds his breath as Ben pulls the trigger so fast, so many shots, and doesn't even blink or twitch or anything.

He holds the smoking gun up to his lips then and blows on it. "Bad ass. That's what I am, bad ass. Come on, junior, let's keep going. We need to get you good. Come on now."

"Don't call me junior."

Laughs, pats him in the back.

"I'll stop it when you grow the fuck up. Now come on, show me some more, lay it down. Give that scarecrow another whallop."

For a moment, Rob pulls the gun up, right up to his mouth, his hands folded around it like he's praying, like he's asking for some saint some angel some god of some sort to come down and take the gun from his hands. Or to just have the gun go off in his face and stop it all for once, just stop it all.

"This is stupid."

"No it's not, come on now. You know what we're doing. You know it's right."

"No, this is stupid. I'm not getting anywhere at all. Come on, let's go, let's get out of here already."

Ben isn't cross. Rob was worried that Ben would punch him and then one of them would fire the guns and it would be over. For a moment he felt death and wanted it. "You just need confidence, okay? That's it. You need to trust it, to stop being afraid of yourself."

"Okay."

"Okay?"

"Okay, already, okay."

—

Later that night they stop by the 7-11 and get some orange juice. They stand outside, smoking, drinking the juice, pretending that they're not doing anything but bullshitting. But in reality they were looking across the street. Looking at the large towering building, filled with computers and software disks on large floppies.

"You sure this is right?"

"How could it not be right, Robert?"

"Don't call me that."

"Oh shut up. I'll call you anything I want whenever I want."

"Whatever."

"You know it's right."

They stop for a moment and a breeze picks up, and Rob thinks of the scarecrow again. Baghead scarecrow shot up and twitching. And he thinks back to the news, about seeing people being taken from their homes in white vans, taken away to who knows where.

The gun feels so cold in his pocket.

"I just don't see the need for this, you know? I just don't see how it's necessary."

"Well, how is anything necessary, huh? How is any of this necessary? What's the point in anything? I say, we make our own points, we do what we want and we make the universe take care of us, take care of us according to our own rules."

"Man, you're not making any sense."

Ben stops and stands still and he breathes in the air and Rob wishes he was somewhere else, somewhen else, something else, anything else. He just didn't want to be him anymore, he didn't want to exist anymore. He just wanted to become the void, to become nothing and be nothing and all things at once. Maybe in death his life would have meaning? Or maybe in life death has meaning, or maybe there is always meaning and non meaning, a fluctuation between void and matter, always dipping and dancing.

Ben closes his eyes. Does Ben want the void as well?

"I'll just pretend you didn't say that."

Then the breathing slows and they finish their smokes and orange juice and walk back to the car. As they drive away Rob looks up and sees the moon caught in the telephone wires and part of him wants to reach out and untangle it. And maybe the moon will fly up then, like a balloon moon, fly up and flitter among the stars.

—

A week later and he's drunk in an arcade. He's got the gun in his back pocket and a bottle of Jack propped up on the cabinet. He screams, yells, puts in more quarters. His hair is greasy and in his eyes and he feels like the world spins and then stops and spins again. Puts in another quarter, drinks some more. With each second his pixel avatar on the screen dies, and with each quarter he is brought back to life. Life and death and void and time. Quarters gain more, get more, extra lives, extra seconds, pushing back the inevitable.

He drinks some more and feels the gun in his pocket. It's cold and heavy and weighs on him like everything else. Like the cycle of the universe, weighing on him, so heavy with each repetition. A crushing weight, an elephant on his chest. His character dies again and he's out of change. By time he goes to the change machine and gets some quarters for this dollar he'll be dead and dead and he'll have to start over again. The game again, from the beginning again, and he will have to perform the same actions again and again.

Futile, futile, he is about ready to pull out his gun, to end this game forever, when he feels a warm hand on his shoulder. He turns around and sees Jen there with a quarter in her hand. He takes it, quickly, muttering a thanks, plopping it in, playing again and again and again.

—

It's pitch dark. You smell something in the air, like exhaust, and hear the sounds of cars driving by and two people talking in the front seat. Man and woman talking, that you can tell. You realize you have a black bag over your head, and that someone had shoved the bag over your head while you were walking down the street. And then you felt something hard and sharp and next thing you know you were out like a light. Now you're awake. You hear the car radio playing Patti Smith's "Summer Cannibals."

What do you do?
>Try to take the bag off.
I don't understand that command.
>Call for help
I don't understand that command.
>Try to remove my bonds.
I don't understand that command.
>Scream and howl and scream and howl

—

Rob's at Jen's apartment, they're on the couch, laughing and watching television. They've talked and talked, and now he realizes it's been so long since he's felt this. Since he's felt light enough to float away and he wonders how his life got so dark lately.

"Okay, now it's your turn. What did you want to be when you grew up?"

"A cowboy."

"Really? A cowboy."

"Yeah, really, no shitting. My dad was a huge John Wayne fan and loved reading those old paperback westerns. He used to read the shit out of them to me when I was a kid, and so that was it. I wanted to be a cowboy."

"What kind of hat would you wear?"

"What's that supposed to mean?"

"You know, white hat, black hat?"

He thinks about the gun he left in her car when she wasn't looking. He thinks about shooting that scarecrow, about wanting to shoot that game, about wanting to shoot Ben. He feels a pain welling up inside of him, knowing exactly which hat he was going to wear.

Instead, the subject changes quickly, quickly. On the television flashes an image of a man being shoved into a white van, a black bag over his head. The picture is grainy and from a distance, and you could tell the camera caught this whole thing on accident.

"Earlier today a film crew spotted another kidnapping while shooting a movie. This is the latest in a large wave of kidnappings that some people are calling the work of a local Satanic cult."

Images on the screen of a pentagram spraypainted over a bridge. Cut to the cover of a heavy metal album being tossed into the flames at a church rally. Cut to the picture of a priest over a possessed little girl, who claimed to be an ex-member of the cult. Cut to pictures of corpses, of little boys and girls, of tall women, of short men, all dead, all dead, with bites taken out of them, with symbols carved into their bodies.

Jen shuts off the TV and holds herself. She is shivering and Rob feels like he should do something, put an arm around her or something to help her out. He never knows how to react to other people's emotions.

"Are you okay?"

"Yeah . . . no . . . I don't know. Why did you quit working with us? Was it me? Did you not like working with me?"

He looks out the window.

"I don't know, I just . . . I don't know."

"Ben's not a good person. You know that, right?"

"Yeah. I do."

She nods and he feels like he should go, he should leave. He gets up and she looks at him with pleading eyes, eyes asking him not to go, not to leave her here. He stops, thinks he should stay, just a little longer. She needs him to stay.

But his hat is black and he goes out the door.

—

The sky is summer-blue even in the thick of autumn and they're sitting in a parking lot two blocks away. Their car is far away from the scene of the crime, making it harder to trace them and get caught. This was Ben's idea, this was all Ben's idea. Rob admits that. Rob knows it's not too late to turn around, never too late to go back and do something else.

His breath is thick and heavy in his lungs.

"You ready, cowboy?"

He mumbles yeah yeah.

"Louder, cowboy, come on. You ready?"

"Yeah."

"Good. Let's go and do this then."

They pull out masks and slide them over their faces. Rob feels confined, trapped under the mask, like the mask is an elephant sitting on his skull, crushing the bones and brain. His breath slows and quickens and slows again. He feels the void everywhere, sees the void everywhere. The void is in the gun he pulls out, the void is the bullets and the barrel and the gun. Ben pulls out his gun too and now they're walking. The pace is slow, as if they could just take their time, walking down the street with hidden faces and pistols in hand.

Nobody seems to notice them as they walk by. The crowd parts and nobody even looks at them. Each person a world in itself, floating by other worlds, never seeing outside of their own atmosphere, not even once. The guns don't even register. No threat, no reality. Only voids and more voids walking. Voids not caring. No one caring.

Rob wants the void to stop. He wonders if Jen could somehow help him get this void to stop, to get everything to stop. He stands still. He is a stone now, a stone in a river of people. Ben turns and looks at him. They stare, face to face, eye to eye, guns poised.

"You sure?"

Rob nods.

"Okay, maybe you're right. Maybe this isn't the way. Let's not do this after all."

They say nothing. They say not a word as a white van speeds past them, off and away. Cop sirens blaring as they take their masks off, put their guns back in their pockets. For a moment Rob thinks of running after them, maybe putting his white hat on, saving some person trapped in the backseat, setting them free from whatever fate awaited them.

But then he realizes his feet aren't that fast, they will never be that fast.

—

Later that night he ends up at Jen's apartment. He has no gun and no mask, he's just shaking as he knocks. He waits for a response, knocks again, hears nothing. He listens closely to the door, listening for sounds of life. Her car was in the parking lot. Why wasn't she there? Was she pretending to be gone? Was she pretending to be missing? He knocks again and again and again and now he's pounding on the door and he screams and howls and then scrapes his hands and kicking and yelling some more and he wishes for his gun, he would just blow the lock off, just like they do on television, he would just pull it out and pretend the lock was a scarecrow in a field and blam blam blam the lock would fall off . . .

But his gun is gone at home and he's got nothing here anymore. *Jen,* he whispers into the door, *come on and open up, come on and let me in, come on I need to talk, come on Jen please I need to talk just open the door.* Nothing, nothing, a void of sounds. He walks outside, down the street, looks at her car. He tries to find signs of life, like she's hiding in the car, like she's laying there waiting for him. All he sees are dirty wrappers from discarded fast food dinners. Nothing else.

He walks away and thinks about white vans and black hoods and now he's running, running down the street. He can't stop running, not with the sun in the sky, not with the cold wind biting his face and skin. He runs and runs and he wants to run away from everything. He pushes people aside, shoves them down as he runs, knocking them out of their voids, making them exist and be real just for once. He runs on and keeps running. He doesn't want to think, he doesn't want to know anything anymore. He just wants to stop, to stop existing all together.

—

You're visiting a grave of an old friend. All the flowers are dead, and the granite is rain-worn and crying out for upkeep. You want to clean the whole area, to make it so nice and clean for her. Like her whole life was defined by this grave, and if her life were to mean anything she should have a clean place to show the world who she was.

What do you do?
>Nothing.
I don't understand that command.
>Nothing
I don't understand that command.
>Nothing
I don't understand that command.
>Nothing

It Tasted Like the Sea

Cathy inspected the faces hung on the wall. Slack, emotionless bags of skin stretched onto brass hooks. Eyeholes, mouthholes, each wanting to be filled with shiny white rows of teeth and slick marble globes of sight. She wondered briefly if she should try one on and decided against it. Josh would not like that. He was very particular about his art.

His apartment door opened at the end of the hallway, sending a shaft of light across the shadows, illuminating his skull with a thick radiance. Josh stood with the light outlining his drunken body, his face half-shaven and a mostly empty bottle of rum in his hand.

His shirt was stained, his hair pulled up into piles of black nests on his head. He stared at her down the hall, his eyes searching for some semblance of reality to transform the world of shadows into a concrete form. "What's up? You okay?"

Cathy sighed and walked through the hall. Briefly, the tips of her fingers brushed the slack skin. She shivered—the skin felt real. Leathery.

"Yeah. I guess. You don't look so good."

He coughed and hung his head. Light like wings danced over his shoulders. Cathy saw the apartment from behind and felt a dread. There were naked female bodies hung and slung over every corner of the room. Their faces missing. Just dolls, she thought. It's his thing. His art.

Just dolls.

"Fuck. Nothing is good. Did you see that review? That fucking review of my latest show? That bitch. That cunt."

Cathy had. That was why she had stopped by—she knew that he would be like this. He was always like this when someone reviewed his work negatively. She also knew that playing stupid was a good tactic right now. "No, I hadn't. It can't be that bad, Josh. Come on. Let's go out."

Josh threw the bottle on the ground. It clinked and rolled against the floor. "Yeah," he said shutting the door behind him and cutting off all light from the hallway, "Yeah. Let's get the fuck out of here. Let's go where they love me, where they appreciate my genius."

Cathy sighed. "Sure thing," she said.

—

They went to his showing. This was the fourth time she'd gone to this show today and she felt the same way each time—disturbed. Broken. Abused. She understood why the reviewer had been so negative—the show was all female body parts. Faces as masks, limbs displayed in dumpsters—the female body destroyed, abused, broken, and mangled.

Then displayed as art.

Cathy hated it. It made her feel awful, horrible and dirty. It made her ashamed to be a woman. And she hated Josh for it.

If he hadn't been there for her when MATT abused her and left her for dead—if he hadn't called the ambulance and stayed with her for that month in the hospital—if it hadn't been for all that she would stop being friends with him. She would have left him and his broken art and gone onto something else.

Yet, he had been there for her. So now she had to be there for him. She walked with him past the mutilated bodies in realistic skin and textured organs. Just art, she kept telling herself. It is just art. She walked with him through the worst parts of the exhibits—the dissected bodies displayed in thin slivers of glass.

And she heard the praise from the art collectors. Those fat and sweaty old men who put fists of dollars against Josh, teasing him like a stripper with a tip. They complimented and condoned this disgusting attack on the female form.

And Cathy listened. Unable to shake the feeling of nausea that rolled around in her stomach like some drowning animal.

—

Later that night she took him back to his room. Josh was barely human, too drunk to stand. He kept proposing to her and she kept turning him down. She had this fear in her gut—a fear that he would be like Matt in the end. That those figures weren't just art—they were corpses. They were others like her who had fallen for him before he showed them what he was truly capable of.

She stretched him out on a couch of female limbs. Severed legs and arms. And then she went into the bathroom and showered, and then fell asleep in the bathtub. It was the only room in the house not filled with limbs and eyes and faces of blank staring female objects.

—

Cathy's eyelids slowly peeled back. Crescents of darkness becoming whole moons of sight. And saw Josh naked on the toilet. His face staring at the floor tiles. His body covered in circular scars. He looked over and saw her.

His eyes like diamonds, full of ageless will and wonder. She coughed and sat up, feeling strangely naked underneath all of her clothing.

"Sorry about last night," he said and stood, his penis flaccid and flapping against his leg, "I was possessed, you know? By regret. By so many things. This art show is perhaps the most personal of all my shows. Even more personal than that bit I did on Sweeny Todd—you know the one. The fat ladies and razor show. With the cave and the bed made of human hair. This one is even more important than that, even more personal. It is why I kept all of the failures here—all the broken and unmade pieces. This show is about me. About the memories of my childhood."

Cathy nodded. She pulled her knees up to her chest, making sure her skirt covered every inch of bare skin. "No problem," she said, "I understand. Critics—they tear us all apart."

He laughed and walked out into the hallway. "I can make you something to eat if you would like. Eggs sound good?"

"Yeah," she said, "Eggs."

She stood up. Her legs shook, like two beams of a house trembling in an earthquake. She wasn't sure why she felt so off, so horrified. Josh had never done her any harm. Never. Yet seeing all those body parts again—all of those scattered limbs—they brought back memories. Memories of a table leg crushing her face. Memories of broken ribs and her eye being jabbed at with a spoon as her ex-husband tried to carve out her sockets like a jack o' lantern.

This show is personal for me too, she thought.

Way too personal.

—

The egg was round, white. A perfect circle, an eclipse. It was held in place on a small ceramic plate. She tapped it with her spoon, cracked it and peeled back the layer of shell like skin from meat. Beneath it she saw the bones of a baby chic suspended in an amber liquid. Staring at her.

She looked up at Josh. He stared at her, as if expecting a response.

"I can't eat this," she said, dropping the spoon on the table.

"I'm sorry," he said tearfully, "I thought that egg was empty."

She nodded, not believing him. "Well," she said, "I should go back home and get ready for work."

Josh ran over to her side. He was still naked, his skin coated with a thin layer of gray ash. His eyes were intense lanterns. He grabbed her hands with his. "Stay. For a little bit longer. You don't have to go to work, right? Just stay with me. I can't be alone. Not today. Things have been going so badly. It's—it's my art. You know? I think I have it right. I have her perfect, the bride and all that. But it ends up wrong, each time. And I need to start over again. I can't be alone."

She got up and moved toward the hallway. She did not want to walk past those masks again, but preferred it to staying here. Staying in his living room, with the cracked and half-collapsed ceiling and the wall-to-wall limbs and grotesqueries.

"I have to go," she said. And almost added, "before I go insane from your art," but decided against it.

He got on his knees, his head rubbing against her leg, his hands grasping hard onto her calves. Out of the corner of her eye she saw knives lined up against the north wall, stained with splashes of brown liquid.

"Please," he begged, "Please."

She kicked him away. Almost stepped on his face with the heel of her foot and then remembered how he had helped her. How he had set her free.

"If you go," he said, "I can't promise I will be safe. I've been seeing things. I saw a naked man with the face of a dog, wandering around my apartment. He had a saw in his hands. It frightened me. You can't leave me for the dog creature—you can't. Remember how I helped you? Remember?"

She sighed. This was a first for Josh—bringing up the past like that. He was the kind that lived in the now, in the today. He must really be messed up.

She looked down at him. "Fuck," she said, "All right. Just stop looking up my skirt. I'll stay. And—and we have to get out of here. I need to breathe. You know?"

Josh made a sound like a panting dog, and then stood quickly and did a little jig. Cathy knew she was going to regret this. She just didn't quite understand how much.

—

To her chagrin they spent the rest of the day indoors, listening to Josh talk about his latest show and reading the latest reviews out loud. Every time she mentioned leaving, going outside, going to a restaurant—he quickly changed the subject.

Later in the day she went to the bathroom. After sitting on the cold toilet for a few moments she heard strange shuffling noises and a dog growling. And then the sound of meat tearing and a woman moaning as if in orgasm. Unable to urinate, she leapt up off the toilet.

She opened the bathroom door to an empty apartment. All of the lights were off. The egg was still on the table, and next to it was a key and a note.

The note told her she was locked inside. That the key was a key that could open any door except for the front door. And that she was free to roam his apartment and do whatever she wanted to until he got back.

What was even stranger than this was that he had signed the note, "your loving husband, lord of these fine estates."

Cathy felt her stomach lurch. She felt her mind darken into stars and her bones quiver under her skin in a messy architecture of unease.

What was going on?

What had happened to Josh?

What had happened to her?

—

The apartment grew four times its size. The rooms became mazes, the body parts scattered everywhere. She carried the egg with her. It glowed in her hands like a tiny amber torch. She found her clothes and hair transforming with each movement—a long white gown with long flowing black hair.

She saw the walls change, distort, transfigure.

With each door she opened she found another horror behind it. A man with mice in his skull. A lady being drowned by monks. A demonic figure who was eating snakes and urinating on a half-nude nun.

Each room more strange then the last. In the final room she saw bodies of men and women skinned alive, flailing and howling on the floor. In the center of the room was a long dinner table. On it were many plates and forks and knives.

In the center of the table was the corpse of a mermaid. The scales glistened in her eggling light, blue and green and gold. The hair was orange and stained with blood, her face half smashed in. The other half of the face seemed so familiar. Cathy could not place it. Where had she seen such a face before?

She walked up to the dead thing, touched the skin. It was cold and stiff. The shoulder and breasts were bare, showing off a half-finished sexuality. An object of male desire with no actual procreation possible.

She sat down. The world spun.

She was still Cathy. She had to hold onto that.

—

She sat in a gilded chair, the mermaid eyes staring at her from the table as she waited for Josh to return. As the hours danced by she saw ghostly figures walk past her. All female, all missing limbs and faces. As if they were the spirits of his art, searching for their missing body parts.

Eventually Josh walked into the room. He wore a black coat with frilly lace choking up his chest and draping out of his cuffs. He smoked a long stem pipe that filled the air with an overwhelming velveteen scent.

"I've been waiting for you," he said woodenly.

She nodded, not knowing what else to do.

"I've had the cook prepare us this little aphrodisiac. It is said to prolong one's life forever. How quaint, don't you think, my dear Valerie?"

She nodded again.

His eyes were still bright, still Josh. Yet—was he still Josh? Was she still Valerie? Or were they being ridden by some obscure half-hidden thing, dreamed into being by a flittering shadow of a spirit?

"Of course. We all know that mortality is a fool's errand. How was your lordship's evening?"

He pulled out a chair and sat down. He clapped. Celestial spirits slid into the room with missing limbs, their ghastly appearance like sheets draped into a breeze. They set bone-filled eggs into lamp posts, lighting the room in a stomach-churning green and golden hue.

"Splendid. I take it, my princess, that you did not overwork yourself? Or were not too bored on these premises?"

She coughed.

"No," she said.

He smiled. He pulled out a bronze knife and began to cut into the mermaid's back, peeling off a thin slice of muscle and then laying it on a plate. "Good."

"Although," she said, "I noticed that my key does not open every room in the house. There is one room it cannot open."

He pointed the knife at her. "And you shall not go in there. Do you understand? That room is off limits."

She smiled.

Of course, she thought. *That room is my escape from this madness.*

—

It amazed Cathy how quickly she forgot her own life and became absorbed in Valerie. She slid away from who she was, her old sense of self slowly falling into a distant abyss. She had memories, somewhere—of Josh being an artist. Of her attending an art show. But they became muddled with this life, this history, this crumbling mansion in which she now found herself trapped.

One without any windows to see the world outside.

She had some other memories—but they had merged and changed. Josh was her uncle, lord of this estate and her husband. She was a princess from afar. He abused her and beat her with a table leg, he tried to scoop out her eye sockets with a spoon. In her mind Josh and the lord and her ex-husband all became merged into a single individual.

And even though her normal life had fallen into an abyss of her memories she felt a pull and a tug toward what was there before. Like she was haunted by something she knew. Something about a room full of body parts. Something about her old life, a life different than this one.

She had dreams about that old life. About going to a job every day. About seeing her friends, and going bar hopping in the evening. About paying bills and scraping by and wondering if she would have enough money to eat next month or not.

She always awoke with a feeling of ghosts running over her skin and the mad nightmare of limbs and torsos and disfigured female forms, and this feeling like she was escaping here. That she had fled here from her own rational existence into one of phantasmagoria.

—

The passages were filled with moving things. Light, shadow, tiny creatures made of clockwork. She saw grubs crawling along the floor, searching for corpses to eat. And she followed them. Followed everything.

She knew that she was a mist here. A princess trapped here. She had not eaten of the mermaid for this very reason—knowing the story of a daughter kidnapped and taken to faerie and trapped after eating the food.

She came to the door—she recognized it. It was the door this key could not open. She tried again to no avail. Tried a third and fourth time. And then she took her own ring finger and stuck it into the lock. Her wedding ring locked against it. Click, click, click.

The door swung open.

She saw the living room of the apartment.

She saw the body parts lining floor and wall.

And she saw herself. Laying on the floor, crawling. Trying to get away. And above her stood Josh. But not Josh. He was dog-faced and had a saw in one hand and a table leg in the other. He was naked. He had her ex husband's back and the lord's penis. And she saw herself on the floor, stoney-eyed and crawling.

Her skirt was hiked up and covered in blood. Her face was distorted, broken, smashed in. She mewled like a kitten as she crawled, a sickening sound that made every bone in Valerie's body melt.

And she saw that she had half a leg missing.

Half an arm missing.

Half her face.

Valerie saw herself on the floor and the creature above her, torturing her, tearing her limb from limb. Howling about his art, screaming about his art. About the ethics of death, about the beauty of the morbid that would transfix the world. About violence as a statement of ethical boundaries.

Her double looked up at her. Mewling. Her whole form like a smashed doll. A broken toy smacked around and tossed out and waiting for the rain and the sun to come and bleach it and destroy it.

She saw herself.

Felt herself splinter, smash, broken mirror.

And.

And she turned.

And she closed the door.

And she walked into the corridors.

And she found the mermaid corpse.

And she sat down.

And started to eat.

It tasted like the sea. It tasted like warm sausages. It tasted like old wine poured over broken glass. It tasted like the sun going down her stomach, exploding inside of her and lighting up her heart and her veins from the inside out.

WINTERLIGHT

Alice, listen:

I know it's been a long time since we put you in the ground, but shit's gone sideways here and I really miss our little talks, you know? So maybe even though you're not really here anymore, maybe I can, maybe I can just talk and you could listen. Just for a little while, you read me? Just so I can go through everything and get it all clean and squared up on my insides.

And oh boy, my insides are all wrong, let me tell you. I need a bit of honey, I need some of that sugar in my skull.

Fuckit. I dreamt about my death again last night.

Tossed and turned and it was such an awful thing, right? Death all around me as I wandered through a damp forest at night. Bodies hung from the trees by their arms, with their heads on fire like some weird lamp lighting my path. A rich smell of sap and gasoline and I knew what waited for me behind the pines. A leviathan of flame. Smoke rising in the air, and then . . .

Shaking awake and I bounced up and Jenny had this horrible look on her face. You remember Jenny, Alice? She was with us when we shot up in the caves and danced until we puked and pretended we were shamans. And she was here now, with me. In the Hollow House, those ruins high up in the mountains. What a messed-up world.

The air smelled of rotting fruit and she kept shaking me, even though I was all awake, and my head was starting to hurt. My temples throbbed, and you know what that's like. Our family migraines, am I right?

"You had that dream again, didn't you? You had that dream again! Tell me, you have to tell me..."

And I nodded and I knew what she meant and why she was terrified. It would all happen again, just like the last four times I had that same dream.

Air raid sirens blasting through the Hollow House and people shouting and screaming. The whole world closed in on me. I knew exactly what they would find, sis. Another dead body all burned up to a crisp. Every time I dreamt of my death they found another corpse, another one of our circle murdered. Burned alive and left to be found by our night watch.

—

See, the last time all that was left was a pile of ashes and some teeth. One time it was a scorch mark and an eyeball and some hair. The first time? Most of the body was still intact, just charred to a crisp and standing upright. A stray breeze and the whole thing turned to ashes and blew away, leaving a sharp red skeleton behind. A skeleton that was precisely posed, hands pointing toward something unseen on the horizon.

My dreams brought death by fire. I didn't even want to consider what that meant.

—

And I need you, sis, oh, dear sweet sister Alice! I need you right here and now. If I believed in such things as *ghosts* I guess you could haunt my ass and I would be okay and all would be right. But I know better, you know? I know that without my kicks the world is a silent place and a lonely place.

But when I, oh. When I. *Oh.* When I had that silk flowing through my veins and my heart full of honey and sugar all kicked into my skull and I'm digging down under a good rush everything comes alive and I could see it, yeah, the air breathing and the world seething and there were ghosts in everything!

Yes, yes, yes, yes!

But alas! Now I'm dry and stuck and the world was silent and I missed the fuck out of you and I wished we hadn't done it at all that one last time, that shit was unclean, you know? Of course you knew, you're dead now because of that shit. You died before I even got a taste of it! I tried, oh god, I tried and I hated myself for trying. Reaching over to touch your numb dead arm and grasping around for a pulse. And oh, seeing it all gone and empty and your mouth so slack and eyes white and rolled back looking for a hole in your skull.

And, and, and, that needle there, lick my lips, just about a few drops left, taste it on my tongue, just enough, I shouldn't, I mean, I didn't want to, but, but, but . . .

Out of body experience: *my hand reached over, just to snag it out and stick that golden liquid right inside my arm.* With the sirens howling and I'm in tears because no, there's not enough. Not even enough for a taste of your death and I wanted to die. I needed to ride that wave right on into death and meet you on the other side.

Lower than low. My absolute rock bottom of my life. The judge gave me a choice—the Hollow Place or prison. Some days I wonder if I made the right choice.

—

Hey Alice, you ever see yourself walking around, just out of the corner of your eye or around the bend like some blurry ghost? I'm not talking about like in a mirror, or like in a dream, or mistaking someone else or anything like that. I'm talking about doubles. I'm talking about seeing myself and that feeling like ice in your spine when you see your own doppelganger and you know, you just know. That. That something isn't right? The way their bones looked under their skin, the way their eyes glazed up and never focused on anything. The double was a broken double, yes.

You ever have that sis? For awhile it happened in dreams when we were younger, though I never told you about that. And then, when we started dipping into honey I would see it like every other time we shot up. At first I thought *oh yeah, hallucinations.*

But then we came here and I got clean and this place was so different. Every day I felt worse than the day before, and in the halls I *saw him.* I did, I *saw me* and there's no missing it or getting it wrong. That's me. My double. My doppelganger.

I told myself the next time I would chase him, but I never did. I just couldn't bring myself to do it. What would you do, sis? Would you do it? Even if he smelled like charred skin and burnt ozone?

—

Today was one of those days where I just wanted the world to end. I told Jenny that and she started picking at my arm hairs, and yeah, she does that sometimes. A kind of nervous thing we all get into after awhile. The little prickles of pain makes you think of that needle sliding in, snip. Splash. Sugar in your skull and the world's alight again. Do you miss it, now that your dead? Do you have any peace from that double glow honey light?

Or does it follow you into the ghostworlds? Follow you and never let go.

"You know what I think? I think it's not a serial killer at all," and Jenny said all this in a dull monotone, like speaking from a dream, as she plucked a bit more at my arm hairs, "I think it's like mass hysteria, you know? Mass hysteria causing spontaneous combustion, it's happened before in the past. I know it sounds crazy, but when you think about it, it's not such a crazy idea after all."

—

"Another dead body, boy! Another crispy corpse! Time to toss him in the pit out in the snow, you hear me? Come on, come on. The charred remains won't move itself, *son*! Come on! Come on!"

It's all up to us out here. Long way, far away from that civilized world. Only a tunnel carved through the mountain that gets us to and through to the world outside, a six mile long thing that's just big enough for one car. And past that? Treacherous snow laced peaks.

This whole place used to be a ski resort, and now it's a safe place to go and get clean. That's right, our addictions brought us here, to this ruin of a place. Yet, still. What're you going to do? You have to isolate the addict from his addiction, after all. And this did the trick something fierce. No one else comes in, no one else goes out. No honey no tricks no sugar in the skull.

So the guy yelling at me right there? The old grizzled vet with trackmarks around his eyes when he ran out of veins in his arm? Yeah, Alice. That's Len, and he's a dick, but he's right. We needed to clean up after the body and get on with it.

"Aren't the cops coming up? You know, to investigate or whatever? They came up last time, and they'll probably want to see the crime scene or something. Should we wait?"

And Len scratched his fuzzy shit of a beard and laughed at me. He kicked that red carpet and pointed at the two-way radio perched over by the windows. "Shit, boy. I called them and everything and they told me to get lost. Just another suicide is the way they put it! Just another suicide. They don't care if we all die up here, we're scum to them. Honey junk scum. Eyes full of pain and nothing else, and of course we burn ourselves up! Of course. They don't give a shit about us, so come on. We need to go to the east end and take care of what's left of that burned-up body."

It was Simon who died this time and I felt like he didn't deserve this shit. Of course, none of them did? But Simon really hurt my heart. Alice, you never met Simon and boy it's a shame you didn't. We were close, he and I, yeah. We were crazy close, and I know you would've just loved him. He spoke in poetry and mystic visions! He's your kinda guy.

Everybody loved Simon, everybody.

"We know better," Len said and laughed again, "Oh, we all know better don't we? It's a damned serial killer, out in the halls hunting us down and burning us up. Nasty business, yeah. Nasty."

I won't lie to you, sis. I felt nervous. Frustrated. I knew what he meant. "The Fireman," I said, my voice all meek and mousy.

"Yeah, that's what they call him. The Fireman."

Because of the way he burns his victims. The Fireman.

—

Once a month we shaved our heads with straight razors and it gave the whole place this eerie feeling. All those bald bodies moving about with tiny nicks and razor burn and blood-stained necks.

This last time Jenny and me traded the razor back and forth (*shiny, shiny glinting in the winterlight*) with what little hair we had scattered across the floor like whispers. I remember how strange she looked bald, like a ghost. Her skin translucent and her lips cinder black and her bones like piles of twigs under a blanket.

After we were done and all cleaned up she did what she always did. She had me kneel in front of her, and spooned my freshly shorn head in her hands. And she kissed my skull with tiny bird pecks and whispered: *I anoint you I anoint you I anoint you.*

This time, her breath smelled like gasoline and gunpowder. And this time, I noticed a few fingers missing from her left hand. They looked cauterized, and I wondered when did she do that? We had no privacy here at the Hollow House at the end of the world. Yet I didn't comment on it. Wasn't even sure it was my place to do so.

—

Yeah, sis, Simon's body was the worst of them all up until this point. We had to scrape what was left of him off the floor and I had to pretend it wasn't him, it couldn't be him. But unlike the others, his face was still intact. Looking like an awful mask, glued onto his red bones. The rest of him was just a mess of charred flesh still smoldering, caked on the alabaster tiles. A few of his fingerbones missing on his left hand. Had they broken off? Where were they?

—

Jenny and me were at the top of our hotel, the ceilings in ruin and looking like a honeycomb. Everything cold and bones all wrong once again. She shivered and we held each other for a moment and teeth chattered in the frost. Yesterday we compared scars, tracklines, all those marks the needles left. She had different scars, yeah. Big one across her stomach where her dad tried to gut her and leave her for dead.

"You ever see your insides outside of your body before? It's so cold and everything feels wrong and aching. But then you're beyond pain, you know? You're somewhere else. And for a moment, you think, how beautiful. There, in the flash bang light of the gunpowder going off and the dead body hitting the ground, how beautiful."

And we're silent then for a moment more. I didn't know what to say, so I didn't say anything.

—

Dreams again, back in those woods again, yeah, following that path toward my death once more. The air rotten and electric and the bodies hung above me, heads like lanterns lighting me away into the deep dark shadow heart. Pines so strong, arms and legs coated in sap and tiny green needles. I sensed it now. I sensed it coming closer, closer.

My death wore a skull mask. Leviathan of a thing. Smoldering ruins of a body. Taller than trees, taller than everything else. It moved slow and laboriously. I saw it there, crush down the trees, burn down the world. It seemed like fire and smoke and I choked on it all. *Wake up wake up wake up.*

When I came to, my bed was all sopped with sweat and I rolled over, and Jenny was gone. And in my peripheral vision I saw *him* in the corners, *him* in the shadows. My double, my mimic, my doppel-ganger. He moved in quick jerky motions and death hung still and naked in the air.

My double darted out the door and the air raid sirens went off yet again. They found another body, and this one was Jenny's.

—

I remembered this one time, a little after we got here and I was still broken down and in the dark deep sad place. Withdrawals coming on fierce and your death still clung to every bit of me, refusing to let go. And we started hanging around each other, me and Jenny, and yeah she recognized me from our shaman days. She tried to help me, tried to keep me sane while my insides screamed out for release.

And then on like the fifth week I was here she started to break down herself. And I was there for her, as she rubbed her mouth with the palm of her hand. Eyes slammed shut, her cheek trembling with ache. "My teeth, my damned teeth they just hurt so much and I don't know what to do, there's no dentist up here and they won't let me go and I have no relief, no relief at all."

And I laughed and told her about what I used to do outside in the world when we were all hard up for cash. "I used to be a street den-tist, not legal you know, but I would help pull teeth that needed to be pulled, by people without insurance. It's not pretty, but trust me the pain of having it pulled out is way less than the pain you're feeling now. And once it's out? Pop! Pain gone."

And she laid against my chest, digging her head into my body, just like she wanted to climb up inside of me. Her words muffled now.

"No, that's okay, not yet, yeah? Not too bad, I don't think," and I felt her wince against me, "It's just my smile, you know? My smile. It's all I've got anymore, my smile. You take my tooth and that's it, you've broken my smile."

And I understood. I won't lie, Alice. Thinking about this now, remembering this now? It brought on a whole lot of hurt. They didn't make me come down and help clean her up. It would be a cruelty too many.

—

Days went by, weeks went by, every day the same day over and over and over again. Numb and in bed unless they made me get out, get up, and do some work. My mind reeled from the way our bed still smelled like her. Dead leaves and raw earth, that soil kind of smell that autumn gets when the world is coated in fog. My head against her pillow, sucking the scent inside my lungs.

I know, Alice. I know. I was pitiful and miserable and I hadn't been this bad since you died and I don't think I could take any more deaths, you know? I just. I just don't think I could take it anymore. And I hadn't had that dream in awhile, and maybe that's okay. Though I didn't want to dwell on it too much, you know? What could it mean, when the dreams of dying stopped. What could it mean.

—

They forced food into me, or I wouldn't eat. They forced me to get up and shower or I wouldn't shower. And I ranted and raved and threw shit against the wall and broke things and screamed. I plucked at my arm hairs and I needed to get fixed, to get a good dream on, to stab in that golden liquid and fill my veins full of honey, yes, honey light and lamp in my skull, sugar kicking around in my heart. I was going batshit angry boy and I kept yelling at Len, claiming he was holding out on me. *You holding out on me Len? Yeah? Give me some shit, I know you're hiding it here, I know it, Len! You can't hold out on me!*

I'm not too proud of this at all, Alice. Len eventually talked me down. He was a good friend, even though he was a dick. We all needed good friends like that every once in awhile. Friends who don't take your shit and smack you until you wake up.

And then. And then. And then.

I think you know what happened next, don't you Alice? You do. Don't you.

—

Hah. Hah-hah. Hah. Sis, sis, hey sis. Did you do this to me? Did you do this, sis? Did you do this to me?

Three fingers missing now on my left hand, look at that, just look at that. Not bloody or anything. They smelled like rosewater and lilacs and yeah. Didn't even feel it, didn't even feel pain at all. Just woke up one morning with my fingers missing and this whole elated feeling inside. Did they feel this way, too? The day before they died? Did they feel so elated and so alive? With that same honey dream of a feeling where it's all haunted by electrical life?

My teeth chattered and maybe it was going to be okay.

—

Surprise, surprise, I dreamt that dream of death again. This time it was a little, well, different. Not too different, mind you, but different enough. The pine trees were there, but the bodies were all gone, and the only light I have are the flickering glow of the fireflies. I follow them further and further and further, deeper into the forest. The ominous weight in the world is gone, just gone! No sense of something stalking behind the pines, searching for me. No.

Everything was silent in that dream, and everything felt dead and empty and hollowed out. As if the very spirit of the world had been sucked away and left this hollow shell of a reality behind. The dream, once kinetic, now volcanic gossamer. Eventually I found my way to the heart of it all. A cave in the side of a mountain, and on the ground were footsteps laced with fire. And nailed to a tree was Simon, Simon sweet dead Simon. His eyes bugged out when he saw me approach, and get this! Get this crazy dream thing.

He started screaming. He pointed right at me and just kept right on screaming, louder and louder and louder, until his screams sounded like an air raid siren howling and I felt something pulling me out like an umbilical noose, dragging me right on out and gasp, gurgle, like I choked on the air, like I drowned on oxygen, and then I was awake.

SUNSORROW

1

. . . and then Beyla sat down, under the lost arch and thought again of Carcosa, and the hidden secrets she'd searched for in its crowded temples and burning libraries. She picked up the rabbit head, deep in her own thoughts, staring into the dead eyes. Wanting to forget. Wanting to remember. Perverse, the way her mind worked. She rubbed the tips of the ears, pushing them back against the head. Slick, like hair. The oracle. She had found him. He was dead, but she had found him.

She ran her hands over the fur of the rabbit head and felt the cool glassy bone jutting out from where the neck used to be. She spun it in her hands, severed from the corpse that sat behind her, large head, rabbit head, head as big as human head. Teeth of human teeth placed in rabbit mouth, dead eyes staring at her. She was pressed between two alleys and under the stained glass arch, the red sun above like a staring eye, dead man eye looking right at her, staring right at her.

—Do you know who I am?

No response. She shook the head. Hoping to revive it. Hoping it would twitch its nose, move its whiskers. Nothing. Behind she heard the caws of the birds crying out and missed the red shores of Carcosa and wished she'd never left the cursed city and she thought again of the sleeping gods and the spiral towers and wanted to go back. But no, no, banished.

—Answer me. Tell me what you know. Do you know who I am, what I've done?

She lifted the skull right up to her lips. Eyes staring at eyes. It did not smell. She expected it to smell. She saw glowing maggots in the eyes, eating away at them, devouring them and laying eggs.

—Can you give me redemption? Can you save me, change me? I'm not my actions, am I? I'm something more than the things I've done, that has to be it. I'm not a bad person. I'm not a demon or a witcheater. I'm a good person, deep down inside. Can't you understand that? Can't you take this away, clean me from the inside out, wash these memories away?

The smile was crooked, human teeth too big for rabbit mouth. She saw a grin at the corners of the lips and wondered if it was laughing at her. She felt like screaming and crying and pounding her fists and she just didn't understand, couldn't understand at all. In life the Loryx would've been able to do these things, been able to see her for who she really was and wipe her mistakes away.

But the Loryx was dead. She let the skull drop to the ground. It rolled around, spinning with worm-eaten eyes glancing at her, weighing her with death. She turned, walked away, walked back into the city where the paper lanterns were just starting to glow and the red light of dusk was washing over the towers like a rag from a wound.

2

The city of a hundred fires, the city of the burning towers, the city of Xylos, the city of the dreaming dead. This was the city where others went to forget, to lose themselves amongst grand and simple pleasures, the city where the red flowers blossomed on the alleyway corpses and the air was filled with the light of glowing night worms. This was a city whose name was etched at the first hours when the sun broke and the world started spinning toward decay and death. It was the first city of the new world, the dying world. The first city born in the age of constant death.

They say that before the sun cracked the world was filled with life and everyone was expected to live forever. They say that before the sun cracked the world was a place of constant wonder, of amazing things that were never seen again. They say all sorts of things about the world before death, but many discount it as idle dreams and escapism. Stories told to pacify the weak of spirit.

3

Beyla ran her hands over the red clay walls as she walked, her head bent down and staring at the cobblestones beneath her feet. It was a pattern of red, white, red, black, red, grey. Maybe she should've kept the rabbit skull. Maybe it would've spoken to her, told her about her life, forgiven her for her mistakes. Maybe all it took was time for the oracle to shake off the cold hand of death and tell her what she desperately wanted to hear.

The clay walls felt like bones under her hand. The red sun was gone now, set beneath the swollen crust of the world. Cold settled under her skin and she kept herself from shivering by wrapping her arms around her shoulders and trying to keep warm. That was the curse of the broken sun: hot sweating daylight hours filled with moist fire and dark cold blue nights that froze and iced the skin. She had to find a place to sleep for the night, before the cold really came in and she was like the many homeless dead on the city streets.

4

Where did Mims want to meet? She couldn't remember. Some part of her didn't want to remember. Remembering would bring back all the life she'd lived until now and she didn't want to remember any of that. She fought against her nihilistic impulses and remembered briefly where she was supposed to meet him. The Shrinking Giant. A house. A grand old place near the edges of the city.

With that memory followed another memory tagging along behind it, grabbing onto it and riding it up into her thoughts. Climbing into her mind before she could forget it, make it go away or make it stop. Clear, clear, clear. Like a bell ringing in her mind. So clear.

5

She remembered:
Shoving little face under the water and it struggled and she held it down and it was flailing and she pushed harder. She couldn't look down. Couldn't look into the eyes. She wanted to stop existing, she wanted to stop being but she couldn't she had to keep on living so she pushed it down harder. Cramming the head against the rocks at the bottom of the lake.

She was crying. She remembered that. Remembered her cheeks wet with tears and she would lift the head up, thinking no, no, I'll let you live, I love you so much I'll let you live and then she would see the face wide eyes and screaming and terrified and she would shove it back down under the water again. And she was crying again. And the body was flailing again.

Why couldn't she forget these things? If only it had been just the once . . .

6

Mims: raven hair, piled up on head. Stick-thin body. Low-lidded, sleepy-eyed. Nose like bird beak, lips plump and crooked in a constant sarcastic grin. He rolled dice in his hands when he was nervous and cheated at cards whenever they stopped for a drink. He had nightmares of snakes devouring him, and had known Beyla since they were young, and lived up in the far north and dreamt of Carcosa together.

He knew of her memories and didn't care. He didn't believe in absolution, and didn't believe in the concept of the soul or a spirit. He believed in finite existences, human beings like fireflies, our lights going out all too fast. He knew she would probably kill the oracle, his cards told him as much earlier on in the day. The oracle was meant to die, and was waiting to die. Beyla just happened to be the one who killed him each time, each repetition of the action creating a greater weight around their necks.

Today his body felt so heavy. And he knew, he knew. It was all about to repeat again.

7

Beyla did not like this place. It had too many doors, too many windows, too many floors and too many eyes. It seemed empty but there was always someone somewhere walking and if you listened closely you heard the voices of people talking in next rooms over but there was never anyone there. It was a dream house, a house built on the ghosts of another time, built on the memories of a world before the cracked sun.

8

Mims was in the center of the room. Table. Cards on the table: face up. He had his head down and was not even remotely looking at the cards. Beyla knew these cards, and she knew that they were used to predict the future. One had a wolf swallowing the moon, and another had a nude woman riding a lion to war. The third and final card had a sword on fire on a field of stars. Beyla knew just looking at the way they were laid out on the table that Mims was trying to predict the future again.

He looked up at her as she walked in, his eyes not going up, not reaching her eyes, avoiding her stare, her guilty stare. As he watched he grinned his own grin and Beyla was reminded of the rabbit grin, the skull grin, the too big for mouth teeth grin.

—We need to go back, she said.

Mims picked up the cards, put them back in his pocket. The room was trashed. It looked like he'd destroyed it the night before, with chairs smashed on the floor, splinters rolling, bed chopped in half with his axe, broken wine bottle spinning, window smashed, stained glass on the ground pointing up like daggers. He rubbed his hands over his eyes. Looked at her.

—We can't go back, Beyla. You know this.

She calmed her nerves by running her fingers along the pommel of her sword: Sunsorrow. The ancient dreaming sword, stuck at the heart of the glass god sea. It was hot under her hands and she thought it was breathing and alive and it too missed Carcosa of all places. It, too, recognized it as the heart home and longed to go back.

—There has to be a way. They can't keep us out, they don't have the right.

He tilted back on the last chair in the room and stared at the ceiling, his eyes closed and his mind deep in thought. He drummed his hands on the table, humming to himself. Beyla watched all this with a calm, detached interest. Like watching a machine slowly calculate the center of the universe.

—This isn't just another mark, right? We can't just waltz in there. Even if we had a back door to the place, they'd recognize you right away.

She pulled a dagger from her boot and threw it at the table and it struck there and stood still vibrating with a sharp note. She barely moved. Mims pulled the dagger out of the wood, rolled it around in his hand and looked at her, stared right through her like she wasn't even there.

—Your existence is my death.

9

Before:

When they first arrived in Xylos their ship was on fire. The crew ran around screaming, people had flames on their backs, spread like wings, ready to take flight. It smelled like burning meat, like burning hair, like burning wood and cinder and ash and decay. Beyla thought about the children of the crew onboard and something inside of her curled up and died.

So she howled and threw stuff and tried to put it out but eventually grabbed Sunsorrow and ran over and jumped into the sea and watched from the clear blue waves as it burned. The air was so hot with fire and the sea was cold, ice cold, daggers of cold brushed against her skin.

She heard the screams and the shouts and wondered when it would stop. The masts crumbled and burst and made noises like thunder and she gulped for air as she swam away, toward the bay where people stood still and watched wearing animal masks.

Fish brushed against her legs. There went everything. All of their belongings burnt to a crisp, money melting into gold pools, loose gunpowder exploding and sounding like giants stepping on the earth. Even all of the memories of Carcosa curling and black with ash, blowing and billowing toward the city. The heat from the flames was too much to bear, even from back here, she felt her skin was burning up like parchment, curling up and ashen. She wanted to disappear, to blow away, to drift toward town like a stray scroll unravelled.

10

Now:

Klack, klack, klack: Mims rolled the dice on the floor. He watched the etched bone spinning, his palm itching, his mind racing. He was trying to pay off their debt and to pay off their room for the past few days. They had no money, no possessions, not a single thing they could offer in trade that they were willing to give.

Beyla stood over the moving dice and watched them rattle and crossed her fingers and thought that she didn't want violence, not now, not just yet. Violence was always there, that she knew, not for once, just for a little bit, she wanted to be freed of it.

The innkeep was a man with a fish's head, and he watched with black fish eyes, waiting to see if he would get double what he'd owed or if he'd be out of everything. His fisheyes dilated, his gills struggling to breathe the air. The dice stopped, crisp and sure, revealing: a skull and a sword.

—Well then. Looks like you owe me quite a bit of money now, don't you? I suggest you two pay up nice and proper. We don't want to get the law here, do we?

Beyla laughed and it was a hideous sound. It looked like she'd have to kill him after all. Sunsorrow stirred in her hands, stretching and waking and yawning. It glowed rust orange in the dim light of the inn, the whispering shadows shying away from it. She walked forward, sword hungry, sword wanting, sword breathing and bloodstarved.

The fish man blinked at her, looked back at Mims and sighed.

—Go on, get out, you thieves. And you best run, once you do get. You best run. I'll have the red and grey in here as fast as I can, and they'll be hot on your tail.

Mims didn't say anything. He scooped up his dice, slung them into his pocket. He then glanced outside, toward the glittering street. Beyla slid her sword back into her sheath, and it fell back into endless sleep, and it dreamed of wars and fighting and violence, and it dreamed of cutting the heads off kings and drinking their blood through its steel blade.

They turned and they left and the fishman stared. His head tracking them, following them, unable to stop glaring at them. His eyes were like two glass marbles, rolling towards them, watching them. Like he was forcing their features onto his memories, forcing them to engrave themselves deep within his mind.

11

A memory:

Beyla, child Beyla, Beyla running and hiding in shadow-coated streets. Beyla with black hair behind her, braided and flying. Beyla wearing oversized fur coat since it was the monthlong night, the snow-less winter, the middle of summer that brought out the cold and the howling wolves crawling through the streets. Her mother was back in the towers, caring after ghosts that thought they were still dying and her father was hung upside down in front of the gates, slowly begging for food, punished for killing four men with his own bare hands.

She saw him now, saw him hung by his feet, saw his face red bright red with blood and his hands swollen and swinging. He laughed as he swung and she saw his lips were cracked and bleeding and his eyes were oozing. She looked up at her father and reached her hand up and he smiled down at her, cracked lip smile.

Around his neck were rabbit bones hooked into a necklace, with rabbit skull as the center jewel.

—Dad, daddy!

—Httthhhhmmmmmm

Muttering, chanting, barely words. Yet his hand reached hers and they held it for a moment, a moment too long and the guards walked over and poked her away with their long spears. She looked at them crossed and then smiled up at her dad and told him she'd get him out of this, she would, she would come and save him and the guards laughed at her for being so small.

Later should would find an icebridge in the sea and walk across it to a castle that grew in the middle. And she would find in the center of it, deep in the center heart, cold and godless and waiting for her, she would find her sword. The sleeping. The dreaming. Sunsorrow.

Next day and the monthlong night faded away, and the icebridge melted and everything was hot and burning in the light of the cracked red sun. She found her father dead and naked and vulture-pecked. They'd slit his throat in the night and stole his clothes and belongings. She went and found the guards from the night before, and she woke Sunsorrow from his century-long slumber.

Death came so easy to her then. It was so much more difficult now.

12

Sometimes she dreamt of her dad and woke up to a feeling so lost and empty and stolen. Like somewhere along her life a piece of her broke. A piece of her childhood, maybe, a piece of her memories, her soul. Something forgotten, lost and left in that ice castle so many years ago. And when she woke she felt that if she could walk backwards in time and find that broken piece and put it back together then, well, then everything would right itself and she would be good and happy and no longer shattered inside.

She'd hoped to find that in Carcosa. Instead she found only masks and more masks.

13

The road was the road of old roads, the oldest of the roads known from before the time of the cracked sun. It stretched across the known world, and was as wide as five people standing shoulder to shoulder. It was grey cracked and yellow lines dashed in the center of it, darting off into infinity. Monks would walk the yellow lines, making the pilgrimage from Yardoza East to the Mazaa Gardens along the western shores. They prayed as they walked, head bowed and shaved and sunblistered, hands working long beads between stick-thin fingers, their mouths low and chanting.

This was the road they traveled. The oldest road, the road that led from sea to sea and from mountain to mountain. At night it was lit by the lanterns of the dead, where ages ago the King in Ywllo walked the road, and hung anyone he found walking there from iron posts he carried with him on a satchel slung over his back. After the bodies became dry and dead and dust, the light that they held within them crawled out and was trapped by the lanterns above.

And now at night every night they turned on after dusk, glowing an eerie bluish white and whispering of the lives they once lived.

14

—That innkeeper was strange.

Beyla was in the front of the line, Mims right behind her, Monks chanting right behind him. Like an arrow pointing backward, toward the sea and the islands of Carcosa. Mims scratched his head, looked toward the red sky and made thoughtful sounds, sounds of wondering, of hmming and hawing, and oh yes, of coursing. Then, he said:

—How was he strange? Because he let us go? I think he feared for his life, and didn't consider four shillings worth dying over.

—No, no, I don't think that's it.

She stopped and the monks kept walking. They would always keep walking.

—His head. I mean. What? A fish's head? Is he a mutant? Under a curse? I don't understand. Is he a living metaphor? A realization? A symbol, a sign from the gods? What does it mean?

Mims looked at her for a moment. rolling his dice in his palm, weighing her, trying to see if she was pulling his leg or not.

—You do know it was a mask, right?

Beyla stopped, stood still, looking toward the edges of the road, toward the horizon, where some sort of future waited for them. She was always amazed at the idea of a future, of a place and time other than the now when she was still existing. She thought about that future, and it felt like the past, like it had already come and gone and left her, and now she wasn't in the middle looking toward tomorrow, she was in the middle looking toward the history.

Even this conversation felt worn and old, heavy with repetition.

—That couldn't have been a mask. He had gills, and the eyes blinked, and the lips moved when he talked. Masks don't move like that. They are still, motionless.

Mims started walking forward again, hoping Beyla would follow. She didn't. It was as if she was frozen in that second, hung still, a pendulum between not the future and the past but, rather, between two pasts that have already happened.

—It was a mask. Didn't you notice the parades, the carnival? The dancing and the lights? Were you so caught up with your quest for the Loryx that you completely ignored your surroundings? The festival of the Whispering Red Wind! It's what Xylos is known for. That, and cheap entertainment, if you know what I mean.

She ran up, grabbed him by the shoulder and she stared into his eyes, feeling this moment, existing completely in this moment. She wanted so badly to be anchored to this moment, anchored and real and she wanted to crawl inside of it, to dig deep down with her fingers pushing against the membrane of the moment, and to lay a nest and live right here and now. No longer swinging through time, but still. Still. Her eyes were manic, wide, desperate. She felt like she was repeating everything again.

—It wasn't a mask. He was real, I saw him.

Mims pushed her hand away, shook his head, walked further along.

—It was a mask. Your memory is fooling you. A mask, nothing more, nothing less. A complicated, clockwork mask maybe. Like a puppet, in a way. But a mask none the less.

15

Later, hours later and red foxes paced on the road, about ten, all told, starved thin with eyes like wild lightning. The monks didn't stand a chance, they fought and prayed and chanted, and their spirits heard some prayers and not others, and ripped the foxes apart, but not others, and the road was covered in red and the bodies were chewed through and bone broken.

Fox corpses and monk corpses and praying hands tilted upward. None of them survived on either side. Beyla had watched, calmly, from a short distance away. Her sword woke to the sound of the violence, and begged her to go out and join it and fight and relish it. She knew that the sword would not tell fox from man, and she did not want the blood of the monks on her hands. So she turned and did not watch, and just looked back toward the silver mountains.

Mims ran forward and joined in and was bit in several places and had a claw scratch right over his eye. It would scar, that was sure, and there was blood soaking his shirt and his hair. But he had this wild joyful look on his face, smiling and laughing as he used his ax to chop chop chop.

He pulled back and walked toward Beyla when the monks summoned the spirits. He did not want to be a part of that. The spirits were angry things, and Mims led a shit of a life, and he knew they wouldn't spare him any more than they'd spare the foxes. And so they both stood with backs turned, and waited for the sounds of violence to finally ebb out and flow away, gently toward oblivion.

16

The Spirits Summoned:

Gold and blue and glory-coated, silver hair like fire on head, skull faced and angry with bodies like mist and dust and ash. Razor fingers reaching through flesh and pulling apart from the inside. Teeth for tearing, tongues for tasting the living, the still breathing, the unworshipped.

When all was dead they were satiated and appeased. The sacrifices pleased them and they walked off the road trailing into the twisted petrified trees, essences disappearing behind the stone echoes of plants and vegetables.

17

A memory:

At the new town, the sea town, the town they lived in after their old home had turned to rust and poison, and the locusts came and devoured all light and all clouds. They were strangers here, at first, at first. Strange people, other people, and they were not used to the sweaty bare backs on the longships, the nets slung in the air and sparkling in the sun, the spears sharp and thrown and pulled back with swordfish stabbed.

They were outsiders here, her and Mims, refugees, wanderers: forbidden. They were not used to the small mudhuts, and they were not used to the spiny-backed crabs the people there rode like horses through the sand and the orange wastes. Everything was different, everything was changed.

This is the memory, here, right after they arrived:

Beyla went down with Mims to the beach. They were older now, old enough still that he yearned and she pushed away. The memory of her father's corpse still clear in her mind from the last city, the locust-eaten city.

Beyla went and stripped and lay flat on the beach while the harpoons seared the sky and she saw millions of fish, all different colors swimming in the waves. The waves crushed and washed over her, over and over again, and she lay there, just lay there and let the sea take her in, drag her in, pull her in.

And there, beneath the waves, floating, floating, she was breathless and free, with the countless fish moving around her, dancing against her skin, and she felt herself being pulled, further and further down, and there, right there, far under the sea, at the center of the sea, at the heart of the world she saw Carcosa:

sparkling city. purple towers glittering. not a ruin, no no. it had a bubble around it. Air bubble. And she saw tall men and women in elaborate masks wandering around in beautiful robes, robes covered in diamonds and jewels, rising up and out of their bodies like cathedrals of fabric.

She opened her mouth in awe and swallowed water and laughed. She wanted to swim closer, closer, but it was too late. She was tangled, caught up in a silverweb strangling. She was pulled now, pulled up and closer to shore, and there her fishfriends were caught as well. And she could breathe again, and she could hear Mims sobbing at the beach, worried that she'd been captured and taken by the sea. But no, it wasn't the sea that caught her, but the fishermen, who laughed and joked about it later, and said that they'd caught a beautiful fish that was trapped in the body of a little girl.

GHOST TECHNOLOGY FROM THE SUN

Master told us that the earth was hollow, and that we lived on the inside of it, clinging to the top of the crust. Below us was another world, a world inside the world, a glowing bright sun of a place. What master called the summerlands. That is where the dead live, he said. That is how we can talk to them, he said. They send us signals across the air, and the mediums pick them up and drink them in.

And when the words came in, we had to speak them. We cannot deny the dead our voices—the dead would be angry if we did. And nobody wanted the angry dead to fly their zeppelins up from the sun and attack us crust dwellers.

That wouldn't do anyone any good.

Master knew this because he is an ambassador to the land of the dead. At night he walked through the door of the dead, and it beamed his body down above us, into the summer sun inside of the earth. That is where he talked to them, worked out trade between our two peoples.

The dead have a lot to offer the living.

He came back with schematics.

Ways of building circuit boards.

Ghost technology from the sun.

—

I remember when Ma first drank in the voices of the dead and talked with the tongue of paper and fire. We'd only been here a week or so and I was frightened of what was going to happen, having heard stories of horror from different members of the God's Foot Spiritulists. I kicked and screamed, refusing to go with her into the lodge, refusing to let her destroy herself for religion.

Eventually I gave in.

They took us into the Dead Man's Tongue. This was a lodge built for dead drinking. It had no windows and was covered in paintings of ghosts and the summerlands. It was lit entirely by the Master's halo, blue light bouncing off of the walls and illuminating the circle of faces in an eerie chilled light.

I remember clearly the shadow chanting and the fingers moving and the feet pounding out that rhythm. Ra-tat-tat. Ra-tat-tat. A hum of sounds: ah-m-m-m-ah. Ah-m-m-m-ah. The air thickened, and we could hear a clear barrage of whispers. Like everything started whispering around us—the trees, the lodge, the stars and the sun. Everything had a voice, and everything spoke in hushed tones.

Mother rolled her eyes back in her head, the marble white of her sclera reflecting the cities in the sun. Her mouth opened wide and out came fire and words and long streams of paper snakes. She danced and spat and spoke, she revealed her breasts and screamed. The chosen inscribers jotted down everything she said into small red and black notebooks.

It is said that past the gardens and into the woods there is a hidden library filled with small red and black notebooks. It is said that the Master goes there every night and reads them. Over and over again. Never sleeping.

"The dead don't sleep," he once told Ma, "And neither should I."

—

The Master was handsome.

The Master was tall.

The Master was a bone setter and an electrician.

We called him he who walks among the dead.

When I turn fourteen I want to marry the Master.

I practiced writing my name and his in a small red notebook. I would run the names together, combine them into new shapes and new words. I hoped that the truth in ink would become the truth in flesh.

I wandered through the garden at night, in hopes I could see him as he returned from the hidden library. I always tried to strike up some sort of conversation with him, flirting with him a little. He acted nonchalant but I could feel something there—a spark, a chemical connection. A magnetic pull from his eyes to my heart.

—

I am scared for the Master when he beams down into the under-sun. The cave made so much noise. The screams of the dead, wailing as he walked between dimensions. I was afraid that he would never return.

And then where would we be?

Lost and haunted by the dead.

With no one to lead us.

—

I was so lonely in God's Foot, being the only child there and with no one to play with. Most of the people in our commune were women, and they were all pregnant with the Master's kin. He called these women the Blessed, and he said that they carried the weight of Angels inside of them.

Last week I noticed my ma's belly was full and shaped like the moon below us, and I asked her if she was Blessed. She said she was, and she said that in a year or two I could become Blessed as well. That made me so happy, I bounced around for the rest of the day. I made extra certain that the Master noticed me, and tried to look my best every time I went out to play.

I wore my blue dress and tied gold ribbons in my hair. He saw me twice, and both times he mentioned how pretty I was and how happy he was for me to be here, living amongst such fine folk. Just hearing the deep rumble in his voice made me feel so happy.

Imagine that! Me! Blessed!
What a wonderful day that would be.

—

The garden was pretty at night.
So blue and full of shadows.
Master said the sun had two sides, one blue and one yellow. It spun beneath us, and that is why we have night and day. And all those stars and clouds—those were voices of the dead, moving through the ether for us to bring into our bodies and interpret.
We used the séance in order to drink in the words.
Our bodies became balls of light.
The words etched into our skin.
Last night I saw a rabbit in the garden.
I shooed him away, but he just smiled at me.
With a mouthful of human teeth.

—

One day the Master came out of the Door to the Dead with a roll of ancient-looking blueprints. He unrolled them and told everyone to begin work on this right away. This would be our greatest achievement. By the end of that week the whole village was lit up with electricity, and we called him the light bringer. Some of the people even compared him to Prometheus or Hermes, stealing the light of wisdom and bringing it down to us poor mortal folk.
I remember the first night we had all those lights up, strung between the trees in paper lanterns. They glowed and hummed and I remember touching the wires, feeling the electricity sharp and alive inside of it. Master says that this was just the beginning.
He was working on something bigger, better.

—

Earlier today the dead came into me and made me paint them. The canvas was stretched out beneath me and dyed brown with tea. I felt a surge of power in my head, and the whispers of the dead in my ears.

The air became thick, heavy. Like a wet blanket around my skin.

Then my hands moved and I couldn't stop it. At first I was scared, my body taken over by an outsider. I tried to keep the dead out, I did not want to drink it in. My hands moved anyway, my thoughts and motions no longer mine. My whole body felt numb around me, completely unresponsive to my thoughts.

I stopped fighting it, and just went with the flow. It was what the Master called the rivers of our soul, which the dead ride like the boatmen. They taint the water inside of us with their fingers as they ride, and we drink in this taint and become the words they speak.

I saw the summerlands as I painted.

I saw the golden sphere within the earth below us.

I saw all of the dead looking at me, their flesh rotting, their teeth grinning. I wanted to scream. The summerlands was no paradise. Not at all. It was all dark and dank architecture and filled with the bones of the dead. They wanted to pull me down, yank on the river of my soul and push it into the summerlands.

When I came to I looked down and saw my painting.

Red, red.

A crow in red.

And that rabbit. With teeth. And his bride in white right next to him, frightened and with a veil of the dead across her eyes.

And there, in the middle of it all was a sun.

Smiling, hungry.

Wanting to eat me whole.

When I was done I ran outside and threw up in the bushes. The Master came by and I was so embarrassed, and I knew he wouldn't want to marry me now. No one ever would. How could he love me when I smelled of vomit?

—

The Master praised my painting. He hung it in the Dead Man's Tongue with all of the others. He said that I had been possessed by Uk-Olak-Ken, the dead god of Atlantis. Gods die too, he said, and they also go and live in the summerlands of the afterlife just like the rest of us mortals.

He said that this painting was very special, and no one had ever been possessed by Uk-Olak-Ken before. He told me he had a secret job for me. One that no one else could ever know about. Not even Ma.

—

I made dolls out of the corn husks in the garden. The dolls were very tall, about as tall as I am, and I dressed them up in my clothes, and took them outside and danced with them. Sometimes I pretended they were real and they were my friends.

Some nights I could hear them whispering after the séance, and I wondered if the dead voices were trapped within them. As if they were possessed somehow. I meant to tell the Master or Ma about it, but during the daylight hours I forgot.

There was so much work to do on the farm, and everyone had to help out. Even those who were Blessed.

—

I once lined up all of the corn dolls in the garden and dressed them in red and black dresses. I called them the army of corn, and made them ready for war against the trees around them. Out of the corner of my eye I saw something brown and furry dart between the rampion.

I stood and walked toward it, following it.

The air felt thick with dreams and whispers. Like it did during a séance. I heard the screams and howls come from the door to the dead, and realized that the Master must be descending again. Going down and above us, into that sun in the center of the world.

I saw a furry puff of a tail peek out from between the cabbages, and two brown ears slicked back onto a mangy skull. "Rabbit," I said as I walked toward it, "Rabbit, what are you doing in our garden? This is our food."

The rabbit turned his head and smiled at me with a mouthful of human teeth. "Get on my tail," he said.

"No, never. Go."

He hopped closer to me, the grin widening into a threat. "Come on. Follow me to the Door of the Dead."

I stepped backward, frightened.

"Who are you?"

He hopped closer, and then stood up. His back uncoiled and he grew as tall as I am, standing on his hind legs like a human. His eyes were dark and troubled, and the center of them looked like suns stuck into his hollow head. "I am the keeper of doorways."

I stepped back and pointed at my dolls. "They are armed," I said, "With the voices of the dead."

They whispered then, the sound out of it filling the air with the smell of turpentine and rotten eggs.

The rabbit hopped backward.

"Ah, then. I guess I'll be getting on. But I will return. You are far too pretty to leave be, and I need a wife sooner than soon."

And then he shrunk down and hopped off, leaving the dust of his footprints across the garden.

—

The Master brought us all together before a séance one night with an announcement. He had brought new schematics from the land of the dead, and we would have new ghost technology in order to build and use. He laid out the plans on the grass and started pointing out different things that would need to be done.

"This will be," he said, "an amplifier to the voices of the dead. No longer will they whisper in the void between our worlds. This will take the ether between us and the summerlands and thicken it—making them louder and more audible to us."

The people cheered.

The Master is taking us into a new era of enlightenment. Humanity will evolve now—faster and more sure, toward the shores of the dead. No longer will we be separate—travel between the worlds will be as easy as riding a train.

—

I was possessed by Uk-Olak-Ken again. He came into my skull and ate away at my mind, forcing the rivers of my soul to become overflowing and flooded. I screamed in angst and my mother said I bit her on her leg. She showed me the rings of broken skin my teeth made, like red moons on her flesh.

I painted the walls of my room in the lodge while in the trance, red crows all over it and rabbit brides. I painted a large sun, grinning and hungry. I painted rivers of black slime and castles crumbling on the moonside of the sun. I painted the hollow earth, and a bridge that moved between it.

And I painted the zeppelins.

The skullish dead riding in them, ready to war with us breathing meatsacks. Their eyes glittered in my paintings, all hollow and holy and wanting to feed on us.

The painting frightened me.

Master said it was a good sign. A great omen. Uk-Olak-Ken had blessed us with this message. It meant that the dead will come to us soon, come and take us to the summerlands where we will be happy and no longer dependant on this crust of a world.

I felt sick and queasy as I realized Master was wrong. This was a warning. The dead are preparing for war. They want to destroy us. They were jealous of our flesh and lives and they wanted to take our skin and wear it, steal our beating hearts and use it to pump the blood of life into their dead bodies.

I slept in the garden after that incident.

I couldn't stay in the same room with that painting ever again.

—

There was a large gathering and ceremony before the Master switched on the newly built amplifier. The celebration started with prayers to the dead, and an offering to the doors between worlds. Then it moved to a séance, with fourteen people all becoming possessed and two whole red and black notebooks filled with the mad sayings of the dead.

He then went forward and turned the machine on. It looked like a vivisection of a robot, all metallic intestines and beating artificial hearts. On top of it stood a brain molded in copper, with black rubber tubes and a spine of bronze spouting out of it. The spine curved up and into the air, and shook and hummed when the machine was switched on.

It vibrated and sang while people celebrated. We danced to the music of the amplifier that night, the voices of the dead a chorus around us. The air felt thicker, wetter. A hot moisture dripping onto our bodies. We all felt possessed, and everyone one of us could hear the voices now, so loud and so clear.

And the smell.

The air smelled of sweetness and ripeness.

—

The next day Ma was outside, laying on the ground in a mud puddle near the back of our house. The mosquitoes hung like a biting buzzing veil around us, hungry in the sticky air. Ma's belly was round and sticking out of the mud like a moon stuck in the center of the void below us. I wondered if there was a world inside of her stomach, with people like us clinging to the crust, and another world in the center with the voices of the dead.

Ma had mud all over her face.

Her eyes looked so tired.

All around us the voices of the dead carried on in conversation, forcing us to speak up a little louder if only to be heard. "Marybeth dear," Ma said to me, "Why did you sleep in the garden last night? I missed you."

I shrugged.

"That painting. It scares me. All those faces, dead faces, looking at us in such hatred."

She waved her arms in the mud, making mud angels. Her face looked elsewhere, toward the ether. *So murky this air*, I thought, *so thick and deadly.* "I can't sleep at night with you gone. Come and sleep with us dear. Or the Master will think something's wrong with you."

I sat down in front of her, the mud staining my blue dress. *Tonight*, I thought, *I will take the ribbons out of my hair. I don't want to wed the Master anymore.* "Maybe there is something wrong with me. This air is suffocating."

Ma laughed. It was a strange and deadly sound.

"I don't feel pregnant. Isn't that weird? It's like what's inside of me is a ghost. Like my stomach is haunted, or even that an insect is living in there, getting larger with time. And I feel like this whole place is a dream, and the dead are the ones that are really alive."

Ma then rolled around on the mud, coating her stomach heavily. It looked like a brown and sticky circle of flesh, hidden under the dark shadows of her dress. I wanted to reach out and touch it, to feel the ghost beating under her skin.

—

It's so hard to breathe.
    The air is so fluid.
    Like trying to breathe underwater.
    And the voices get louder and louder every day.
    They sound like shouting snowflakes in a blizzard of sound.

—

The Master changed. I don't know if anyone else noticed it, but he started glowing brighter. So bright that the daylight gave way to his glow. And his skin peeled and cracked. Beneath the holes in his skin more light throbbed and glowed, even stronger and more radiant than before.
    He called himself Xansu.
    Lord of the Lights.
    And he would talk to people in half-heard whispers. I saw bits of paper stuck under his fingernails, and I saw him at the library more and more. He must be constantly reading those notebooks.
    He stopped going to the séances.
    And the séances became more violent, more disturbing. Almost everyone became possessed, and they attacked each other, the ghosts burning holes in their eyes and poisoning their soul rivers with rot and plague. Yesterday Erica blinded her husband. Ripped out his eyes with her own fingers.
    The dead made her do it.
    The dead make us do everything.
    Their presence is overwhelming.

—

Master came by to visit me while I played in the garden one night before I went to sleep. He looked at my corn dolls and smiled. Their voices are louder now, I realized. They are practically screaming in the language of the dead.

The Master's body glowed as he approached me, sending away the light of the moon with his own disturbing blue illumination. He held his arms out to me. The closer he got, the more disgusting he looked. His face had holes in it, and his eyes were falling out. His hair was unkempt and decrepit, and I wanted to scream at the sight of him.

Instead, I stayed silent.

"Hello, my child."

I nodded.

"I have a secret job for you."

I moved a little away from him. The corn dolls hissed at the Master as he moved, trying to send him away. Their voices clattered out insults, trying to move their corn husk bodies to get close enough to attack him.

"Don't you want to know what it is?"

I stumbled back.

Still covered in sweat. This heat was unbearable even at night. No reprieve from the thickness of air. "No, it's ok. You can tell me tomorrow."

The Master smiled.

"Tomorrow might be too late," he said, "I need you to summon Uk-Olak-Ken. I need to talk to him."

I shook my head no. "Why can't I do it during the séance tomorrow?"

The Master moved closer to me, his body gliding across the ground. "Too many people. I need to ask him secret stuff. Only stuff I need to know. Something is being hinted at in the notebooks. Something dark and terrible. I need to talk to him and learn what."

I looked at my corn dolls. I only wished I could give them life, let them move and protect me. "I don't want to. Have someone else act as your human puppet."

He grinned and then chanted and clapped under his breath. My mind swam and my body felt moist. I rolled in the rivers of my soul, falling over the earth and up below us into the undersun. I could see the curvature of the crust above me, and Uk-Olak-Ken taking over my body.

I fought and tried to swim up through my mind and back into my flesh. I did not want to be trapped in the cellar mind anymore. I wanted to be out and stopping him. The Master was doing dangerous things, and we are going to pay for them soon enough.

I crawled against the currents, and fought against the rebellion in my mind. I forced that Uk-Olak-Ken back into the sun, forced him back into the ether and the dank cities of the dead and out of my body.

When I came to I realized I was sweating, naked.

A light was flowing out of the Master. It flew into my body in streams of fire. I started to cry as I realized what was going on. The light of him spun inside of my stomach, weaving against the walls of my womb.

When he looked down he realized it was me in my body and no longer Uk-Olak-Ken. "My child," he said as my stomach spun inside of me, "You are one of the Blessed now. You carry my seed, and the weight of Angels inside of you."

I wiped my tears away with my hands.

"Did you get the information?"

He nodded.

"Thank you, my child."

Good, I thought. *Maybe you will do something to stop this, stop all of this. We are in danger of being eaten by the dead, our bodies used as costumes for them to parade around in and pretend to be alive.*

He walked away, and I felt sick to my stomach, and certainly not blessed.

—

The next day I decided to wander through the woods and find the library. It took me a few hours, but I eventually found the ruins of an old catholic church, and inside of it notebooks upon notebooks scattered in the pews. The walls of the church looked like old bones, bleached and full of holes.

The notebooks were mostly arranged by importance and relevance. Most of them had pages bookmarked, and some were impossible to read due to water damage. I flipped through a few of them at book-marked pages, and started to find an unsettling pattern.

Every bookmarked page mentioned a war of the dead. It mentioned fire from the sun, and the destruction of the crust dwellers. It mentioned war machines of unbelievable power, and of ways to travel between the lands of the living and the dead.

I felt something slick move in my stomach.

He knew all along.

And was going to do nothing.

—

It wasn't long before my stomach extended.

Fast, I thought, *whatever it is, it grew fast.*

I knew what Ma meant—it felt haunted. More of a ghost inside of me than a child growing.

—

A night or two later I saw the rabbit again. He walked up to my corn doll army, staring at them as he went by. When he saw me he stood upright, his teeth shimmering in a grin beneath the moon. "Marybeth," he said, "Will you get on my tail and join me?"

I had nothing else to lose.

"Where are we going to go?"

His grin deepened, wide and wider still. "Someplace you need to see. The Door to the Dead."

I climbed onto his tail.

"Let's go then," I said, "And when we get there, if you still want me to, I'll marry you."

The rabbit turned his head almost fully round, his mouth full of human teeth. "I would and still might. But what grows in you is dark and deadly, and I will not raise it. Not I, not ever."

He turned his head and got on all fours, his body shooting out and darting with me on his tail towards the cave known as the Door to the Dead.

Above us I saw the light of red crows, dancing under the moon.

—

The cave was empty. The door was a chalk drawing, and the sounds of screams and horrible noises came from a cage full of geese that the Master poked with a red hot poker. Rabbit showed me these tricks, how he deceived the people. In the corner of the cave was a series of diagrams and maps. All these schematics, all this hollow earth—he did not get this from the dead at all.

He came up with it himself.

Using us to get information about the dead with his séances, never once putting himself in any danger.

I saw rituals described in other pages, tales of sacrifices and stones that make you immortal. I realized than what the Master was doing—that each of us would be used to make him live forever. Even if meant to bring the dead here, and put us in danger.

I looked at Rabbit.

"Thank you," I said.

He held my hand in his paw.

"I love you. Come back to me when you are free from this burden. I will marry you, and we will live together in perfect harmony, far away from this dead world."

Outside of the cave I heard the red crows cawing, and the voices of the dead getting louder and louder still. It was so full in the air, and it corrupted our thoughts and poisoned our soul rivers. Outside the moon became bright and turned into the sun, and the sun became bigger and bigger, like it was coming right toward us.

And I could see cities on the surface of the sun.

Bright, brilliant cities of light.

I held the rabbits paw in my hand.

So soft, so comforting.

"It may be too late," I said.

He nodded and then I jumped on his tail. Back to God's Foot we flew, fast and with the trees blurring around us.

—

In the sky above we saw the Zeppelins of the dead, flying from the sun cities to us crust dwellers. The voices around us floated in the air, angry, yelling. Wanting their light back. Wanting the stones of immortality back.

I searched for Ma when I got back, the rabbit following me, making certain I would be okay. The air felt like drowning, the water of it entering our lungs and corrupting our breaths. We could not talk, not over the voices of the dead being amplified in the world around us.

My head was filled with so many thoughts.

So few of them were my own.

Rabbit helped keep me calm.

Helped keep me sane.

The creature inside of my stomach swam through me, licking my blood and grating against my bones. I wanted to flush it out of my system, to destroy it whenever possible. I was afraid to give birth, fearing that it might rip me apart as it crawled out.

—

I found the body of my mother with the others. Her stomach a mess, her ribcage poking out from her flesh. They were all stacked there, back behind the Dead Man's Tongue. They had all died in childbirth, their bodies destroyed by whatever lived inside of them.

I saw the shadows of giants as they slouched about town, and heard the voice of the Master screaming and singing songs to them. The Master seemed to be almost completely light now, his skin discarded on the ground at his feet.

I wanted to tear this thing from my stomach.

I did not want to die like that.

I turned and looked at the stack of bodies. Standing next to them, all in a row were my corn husk dolls. The dolls turned and looked at me, and spoke in unison.

"They are here," the dolls said.

"The dead have come."

POSTFLESH

1. Captain Found Us a Ghost World.

Shadrim. It was a grave of space, a planet of bones. It was the endless all and everything. Shadrim. When we discovered it, we found it full of ruins and corpses. Shadrim. When it discovered us, it was thinking. Shadrim. It had the grave thoughts. Thoughts that only the dead could or would want to think. Filtering through the entire planet.

When we found it we were lost. It sent out beacons, psychic signals across the radio waves. Old Gray Mack thought it was perverse. We all laughed at his thoughts. Mack could fly the darkness like no one else. But he didn't know anything about the human mind—the world between the waves.

When we landed we saw the big bronze skull city states, we saw the machines that they had left behind. Large spider beasts. Evolved, transfigured. Machines with alienskin stuck to the grindbones, scuttling through those ruins and making the corpses dance. First time we saw that sight we wanted to leave. Big alien bones with zombie skin still stuck on them, prancing around in nightmare waltzes. We ran like hell away from them. They didn't follow. They stayed behind, dancing and staring with ghost eyes.

When we got back to the ship it was dead. Buried in the ground with a grave on top. All that was left was ash and a skeleton. A breathing thing that sustained us gone and dead now. Like manhome itself.

Carit wept and Sunday Jay said a prayer in Pascal. It was the way Sunday Jay talked to the onboard systems. Through Pascal. Sure, it was an old language, but we are an old people, wandering the restless void of space and searching for ourselves in the reflection of the cosmos.

The next day we found that dog that did our ship in. Giant machine thing that kept piecing itself together out of the ruins of the world around us. He was a sea of corpses and machinery. He looked at us with alien eyes, and Good Day just smiled at him and offered him a smoke.

Carit cursed it. Claimed it killed the ship and kept us trapped here. We couldn't look at that alien thing, covered in ship blood and the strings of organic machinery. It kept trying to talk to us, talk to us over the radio sounds of the dead. It was so lonely.

But we couldn't. Not now. Even though it promised us so much. Faster-than-light travel. Becoming transhuman. Existing beyond the realm of mortality. We couldn't let it know how we felt. How it hurt us and stranded us in the depth of space. The captain even went out and got the zox box and shocked it around. This machine seemed to love it. It squealed with delight, and then asked us if we had anything yet for dinner.

Good Day stepped forward and told it we were all starving. The creature had a few nanokin whip us up some good stuff. It tasted all right, for alien metal food. And we thought, this giant postflesh space-cat couldn't be all that bad. Sure he killed our ship, but that space trawler was dying anyway, maybe it was a mercy killing.

Later that night we slept under the frozen purple light of fourteen distant suns. They were moon-sized in the distance, spread across the sky and shouting out the light of the stars. The pull of this world was dizzying and complex, it weaved through the orbits of so many planets and suns. It was like a drunk fractal nightmare of astronomical physics.

When we dreamed, we dreamed in ghost voices. We dreamed of ghost algebra in a ghost planet. This world, it spoke in our sleep and screamed in our waking hours through the radio towers broadcasting around us. The bones are restless, dancing. When the last hour of sleep washed away, we were greeted with the beating of techno drums and the dancing of the alien corpses.

And this time, they sang.

2. We Discuss Ghost Dreams

Spillgal was the first to do it. She just sat up like a white cat with black eyes, stretched out her tail and started talking. Her voice meandered at first, wandering over our heads. But then we realized what she was talking about, and we leaned in and listened.

Even that big A.I., that giant shipkiller corpse monster, it bent the massive head down dripping with columns and garbage and rotting alien flesh and listened. We had to filter out the screams of the dead in order to hear her properly.

Her voice was like static, noise in the broadcast of Shadrim. "I dreamt of endless space, and vacuum tubes. I dreamt of a doll without eyes, and a lady without teeth. I dreamt that I licked the feet of secrets, and they gave me bones to pay for a ship. I think I dreamed memories, but I can't be sure. So many voices, lost in my head. Even as I am awake now, I am almost certain I am still dreaming."

We talked about her dream for a bit, discussing its contents but coming to no conclusion. Whisper Kid went next, talking about smoke and a guy named Kagaratz. Each of us went in turn, and each dream was discussed but without any answers. Finally, at the end the captain sat up and proclaimed that he would build us a new space ship, one to take us home.

The dead aliens scuttled away screaming. Our dreams were a gift. They felt insulted that the captain would not stay and experience more of them. The giant machine that was our host ticked his head to the side and sighed, getting the nanokin to make us a meal of tin and scraskin. It tasted worse than it looked, but we ate it.

After that, we were less welcome in the planet of the dead. Our host kept ignoring us, and the broadcast screams of the lost world got so loud we became just static and noise in the background. It was hard to think like that, but we had to. It was a learning process, a way of filtering ourselves out from the void that tried to swallow us.

3. Skullchic Finds Material

We scavenged the world for parts and pieces, but of course we couldn't go too far. There were a lot of alien machines, but we couldn't make sense out of any of it. And our host wasn't talking to us anymore. He kept towering over us, watching and recording us with thousands of nanocams. We could see them scuttle about his massive body like living dust.

And the corpses—they were mad. They hung out on the edge of our vision, running through the ruined city and howling in a dead tongue, their voices projected just barely above that load broadcast of ghost voices and ghost memories.

And we starved. Hunger laced through our veins, spilling over into our thoughts. All we dwelled on was the memory of food. Of great things like pancakes and waffles and syrup and strawberries and tomatoes. No vegetation was on this planet, nor any living meat we could kill and fry up.

In the hour of our greatest hunger Skullgirl found some parts. At first we weren't sure what she had—it looked like some skeleton from an alien body with a glowing orange heart. But metallic, and carved with cold foreign pictographs.

The captain knew what it was, knew what to do with it.

He kissed her in joy and we all screamed. The voices got louder, and that A.I. started to crumble into smaller pieces around us. We fitted each part in and assembled it right and proper. The captain got Old Grey Mack to study the controls, and then to figure out a way for us to interface with it.

Old Grey Mack was great at that sort of thing. He was a xenoarche-ologist, a regular alien retrofitter. He could sew these things into the right pieces of his mind, find out exactly how their propulsion system differed from our ion drives. He was used to this sort of thing—rear-ranging his mind into alien shapes and geometry.

Soon we had a working model up and running. Time for a test drive, and then off to freedom.

4. We Gasp, We Sigh, We Say Goodbye

It was a rough-looking space vessel, made from the alien boneparts we found and some old stuff from our ship, strapped on so that Old Grey Mack could pilot it without a problem. More like a shambling half-dead animal than a cruiser, it spun around the atmosphere and screamed as it flew in chaotic messy lines. Our host watched, his body slinking into sludge parts, the air filtered with his nanodust. He tried to get the alien corpses to dance a goodbye dance, but he could not get them to come near us.

On the moment of the test departure, those dancing corpses came out again, screaming and running toward us. Mack was flying low in the sky, looking down. The machine worked, leaving trails of blue light behind it in whirling vapors. Mack smiled and gave us the thumbs up to say that everything was okay. He flew a little lower, getting ready to find some open ground to land on.

Our host collapsed into thousands of tiny bodies, trying to restrain the living dead's nanosystems. They surged and came forward, crying out and scurrying across the floors of the world with many thin and angular limbs. Like undead spiders, with big bulging eyes and tiny puckered lips.

The planet shook, the radio systems picked up. It was all one voice now, the voice of Shadrim, that zombie planet that wanted us to stay here and be assimilated into its nightmarish ecosystem. The voice of the planet spoke in strange tongues, and the nanomachines obeyed. We tried to get Mack to land, to drop down something we could cling onto and escape. He only hovered low, a look of shock and horror on his face.

The dust of the world poured into us. Living things, tiny A.I., pieces of that host that kept us here for so long. Mack just circled about and watched as we were disassembled, our parts and pieces connected to the ruins now. They strung up our bodies like art, our intestines and bones collected with bacterial computers and small nanomachines that somehow preserved us and made us do what the world told us to.

In our mind we could hear it all the time. The thought, running through our veins like the whispers of space. Commanding us. Telling us what to do. Our we had gotten bigger, engulfed us. We had one mind now, the mind of the world. The mind of the ghost planet. It sung in our skin, set our nerves on fire.

And now we danced. We danced, and our voices broadcast from those old radio waves. This was the radio song, the voice of planet Shadrim. This was us and who we were. Mack sped off, and we would have too. But now we were dancing, our corpseskin cold. Soon we would transcend. Transcend and be like our host, postflesh.

The Skinless Man Counts to Five

The first corpse rode the waves to the beach and greeted the librarian on the shore. It was tied to a chair with catch ropes, skinless with eyes popped open and mouth gaping wide. Inside the mouth was a speaker, connected to an old ghostdrive in the corpse's chest. The speaker said the same thing over and over again, in a rusty metallic voice. Clear and sharp as a bell.

"Five. Five. Five. Five. Five."

The librarian snapped her fingers, took a quickpic, and uploaded it to the emergency datamines for the police to see. Now she just had to wait for them to arrive and take the body elsewhere. Goosebumps dotted her arms as the spiralsun slowly glittered to life, chasing away the starlamps, and finally bringing bright daylight to the generation ship.

After this, she would have a headache that lasted for days. Blistering. The two detectives that eventually arrived barely listened to her and were no help at all. She spent the next few weeks muttering the number five to herself over and over again. It had gotten lodged into her thoughts, unable to escape. The dreams were gone and replaced with white noise and a shadow moving slowly toward her, just at the edges of her peripheral vision.

—

Back at the station the detectives wound into the hivemind and pulled up the feeds from earlier that day. The first detective looked closely at the collection of images, magnified them as best as he could. A large ominous shape rose from the waves in a constellation of stars. The second detective had his back turned and was trying his hardest not to vomit. A low hum buzzed about in his head, and his knees ached. This was worse than rain. It was something else.

Maybe a solar storm outside of the ship? Wouldn't be the first time it messed everything up.

The first detective said, "Look, here, see? See? He almost has a face, but it's not a face. It's like every face I've ever seen all at once. Like the memory of a face made manifest. See? Turn and look."

"No," said the other detective, "I don't have to look to know what you're seeing."

The first detective spun around in his chair. Stars flung themselves past the windows overlooking the galaxies beyond, making a celestial halo around his head. "Tell me, then. What do I see?"

"A shape made of stars. A face made of faces."

The first detective stood up, shook his head. "How do you know that?"

"No. I mean. I don't know."

The second detective leaned over and vomited. It was clear and blue and smelled like raw exhaust from the thermal engines. In the center of the pool of sick was a skinless finger encircled with a small glass ring. "What is going on with me . . ."

"Come on, let's get you to the pharmhounds and see if they can fix you up."

"I don't know if they can. Something is rotten inside, I feel it. This is a deep, in-the-bone feeling."

—

They found an eyeball and several teeth in the second detective's stomach. At the same time he was in the pharmcages, another body was found. This time it was in the night forest, high up in the pines. The branches brushed against the wind and made a soft whistling sound. Two little girls found it and called the cops, terrified. They kept saying that they didn't know he was real, that there was no way he could be real. Was this another dream? Or something else?

The second body was much like the first. He was tied to the branches upside down, with his head pointed to the ground. He was missing some teeth and an eye and a finger. And, just like the first one, he'd had a ghostdrive placed in his stomach, and a speaker in his throat.

"Four. Four. Four. Four."

—

After a week the girls stopped speaking altogether. At night they would pace their apartments near the westernmost quadrant, unable to sleep. Their minds repeated the music of fire in their thoughts, keeping them awake and restless. Until their quadrant was burned barren and destroyed by a freak accident.

Thankfully, the zoombots put an end to it and only a small handful of people died.

—

Right before they found the third body, the machines of the ship began to act erratic and uncertain. Cleaners spun in the dark howling of their wheels. Datacrunchers vomited numbers and letters in random order, unable to make sense of anything any longer. Their entire purpose in life wiped away in a single instant. The spiralsun flickered and burned with a low buzzing sound, while the moonlamps lit up brightly during the daylight hours.

There were even moments when the gravity went south, and the passengers of the slowship floated about weightless and lost. That was when the third body was discovered, right before gravity righted itself. An elderly couple was floating hand in hand when the husband screamed and turned inside out, his skin drifting around them like feathers. When the gravity turned back on, they fell and smacked hard on the ground. There was a speaker crammed in his throat, chanting.

"Three. Three. Three."

His wife did not know how the speaker or ghost drive was inserted into her husband. It made no sense; they had never left each other's side. She could not answer the detectives' questions. Everything inside her was broken now, terrified of breathing and thinking and sleeping.

—

People ran through the halls and corridors and screamed. Panic was everywhere. It moved from body to body and sang through the hive in electrical streams. What was it counting down to? The people demanded to know. Someone had to know! They rioted and tore out entire walls, ripped circuit boards to shreds. They yelled at those in authority, people who must know what would happen when the last corpse appeared (oh, bright angel of death), and said that final number . . .

One

People argued, hypothesized, philosophized, but had no answers, only fear.

—

The detectives wound through the archives back at the station. They followed the elderly couple, viewing them from all these different angles, from the week that led up to the husband's demise. And just like the last two bodies, what they saw raised more questions than answers. It was like each one was a riddle, daring to be solved. They saw restless shadows in the night, filled with stars, shuffling around the old man's body as he slept.

The shadows placed things under his skin, in his eyes, opened his mouth, and put shadow hands in his throat. The second detective paced around the room, muttering the number four to himself and saying repeatedly, That could have been me. That could have been me.

"Do you want to watch your vidfeeds from that week? Maybe something similar happened?"

No, no, no.

They kept watching. Each night, every night, the shadows came and did the same thing. Opened mouth, hand down throat. Tiny scalpels making incisions, placing stars under his skin. For a moment, the bones glowed, flickered, and then went silent.

—

Elsewhere, dogs barked, and a pandemic reared its ugly misshapen skull in the darkness.

Very few people would be spared. Even the first detective fell ill, his body slowly wasting away with each day until there was nothing left. Just ashes under loose flaps of skin, propped up by an architecture of brittle bones. The second detective did not stop his investigations. He only grew more determined to uncover what was going on.

—

Right after the fourth skinless body was discovered in the ponds of the northernmost quadrant, a ship was seen outside of their windows. Long, slow, it seemed to be devoid of life. No light flickered, no bodies moved; it was a ruin in space. It also made no sense. How could there be another ship outside, so far away from their own galaxy? Had they turned around without realizing it?

And why was it dead?

Some people thought that maybe it was an alien ship, and they weren't alone out here in the universe after all. Others postulated it was faster ships built to grab near light speed in bursts of powerful nuclear light. And since their own ship was such a slow one, it could easily surpass them.

Yet, it was not surpassing them. It was still, motionless in the void of space, while their own ship crawled past it. They sent drones out to take pictures and study the inside with new recordings. At first, there seemed to be bodies moving in the shadows. But no, those were only corpses of giant humanoid creatures, propped up and mummified. They were posed specifically, but for what purpose? The humans could not figure out.

Were they dancing? They looked like they were dancing.

Then the feed cut out, and the ship vanished. It was as if it had never been there at all. Some people came to believe it was nothing, just a mass hallucination, and yet the feeds stored on the hive did not lie. They were preserved there for all time, for anyone to pull up and prove them wrong.

And all this time, the fourth corpse in cold storage still chanted out:

"Two. Two."

—

The final detective would not give up. There were clues all around him, patterns and sequences that he knew could fit together in some morbid puzzle that would explain everything that was going on. He took notes, conducted interviews, uploaded massive troves of information into the hive and fed it advanced learning platforms to see if it could see any links between the data that his feeble meat mind could not.

Instead, it spewed back gibberish and images of the dead around him. One day, it showed him the corpse of the first detective hung from the rafters of the artificial sky. Behind him starlamps twinkled on and off in rapid succession. Maybe the lights were a pattern. Maybe not. Would these be the constellations of the dead?

—

Somewhere, children walked into the waves, singing. They could not swim, and they died, clogging the lakes with their bodies. The lower levels flooded from the backed-up water, sending mile-high waves across the biomes. The spiralsun had been off for days now, or was it a few weeks? Maybe it was even few months? Time didn't matter anymore. The days ran together, while the starlamps flickered overhead in a forevernight.

—

Many generations ago, when they were near the edge of the solar system, they were in a fleet of a hundred or so generation ships, linked worlds with massive star bridges extending between them. They could see something at the edge of the known system. The ship's sensors sent off warning signals, the feeds filled with a pressing darkness that hurt the eyes to look at.

They were told to turn around, like the others. But the AI captain of this generation ship calculated no risk. It overrode those errors, called the humans silly emotional meat machines, and demanded that they stop being foolish and to just look at the raw data. There was nothing to be afraid of.

It severed its bridges, cut all ties to ribbons, and pushed on forward. For almost four hundred generations it seemed to be working just fine. Until . . .

—

The last corpse was the final detective. He was found by a gang of rudderless teenagers, covered in tattoos and body piercings. A few of them had been genetically modified and were covered with soft blue fur and had large rabbit ears. One of them had a pair of tusks sticking out of his craw. They were on the edge of nihilistic despair after they had watched their parents commit suicide together in the center of the town, under the dead lights of the spiralsun.

Now the corpse was their trophy, their own little toy to play with. A razor blade snicked out; a baton dropped down. It had been a while since they had a fresh corpse to kick around, and watch ooze out some sick liquid. But before they could do a thing, it simply said "ONE" in a very final and aggressive tone.

"Guys, hey, guys, stop that for a moment and look. Look!"

They all turned and stared at the artificial sky as the constellations began to go out one by one, the engines wound down, and the machines went into a restless sleep. It wouldn't be long now before the trees started to wither and die. When the oxygen tanks slowly dried up and rain stopped misting on the ground, the gravity would lighten up a bit and then a bit more, and they would all float in the center of the ship, suffocating in silence.

A ruin in space. One that waited for another lost generation ship to come find them and hear the chanting of their bodies as they counted down to a new number, a new warning, a new oncoming apocalypse.

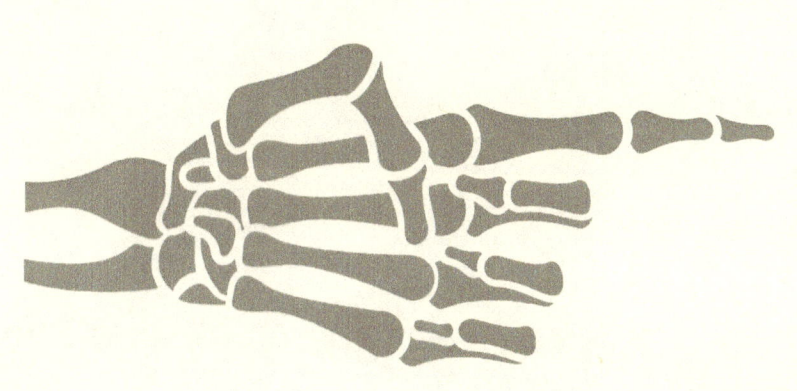

Acknowledgments

It's impossible to remember all of the people to acknowledge in a book like this, but I'll try my best.

These short stories were collected over the last 25 or so years, in various publications, and I want to thank all of them, each and every one of them, for buying these fantastic stories. I especially want to thank the editors who have supported me the most during the start of my career, most specifically Jason Sizemore of Apex, Peter & Nicky Crowther of PS Publishing, Darin Bradley of *Farrago's Wainscot* (also my editor for this book here, so he gets double thanks!), Silvia Moreno-Garcia (then editing Innsmouth Free Press and countless anthologies I was in), and Nick Mamatas (who published me in both *Clarkesworld Magazine* and the *Big Click*).

I also want to thank Jeff Vandermeer for publishing some early short stories, as well as doing the introduction to *Glass Coffin Girls*, which share a lot of stories with this excellent collection.

Thank you, to everyone, and to Mark Teppo for being insane enough to publish this collection and give it such a fantastic cover and layout.

ORIGINAL PUBLICATION

- "The House at the End of the World" — *Farrago's Wainscot* [© 2009].
- "Light Like Knives Dragged Across the Skin" — *Psuedopod* [© 2007].
- "Apple Magick" — *Farrago's Wainscot* [© 2008].
- "The Happiness of Pinned Wings" — *Graveyards Yawn* [© 2006].
- "Last Stand of the Antmaker" — *Apex Magazine* [© 2010].
- "Watch Me Burn with the Light of Ghosts" — *Nox Pareidolia* [© 2019].
- "Fingerbones, Hung like Mobiles" — *Pseudopod* [© 2007].
- "Glass Coffin Girls" — *Glass Coffin Girls* collection [© 2010].
- "Red Hairs" — *Glass Coffin Girls* collection [© 2010].
- "Stone Dogs" — *Glass Coffin Girls* collection [© 2010]. Reprinted in *Candle in the Attic Window* [2011].
- "Secret in the House of Smiles" — *Clarkesworld Magazine* [© 2008].
- "When Max was Hungry Again" — *The Harrow* [© 2006].
- "This Hunted World" — original to this collection [© 2024].
- "Jars of Rain" — *Glass Coffin Girls* collection [© 2010].
- "Wire Rabbit"— *Glass Coffin Girls* collection [© 2010].
- "Fake Plastic Trees" — original to this collection [© 2024].
- "A Gift of Teeth" — original to this collection [© 2024].
- "Summer Cannibals" — *Big Click* [© 2014]. Reprinted in *Great Jones Street* [2015].
- "It Tasted like the Sea" — *Glass Coffin Girls* collection [© 2010].
- "Winterlight" — original to this collection [© 2024].
- "Sunsorrow" — *Swords and Mythos* [© 2014].
- "Ghost Technology from the Sun" — *PostScripts Magazine* [© 2007]. Reprinted in *Apex Magazine* [2009].
- "Postflesh" — *Apex Magazine* [© 2008].
- "The Skinless Man Counts to Five" — *Apex Magazine* [© 2022].